Shane Kind is a native of the northwest of England and moved south to follow his work as a postal worker, now retired. He began writing novels in school but never took then any further until late in life when he was greatly encouraged by the reception he received for a fanfiction-based story he submitted online; the rest, as they say, is history.

To my two dear friends, Richard and Mike, who never lost interest.

Shane Kind

THE SHATTERED REALMS
BOOK 2: THE GREAT DIVIDE

AUSTIN MACAULEY PUBLISHERS®

LONDON * CAMBRIDGE * NEW YORK * SHARJAH

A CIP catalogue record for this title is available from the British Library.

ISBN 9781035871001 (Paperback)
ISBN 9781035871018 (ePub e-book)

www.austinmacauley.com

First Published 2025
Austin Macauley Publishers Ltd®
1 Canada Square
Canary Wharf
London
E14 5AA

Table of Contents

1

Preparation

Brother Bryn Cuthbald considered himself to be a spiritual advisor and friend of Rogan Ragisson, and would under normal circumstances have been happy to run a 'small errand'. This favour though went against all that Bryn stood for; Rogan wanted the promise of warriors ready for war. "What did we read in the book of Esaias?" The preacher asked Rogan.

"I don't remember, priest!" said Rogan like a sulky child.

"And he shall judge among the nations, and shall rebuke many people: and they shall beat their swords into ploughshares, and their spears into pruninghooks: nation shall not lift sword against nation, neither shall they learn war anymore."

"Brother Cuthbald, I can't ask anyone else, you know how thinly we are stretched, every trusted man is needed elsewhere."

There was an impasse, a silence between two dear friends, but Brother Cuthbald knew how unbending the younger man could be, and he did not wish to test their relationship. Rogan turned to look directly into his eyes. "Gufi and Arn love you visiting, they will throw a feast in your honour and who doesn't like good food?"

"I will deliver a message only if you write it down and don't show it to me, and if they press me on the subject matter, I will eat and stay silent!"

"Bryn, you are a good man, no a great man, fetch me parchment and I will write this very important message, then I must let you get on your way!"

The day was pleasant enough and as the preacher wound his way along the road he began to whistle as the two ponies pulled his small cart at a reasonable pace. The village of Hundsnes lay 102 miles away from Kaldakinn, where he was currently, which would take roughly nine hours if Bryn did not stop off anywhere along the route for more than the time it would take to feed the ponies.

The route was remote but for the seven small communities dotted along it, each place would have welcomed a preacher, more for the news of other places than to hear a sermon. Ordinarily, Bryn would have relished the opportunity to speak with the farmers but for the fact that after Hundsnes he was expected to continue to the village of Langaholt, which lay a further 15 miles to the west, or an extra hour and a quarter journey time.

Night watchmen guarded the wooden walls around Hundsnes as it was past 10 o'clock in the evening when Bryn finally arrived outside the village gates, and they were closed for the evening. "Who be there at this late hour?" called one of the guards.

"It is Brother Cuthbald, and I do apologise most profusely for my late arrival, but I am here with a letter from Rogan Ragisson for Chief Gufi Grettersson."

"Open the gate!" called the guard. "I'm afraid you are too late even for supper, my good sir!"

"Hmm, I was promised a feast as well, oh well, never mind!" grumbled the preacher under his breath.

The guards outside the Chieftains Hall did their best to welcome the preacher, he was after all both a regular caller and friend to all in the village. "I am sorry, Brother, but the chief has taken to his bed for the night and everyone in the hall will most probably be asleep as well, perhaps you can find lodgings at the inn, I don't think the landlord sleeps!"

Bryn took the advice and turned his ponies right down the main street towards the Wood Cutter's Inn, and just as he was informed, the landlord was busying himself wiping down tables and clearing away empty flagons. "A very good evening to you, master preacher, are you looking for food and lodgings or can I get you something else?"

"Oh, thank you, good sir, I require hot food and a bed for the night…"

The following morning Bryn was awoken by the sound of a Cockerill crowing somewhere nearby, it must have been shortly after dawn because the room was still quite dark and when he raised himself, the preacher felt cold, but he could hear movement out in the street below and he knew that fishermen would be already making ready to launch their boats out on the river Snes, which gave its name to the village.

The preacher got up, washed his hands and face in a basin of warm water that was brought to his room by the landlord's wife, and afterwards, he got dressed, once downstairs he tucked into a freshly cooked breakfast of eggs on bread, with a thick spread of lard between the egg and the bread.

"You are wise to be up early if you want to catch the chief, he likes to ride out with the tree-cutters early and when he does, we don't see them again until dusk!" the landlord's wife said as she began clearing his dirty plate and crockery away.

Bryn left the inn about one half-hour later and was within minutes drawing up outside the hall once more. "Hey, don't just leave your cart there, old-timer, we don't want to be cleaning their dung up all morning, thank you very much!" advanced one of the two guards.

"Don't you know that my ponies only drop blessed dung, it works miracles on your crops, literally!" the preacher quipped.

"Oh, sorry there, priest, I didn't realise it was you, the night watch left word you might show up early, his lordship is just partaking in a spot of breakfast, just leave your cart, I will shout one of the young boys to look after it for you."

"Brother Cuthbald, as I live and breathe, how are you, old fellow?"

"Er, not so much of the old fellow, if you don't mind!"

"Have you eaten already? If I was informed sooner, I would have got the cook to rustle you up a full breakfast."

"I have eaten, yes, thank you…"

"So, am I correct in thinking young Rogan has sent you on an errand?"

"You know him so well, yes, but please, neither ask me nor tell me anything about the reason he sent me, I have a note and while I will await a reply, I told him, I didn't want to get involved."

"Give the parchment to me and let me see what all this intrigue is about?"

Gufi Grettersson 'hummed' and 'erred' to himself as he read the note. "Will you make your way to Langaholt next, Bryn?"

"Yes, with the exact same request, judging from your tone, all you need do is say; 'yes' or 'no' and perhaps include an amount!"

"I thought you didn't want to know what this was all about?"

"I don't but at the same time I'm not entirely stupid, you know!"

"Never doubted that for a moment, Bryn, now shall I write back or will you be happy saying 'yes' on behalf and give him the number, five hundred?"

"It would be better if you wrote it down and sealed the message with your seal, that way I can deny everything."

"I thought Aru was the all-seeing God, preacher!" the chief joked.

11

"He does have a name you know, Gufi, and yes, he is, so hurry up while I distract him!"

"To be serious for a moment, Bryn, Rogan was among these 'Orsk' for years and knows them better than anyone, but does he think he can defeat them in battle?"

"If there is one thing I have come to realise about Rogan Ragisson, it is his drive and determination, I may not always be able to agree with the way he goes about the things he does, but I know him to be the most selfless person I have ever met, and that is while 'Eliyah' loves him and uses him as his instrument in this instance."

"Wow, that's deep Brother Bryn, and I know you would sit me down and tell me everything you have learned, but you, dear fellow, have work still to do!"

"You are correct, forgive me, Gufi, I must reach Langaholt before noon if I am to return in time to give your replies to Rogan."

Gufi had a few fruits and some dried food and water packed onto Bryn's cart and delayed his departure to wave goodbye to the preacher.

In little over one hour, Bryn Cuthbald was entering through the open gates of Langaholt. Langaholt was built in a similar style to Hundsnes, with one major exception, Hundsnes was almost completely constructed from wood, whereas Langaholt was almost built entirely of stone, there were the odd exceptions.

As it was nearly midday and traders were coming in and out of the main gates, they were open, and the guards relaxed, those who knew the brother personally waved and shouted a greeting, others just smiled and some even bowed their heads as a mark of respect for the preacher.

Arn Ironside was the chieftain of Langaholt, which lay further down the river Snes but on the far bank, he was a much younger man, possibly by ten years than Gufi. It was hard to tell because they both favoured the local custom of facial tattoos and bore thick moustaches and beards, if it were not for the fact that Arn shaved his head whereas Gufi shaved only the sides, they may have been mistaken for 'blood' brothers.

"Brother Cuthbald, it is always a pleasure to see you!" welcomed the chieftain.

"As is a visit to your fine village, dear Arn."

"Now, let me see, a preacher of such note enters my village full of the joys of spring, and alone, for what purpose, I ask myself?"

"Oh, listen to you, young sir, you have been spending far too much time with your neighbour, Gufi and it's making you cynical!"

"Why else, old man, would Rogan Ragisson send such a trusted friend and confidence, as yourself, and a man of the one true God, if it were not to ask for a favour, a very big favour, and one where Rogan the rascal is quite clearly saying, under the watchful eye of our Lord God?"

"You are a man who speaks wisdom, Arn Ironside, and you have me at a disadvantage for words are spoken truthfully, and yet there is a part in them that I did not even see for myself, and for that, I apologise."

"No apology needed, brother Bryn, we have all fallen to the charms of that young wiper-snapper, now if it is wisdom, you deem me to have, then let me go further and say why I think you are here on his behalf…"

"No, no, I have no wish to be anything other than the messenger in this matter, so please do not on this occasion bless me with your insight!"

"As you wish, preacher, then hand over the parchment that he has sent and I will reply immediately."

Brother Cuthbald handed a second wrapped piece of parchment that was sealed with the wax seal of Rogan Ragisson.

"Hmm, how did Gufi answer?"

"He uttered just three words, my lord chief, 'yes' and 'five hundred'."

"Five hundred indeed, does he wish for my village to be bereft of menfolk?"

"Chief, I can assure you that I did not come here to put undue pressure on you, and neither did Rogan, he requires…your services, and anything you can spare would be gratefully and sincerely received, I can assure you."

"Poppycock! That scoundrel has sent you knowing two things full well, firstly that I would dare not displease a man of God and that I would not allow my dear friend Gufi to without at least equalling his gift in total, so here take my reply to that sly young fox, and tell him they will be with him before the week is out!"

"I do thank you, sir, on his behalf, truly I do."

"Yes, but on whose behalf are we talking about, your sovereign Lord God, or your sovereign lord Rogan. Och, pay me no heed, Bryn, for I have a large order of stone to quarry for Ingolfsfell and that too is expected to arrive before the weekend, prey for me, preacher, that I can fulfil both promises."

Brother Cuthbald set out on his return journey as soon as he received the chieftain's reply, knowing full well that it would be turned midnight before he entered the gates of his adopted home, Kaldakinn.

The late evening air was brisk and Bryn was thankful for his thick sheepskin robes, they kept the heat in and the cold out, even though he knew that he could expect a hearty meal once he was in his favourite chair in front of the fire at home. Gertrude, his long-suffering servant would already be readying the oven for bread baking, and once she heard the garden gate open, she would be preparing fresh eggs and cheese and possibly cod or herring for her master.

It would seem as he walked his two ponies towards the village gates that there was a bit of a commotion going on in the village. *Oh dear, and when everyone should be tucked up safely in bed*, Bryn thought to himself before shouting to one of the guards, "I have only been away a couple of days and the place is in an uproar."

"Brother Cuthbald, how fortuitous is your timely return, let me get the gates open, and hurry you inside."

Bryn flicked his reigns up and forward to motion to his two ponies, where he then continued into the village centre where he was greeted by a gathering of very angry people, who threatened to turn ugly in a heartbeat. As he surveyed the crowd, he noted many of his flock both old and young, wealthy, and poor, and most were armed with pitchforks and other farming or fishing implements.

From his vantage point on the cart, he could just about make out that the villagers had someone in an iron cage and they were prodding and poking him with staves while others were throwing small stones at him, but was it indeed a man, for unless his eyes deceived him the shape although manly could also have been a bear.

"Make way! Make way!" Brother Cuthbald shouted at the mob, but they were in no mood to listen and so they just ignored him, leaving the brother no other option than to push through the crowd using the weight of his two ponies as a buffer to prize them apart.

After 'bonking' some on the head with the bottom of his staff and shoving others out of the way with his ponies, Brother Cuthbald eventually made his way to the centre of the village green and the mob. "Back away, move out!" he bellowed as he brought the cart to bear in front of the iron cage.

Slowly and reluctantly the angry villagers began to move back and there was open ground all around the circumference of the cage. "Now will someone kindly tell me what is going on, and why this fool is locked in the cage and wearing this ridiculous garb!" the preacher asked, not wanting to add that the smell was nauseating, to say the least.

"It ain't no garb Brother Cuthbald, it is his real skin, he is the devil incarnate!"

Shouts of, 'the devil' rang around the crowd and they started to push forward once more.

"Stay back you idiots, if this is the devil then he will damn you all, especially those who keep poking him and throwing things, do you all want to go to the burning lake of fire when you die?" Not that for one minute did Brother Cuthbald believe in any of that nonsense, there was no mention of such a place in the scriptures, only the loving embrace of our heavenly father.

The villagers thought carefully about what Brother Cuthbald had just said, and it made sense, which spoked them, and before he could speak again most of the villagers were running for their homes and bolting their door shut behind them. Some of the more sceptical or downright stupid villagers refused to move an inch.

"Where did you find this creature?" demanded the preacher.

"Out by the western wall that faces Obreā, we thought he is an Orsk spy but look at him he isn't just black-skinned, he's covered in thick black hair, he's a devil I tell you Brother Cuthbald, a devil!"

"Simkin's isn't it? Since when have you been an expert in what a devil does or does not look like, now bring me that spear you were prodding him with, come on, bring it to me, I want to examine it."

Then the preacher climbed down from his cart and took hold of the spear, suddenly his ponies reared and stamped their hooves on the ground before bolting away towards Bryn's Hall of worship.

"You see that! Preacher? The thing put a hex on your ponies…"

"You lot probably spooked them gathering in so closely, stand back I say, and let me further examine this object, look what is this stone set a top of it?"

"It's some kind of stone looks like it has very sharp edges and it glows in the moonlight!" stated one of the onlookers.

"Take a closer look at the thing, and look he is naked, you can see is…" started another before being interrupted by a third voice.

"Everyone knows that the devil goes about naked!"

"The devil does not roam about naked you fool; the good book tells us he is like an angel of light, covered in beautiful jewels that is how he seduces people, although I'm not so sure he need bother with some of you imbeciles!"

"He has a precious stone on the top of his spear!"

"That is a piece of sharpened crystal, but I doubt it has any special qualities, I rather suspect that he uses it just to catch his food, although it is clean it does rather smell of dead fish and rabbit!"

"Catch his prey more like it, I say we burn it"!

"Do you want me to call fire and brimstone down on your stupid head?"

"You can do that, Father?"

"No, I can't sadly but the thought made me feel better, now please either help me or shut up and just go away!"

"What can I do to help, priest?"

"Fetch me some chicken or pork, quickly!"

Brother Cuthbald turned to the naked hairy creature and said, "What am I supposed to do with you, I don't even know if you can understand a word I am saying."

The creature grabbed hold of the bars and tried to push its face through two of them, then it made a low guttural keening sound, before abruptly stopping and then either mimicking what Brother Cuthbald had said or trying to talk or it was just making random wild noises.

The man returned with a whole cold, but, cooked chicken.

"You must be rare hungry Brother Cuthbald."

"Just give me the chicken here before I feed you to the creature…"

Cuthbald swiped the cooked bird out of the idiot's hand and held it up in front of the creature and said only the one word, "Chicken."

The creature tried to form the 'Ch' sound in a desperate attempt to copy Brother Cuthbald.

"Chicken," Brother Cuthbald repeated.

"Ch-e-kin," the creature said.

"Ah! So, you do speak, just not well, now let us see, ah yes."

Brother Cuthbald offered the chicken through the bars of the cage, to the creature, and it snatched the bird out of his hands causing all who were still watching to flinch, sink back a step, and begin to murmur once again.

Next, Brother Cuthbald raised his index finger on his right hand and pointed to himself and then prodded his chest and said, "Hu-man."

16

The creature stopped devouring the chicken for a moment and made a scoffing noise before beating his chest with his free hand, and offering the word, or sound; "Och!"

"Och?" Brother Cuthbald turned to the man who had furnished the chicken, I do believe he is trying to tell us that he is an Orsk, what do you think, if you say, burn him, I will burn you instead."

"I dunno, Brother, I'm just a poor fool after all, what do I know about these matters?"

"Right, this is what we will do, fetch some sheep skins and enclose the cage on three sides with them, then push one through the bars to give him some comfort and arrange for him to be fed three meals a day, I will pay and you will stand guard until Rogan returns and we figure out what to do properly."

"And what if he turns out to be one of these Orsk, what then priest?"

"If he is one of the Orsk, then he might speak the language of the Orsk which Rogan understands and speaks fluently himself, he might even provide important information, which of course means, that you, my friend, might just be in for a substantial reward!"

"A substantial reward…just how much are we talking here, priest?"

"A lot of coins, but only if he is kept well-fed and safe, do I make myself clear?"

"Yes priest, I shall stand guard and no man will get close enough even to smell his filthy hide!"

Brother Cuthbald returned to his house by the Hall of worship to look for a book on demons and other beasts, but he was met with a scolding from his servant, who had done all he expected she would do in cooking a tasty hot meal for him, and it had all gone cold or spoiled.

"Life is never dull in this parish that's for sure," and off he went with a flea in his ear to find that elusive book that might give him some more information on the creature who thinks itself an Orsk, a rather hairy one, but then winter is coming and he supposed that even Orsk must feel the cold some of the time.

If Brother Cuthbald thought that he had everything nicely under control, he was sadly mistaken for the next visitor to his door, did bring the roof down. Father Oswald Dansson, from Ingolfsfell, had come at the behest of a group of villagers who had held on strong to their faith and shunned the things Cuthbald taught about what the holy writings said.

This new minister had brought with him plenty of coins and the full backing of the powerful Katholoanian Church. The Father told Bryn that he was sent to construct a new church was being was to be erected on the outskirts of the town just outside the jurisdiction of Rogan Ragisson's village, and out of the reach of this misguided fad Cuthbald called, 'the way'.

This priest had in his possession an official land registry form signed by Jarl Gudrod Sigfusson of Ingolfsfell, the regional capital, and bearing his seal. Brother Cuthbald wanted to know what values this new church would stand for, suspecting already that many of its followers were those who had been calling for the destruction of the beast in the cage.

"You do know the name of our Lord Iesu's church, and we will not tolerate your continued alliances with people or foul creatures that are not put on this earth by our heavenly father, and our order has dedicated our lives to ridding the earth of those blasphemers and abominations." The Father stopped short of outright accusations against the preacher for fear of having him burnt at the stake and martyrised by the more exuberant among the congregation.

"I do wonder just what filthy creatures they would be precisely, and why you and your followers insist on building a church in the name of God's own Son, without giving any glory to his Father?"

"I am not here to bandy church doctrines with you, suffice to say, God and our Lord Iesu are the same, and every Orsk, Half-breed, Elf, Halfling, or any other Godforsaken creature, including anyone who is found guilty of cavorting, carry on relations with, or generally dabbling in things that don't concern, will be hunted down and sent back to whence they came!"

"So basically, anyone you choose not to like?"

"Anyone who takes the Lord's name in vain!"

"What is that supposed to mean?"

"If you insist on using God's actual name when you are not ordained to do so, it will be considered an act of blasphemy, and you will be brought to task over it, consider yourself warned!"

"Alright I get the picture, now if you don't mind, I have some actual work to do, and take my advice, read the good book, preach the message of love and tolerance or risk sowing only division and bitterness, which will result in people getting hurt!"

"You have been warned!" said the other priest as Cuthbald's door slammed in his face.

Over the next few days, public unrest became manifest on the streets, fights broke out between opposing factions, some had their homes and businesses set on fire, and the half-bloods, endured the scourge of the mob, some being physically attacked and even beaten. No longer made to feel welcome in the village they had helped get back on its feet.

The following day began with the body of one of the four half-bloods, who arrived with Rogan over a year ago, was now found hanging from a tree near the whale processing factory, the other three who had not been on an assignment for Rogan had disappeared completely from the village.

Cuthbald decided that the creature should be removed from public sight and he discharged the man of his duties who had been looking after it, paying him handsomely for all he had endured these past couple of days.

The creature was secretly taken down into the catacombs under the preacher's Hall of worship later that night and under the cover of darkness. The villagers were led to believe that the 'hell spawn' had returned to where it had come from and the Katholoanian Father said they should praise the Lord for removing it from their sight.

The day after, when Bryn had hope things would calm down, Father Oswald Dansson was seen going around the whole of the village blessing anyone who would give him the time of day, he carried a silver sprinkler in his right hand and a small bucket of water in his left. The sprinkler, when dipped and swung about dispensed water in the form of a mist-like spray, which the Father called 'holy water', and suddenly he was the most popular man in the village.

Simple people wanted peaceful lives, they wanted to feel protected and the Katholoanian certainly did not disappoint. "Soon," he would say, repeatedly, "we will prevail and all of the filthy grey-skins will be annihilated, wiped completely from the face of the earth!"

Cuthbald wrote to Oswald's bishop in the large church in Ingolfsfell and to the jarl detailing the disunity and discord that Oswald was sowing, but he waited each day for a carrier pigeon to return with a solution but none came, instead the word of war spread like wildfire, words that said that the king was gathering a mighty army to smite the Heathen Orsk and their godless off-spring once and for all. Cuthbald was on the edge of despair.

Renwick Heldursson, head Alderman of the village council had been, for three days at least, conspicuous by his absence and at such a critical time, however, today brought an answer to a father's prayers and an explanation for

19

his disappearance. Renwick walked his horse through the gates of Kaldakinn followed by twenty-four heavily armed and armoured, former royal guard housecarl, and each a close friend of Captain Brecott.

Renwick had the foresight to see what was unfolding in his village and took immediate action. The ex-royal guards were festooned in their colourful uniforms with deep green cloaks, and rich green tunics with highly polished iron armour, overlaid with gold detailing. Unmistakably and instantly recognised by all, except perhaps a few, but soon even they became informed as gossip spread through the village like wildfire, and everyone turned out to welcome them.

Speculation was already rife that Rogan had put out the clarion call to arms, for an invasion of Obreā and the destruction of the Orsk, and who was even now away raising an army the like of which the world as not seen since the days of the conquest of the Shattered Realms by the Holy Rhōmaíōn army, some five hundred years previously.

Brother Cuthbald was open-mouthed as the procession of men and warhorse trotted past where he stood, with Renwick Heldursson a full horses length out in front, waving at the people as he passed by, The Headman of Kaldakinn was the saviour this day and he wanted to bask in the glory of it for as long as he could, but not in any self-proclaiming way, he was not that type of man, instead, it was a deeply personal moment, a sort of thank you from the people he adored and looked out for.

Renwick dismounted his horse and flicked the reins to a nearby servant, before storing casually over to Brother Bryn Cuthbald and embracing him tightly. "You look like you have seen the second coming of the Messiah, Cuthbald, is everything alright?"

"I think it will be," he nodded as he looked around at the twenty-four guards as they dismounted and reined in their horses. Each guard was resplendent in highly polished armour that gleamed gold and silver in the afternoon sun. The segmented sections overlayed and etched with the outline of dragons rampant, the visually stunning display caused quite an emotional display from many and even Brother Bryn Cuthbald cried and laughed at the same time. "Thank you, Almighty God, the hearer of prayer and praise to your Son who delivers us from the temptations of the wicked."

Renwick introduced Captain Benardin Faucon and Captain Henri Damours before passing on to every other soldier in turn and introducing them so that Brother Cuthbald could personally welcome them to Kaldakinn. The soldiers were then taken across to the large village hall where they were told they would billet until further orders.

After speaking candidly with Brother Cuthbald, Renwick and the two captains agreed that patrols should be set up to calm the fears of the people and they came together with a plan that would have six units of four guards each, out on the streets of the village each day and each night in shifts, to accompany them they would each have an additional member from Rogan's housecarl guard who had been left behind.

The plan was to demonstrate that the Royal House of Råvenniå was standing shoulder-to-shoulder with Chief Rogan Ragisson, and even to some small degree, with the preacher Brother Bryn Cuthbald who was a known friend of the chiefs.

On the last day of the week, those guards who were able to attend Brother Cuthbald's religious meeting at his hall a bid to show further solidarity with Brother Cuthbald, and 'the way'. And not the other church which was being laid out outside of the village wall.

One of the biggest surprises of all and one which garnered the biggest 'gasps' in the hall, was reserved for one of the royal guards who when removing their helmet, as a mark of respect, was revealed to have been a woman, Madelaine Bordel, another flaxen haired beauty who immediately won the hearts of many an admirer, because the royal guard did not recruit just to make up the numbers, you earned that right to be there.

However, it was her skills as a diplomat that would win the hearts and minds of many as she volunteered to clean the church each day, after her shift, with the other women who helped with the daily routine of keeping the house of God clean and tidy. Madelaine walked around the market buying flowers for the hall, and she always made time to stop and talk to interested people who had many questions.

Father Oswald Dansson, was conspicuous by his absence, sending others into the confines of the walled village to purchase material from which to have his church constructed, along with other things needed like food and water and the mundane things of everyday life.

The royal guards had hardly been in Kaldakinn for more than a few days when in dribs and drabs' newcomers started to appear outside the village walls. The Headman was called by the wall guards. "Hail, to you all, what can we do for you here in Kaldakinn?"

Now the clouds of war loomed over the village, and men came to quench their lust for battle and blood, others the chance to make a name for themselves, and yet others who came because it was the right thing to do, and they all needed somewhere to sleep and to eat and to just congregate before they were allotted military positions.

An emergency meeting of the village elders was called and an urgent decision on what to do with these folk was called for. After much deliberation, it was decided that all these uninvited guests would be billeted on the southern outskirts of the village near the new church, of Iesu the Redeemer as it was becoming known, even though this meant that the newcomers would be pushed into the arms of a very willing and able, Father Oswald Dansson.

It was considered the lesser of two evils, as many of the 'uninvited', as they were being called, were an unruly and belligerent lot, prone to arguing and fighting and getting drunk most of the time. What little money they had seemed to be won in a contest of strength or by gambling or other nefarious ways, none of which contributed anything to the upkeep of the village.

For a chosen few, the church gave them a living wage, mostly to mimic the twenty-four royal guards whose presence had stabilised tensions within the walls of the village, they now served as bodyguards to Father Dansson. Everyone else lived off the charity of the church, in hastily arranged tents and poorly constructed wooden huts, which were made from driftwood washed up ashore, or from refuse discarded by those inside, what was becoming a real problem was that the outsiders began using the ditch that ran alongside the base of the northern wall as a latrine.

It was during this time of the uneasy truce, that Brother Cuthbald asked among the royal guard soldiers if any of them had picked up the Orsk tongue as he was in dire need of a translator. To his surprise, one of the captains, Henri Damours came forward and said that in the early days of the inception of the queen's royal black guard, he had the opportunity to mix with some of those soldiers and learn bits of their language.

The captain was soon squirrelled away from his day-to-day duties and found himself almost being dragged to the church undercroft, it was about as uninviting a place as it was possible to find, where roots regularly pushed through the roof threatening to bring the whole place down, and it was dark, damp, and frigid and the captain had wondered why Brother Cuthbald had dragged him down here.

Bryn walked quickly with a torch in his hand, meandering his way past all the hanging objects and it was all that he could do for the captain to keep pace. However, all became clear when the preacher finally stopped and his eyes eventually adjusted to the torch lights and the light from a lit brazier. That was when he saw the creature, with its jet-black thick hairy coat from head to toe.

"What manner of creature is this brother Bryn?"

"It is called a 'Troglodyte' in all the references I could find about it, not that my library is extensive, but look, and I am sorry to do this to you, but it has to be our little secret. Many in the village would drag this unfortunate soul out of there screaming and kicking and not hesitate to put it to death with fire. However, this creature has, I think, valuable information about the Orsk under the mountain, we just need to get it talking!"

That evening unbeknown a secret meeting took place between a group of mercenaries outside the northern wall, like so many other times the meeting turned into another all-night-long drinking competition but one that this time resulted in this group of over twenty, steeling a flat-bottomed trading barge and somehow navigating it northwest along the shoreline of Råvenniå.

The group was fortunate that they had a fair wind blowing their sail in the right direction and by the time they had sight of the southern tip of Obreā, some at least had managed to sober up enough to take control of the vessel. It was then that they realised the old man sat at the tiller, he was smiling happily away at anyone who happened to look his way. "Who's the old man?" one of the mercenaries asked.

"Don't know!" seemed to be the consensus.

"Hey, you there, why are you here, and why do you keep smiling?"

"This boat, it belongs to Alnoth…"

"So, what old man, why does that make smile?"

"You guys asked me last night which boat you could take, and pointed to this one."

"Yeah, I still don't understand…?"

"Alnoth, he thinks he is the greatest fisherman in all Råvenniå, and you stole his boat, ha! What I would give to see his face this morning when he finds it gone."

"That's it, that's why you came with us?"

"Oh, no, last night you were talking about all the gold and silver you were going to find, that's why I came, and it's just as well because none of you would have survived this far without my seamanship!"

The old man did seem to have a knack for sailing, and it wasn't long into the morning that the boat was cutting through the waves in the mouth of the river Tawa, that bordered Obreā and Råvenniå, the mouth of the river was over a league wide and difficult to traverse even with a well-trained crew, but today the gods smiled on the twenty-one, a crosswind had pushed the boat on to the southern shores of Obreā.

The first thing that the group needed was a leader, someone to take charge of the whole operation, and that almost cost this motley crew the whole purpose of the expedition before they got off the boat. Only five or six men put their names forward but not one of them could get even three other people to support them, then a fight almost broke, instead, one bright spark who had sobered up faster than most it would seem came up with a rather good idea.

The old man was sent ashore, having had to be lowered down over the side of the boat, he was to pick twenty long pieces of dried grass and snap one of them so that it was shorter than the rest. After scrambling back on board, each of the twenty was then asked to draw one of the lots from his hand, and the one with the shortest lot would be elected as their leader.

Harek Kormak was the winning picker and declared leader of the expedition by all, in a rousing shout of cheers and shield banging, and so he, Kormak chose to walk across the open scrubland as far as the base of the mountains and once there they would look for suitable caves where the Orsk might have hidden their treasure, as rations were low and none of them had much other than the clothes on their backs and their weapons and equipment, everyone agreed and they set off with enthusiasm.

Soon enough they would feel the wrath of an Obreā welcome, the wind was almost gale-force across this desolate open, Icey land, and then came the driving rain, so dense it made it hard to see, some who knew the story of Rogan Ragisson wondered how he and his fleeing warband had survived any of this never mind the women and children that fled with them, but he did, and so they too pressed on in his spirit.

Some of the brighter fools came up with the idea of catching the rain in their cloaks and then squeezing out the life-preserving liquid into their helmets, while others were more adept at scavenging and managed to find eggs in the birds' nests, which was not too difficult as they littered the ground in some places at every turn or step that was taken.

After two days, they finally saw their target location coming into view, and they had only lost five warriors along the way. Alas, what the remaining sixteen saw next surely dented even the hardiest of the fools, no longer was there just the bottom of the enormous mountain range with wide-open tunnel mouth's that Rogan had spoken about.

However, now it would appear the Orsk had built themselves some defences, in the year or so since Rogan escaped. A rough drystone wall about ten feet in height sat atop a ten-foot ditch and hill, the ditch being filled with a black gluttonous liquid that looked and smelt like pitch, or tar.

It was around midday, on that second day when they got close enough to lean down and stick a finger into the black gloopy mass, and they suddenly realised why nobody had bothered to halt their progress. There was nowhere to cross this black morass and the defences appeared to run in both directions as far as the human eye could see.

The group pulled back to a safe distance to re-assess the situation, most of the men were dejected and angry, they had come here in search of fame and fortune and instead, they would go back to the village with their tails between their legs, quite penniless, and possibly facing criminal charges, but what other choice did they have.

Then a flash of inspiration hit Harek like a bolt of lightning! "All is not lost my friends, if we go back and tell Rogan Ragisson about these defences, this has got to be worth coin, no?"

"Then he can make plans before he sets out with his army, they can make ladders and things to cross the ditches, oh my friends we do not return empty-handed but with information that is worth a king's ransom I think!" said another.

That brought a loud cheer from all who still lived and at the same time it gave them the strength and courage to endure the hardships and return to the boat, and to help them on their way, if an incentive was required, there was a sudden flurry of arrows that had been fired by the Orsk defenders who had finally been alerted to the group's presence.

The return journey was very much the same as it was going, cold, wet, uneven ground, and generally miserable which accounted for the lives of a further three men, now sailors were a superstitious lot and looked for omens in everything from a feather falling from the sky to the distant cry of a sea bird in flight, so when they arrived back at the boat and the old man counted out thirteen survivors, he refused to get in the boat with the rest of them.

"What is wrong now old man?" asked Harek the leader.

"Thirteen is an unlucky number we will all be doomed if we try and cross the water, someone will have to remain here!"

That was not a statement that went down well with the others, and when Harek told the old man; "Fine you can stay here and wait for Rogan to come!" the others began brawling once more. "You can't leave him behind he's the only one who can navigate the channel!"

Once again, the old man was sent out to collect dried grass, and he was asked to hold the pieces while the others drew lots, the one who would draw the shortest would be left behind, with the promise of a boat returning for them at some point shortly, of course.

The unfortunate one was called Plechelm, and reluctantly he got off the boat and walked a shore, with nothing else to do he plonked himself down in the sand at the edge of the scrubland and he sat and watched as the boat was pushed out into the river mouth, and he stayed staring into the distance long after its sail had disappeared from view.

In Kaldakinn people were getting restless, the numbers outside of the village walls were swelling and with nothing much to do each day fights were breaking out and crime was increasing to epidemic proportions, so much so the Kaldakinn guard refused to go outside and investigate anything that was being reported to them, including the theft of Alnath's fishing boat.

Renwick Heldursson came up with a solution, it was only short term, but surely, he thought to himself, *how much longer could Rogan Ragisson take before he returned, as though his return, of course, would magically put everything right.* "Captain Faucon, take half of your men out into the camps and tell them to form small groups with which to walk along the shore for the missing boat."

"Do you think that it will defuse the tension out there?"

"It will if we offer them a reward for its return, don't you think?"

"Perhaps it would be better if we offered to pay them for each hour they stayed out looking?"

"Hmm, you might have a point, if just one group gets the reward, they all might have cause to fight over it, what would you say is a fair amount for their pay, captain?"

"Perhaps a penny for every six hours they stay out?"

"I just hope that the treasury will stretch that far!"

"Hasn't Rogan got fund enough to pay for an entire army?"

"Yes, but in case you hadn't noticed, our dear leader is not back yet, and I have no idea where he keeps his war chest!"

"If we are serious about this whole situation, why don't we ask the people in the camps if any of them have any knowledge about making weapons, surely the mercenaries alone would know how to fletch arrows, but there might be blacksmiths, carpenters, and the like if we could offer all them that sort of employment then that might help," hypothesised the other royal guard captain.

"Why don't we offer them the opportunity to train with the royal guard, you know people just need something, even training could help?"

"How quickly would you like to run the treasury down; they are all wonderful ideas but we simply don't have the finances to back them all up!" Renwick Heldursson postulated.

"Why don't we consult Brother Cuthbald, if it's a miracle we need…"

Captain Faucon said that he would go and ask the preacher's thoughts on the matter, and as he had been seen to have been spending a lot of his time with the holy man, the others agreed that it might be best coming from him. The captain for his part was only trying to buy time before Rogan returned, the preacher's 'guest' was proving to be very tight-lipped about everything other than food and water.

The royal guard captain apologised to Brother Cuthbald for asking about funds, but Bryn, jovial as ever, said that while it was a difficult question the Lord would provide an easy answer. "Follow me and pick up that bucket over there by the door!" the preacher continued.

"I don't understand Brother…"

Bryn led the captain down the stairs and into the catacombs once more but this time instead of going straight on towards the hidden guest, he turned down a narrow and cramped tunnel that led off to the right.

The captain had to remove his helmet to even be able to crouch comfortably.

"Enter through the narrow gate. For wide is the gate and broad is the road that leads to destruction, and many enter through it. But small is the gate and narrow the road that leads to life, and only a few find it. Maththaîos 7:13–14," muttered Bryn as he came to a halt by a wooden door.

"What's inside, brother Bryn?"

"Why, the answer to all of your prayers of course!"

"If only I could have faith like you have brother Bryn…"

"Past the bucket to me, please!" announced the preacher, who then disappeared inside the small room with his torch. The captain heard the strangest of sounds, like falling pieces of metal and a dull thud.

"Is everything alright in there?"

Suddenly the preacher was there, standing with his head poking out from the doorway. "Everything is fine, thank you, here you are, take this!" Bryn pushed the bucket towards the outstretched hand of the captain.

The captain, taking hold with just his right hand, almost dropped it, such was the weight of it now. "What on earth…"

"You required coin did you not?"

The captain had to hold the bucket with both hands as he waddled his way out of the narrow tunnel.

"How much is in there?" asked the bright-eyed Headman of the village, once the captain had returned to the village hall.

"Clear the table and I will tip it all out, then we can count it and see."

"Did the preacher say how he came by this?"

"He said that Rogan had donated it to his religious order, but the preacher hid it away just in case there was a more pressing need for it here in Kaldakinn."

"So did he just give it to you, to us I mean?"

"He just handed it to me, yes, and didn't say another word about it, why?"

"Why, obviously if we have to repay him…"

"I think he gave it in the same manner in which he received it so that we might realise all the things we talked about earlier."

"What better way to show Rogan when he finally returns, and we have an army trained, ready, and waiting for him to lead."

"Then what are we waiting for, let's get signing those folk up, at shilling a week for foot soldiers and sixpence extra for mounted men."

Over the next few days, the men and some of the women trained hard and others set up shops as farriers, fletchers, spear makers, and blacksmiths suddenly new houses were being constructed once more within the village walls and the whole village was slowly coming together in the spirit of unity. Nearly two weeks later, the missing boat reappeared and those who survived the ordeal had quite a tale of their own to tell.

2

The Audacious Plan

There is something about returning home from a long and dangerous mission that fills an individual with pride, for a job well done, and relief, relief that everyone returned safely as well, that and the strange thought that the return journey always seems to take less time!

When Gunnar Helgisson first sighted his friends from the footplate at the bow of the ferry, he was so pleased that he almost fell off, and into the water, before it hit dry land. There was no need for any words at this point, Solveig, Atli, and Sigrunn, all just embraced each other, they too were as relieved to see him as he was them.

It was just afterwards, after a brief exchange of words, that Gunnar realised that one person was missing from the group. "Where is Olpaz, why is he not with you all?" Gunnar queried.

For the next few moments, there was nothing but an awkward silence, the sort that only occurred when nobody wanted to speak for fear of being held responsible for the bad news which was to follow. So, Gunnar asked the question again.

Another awkward silence, the only difference this time was that Atli and Sigrunn both looked towards Solveig before averting their eyes entirely. Gunnar stared at his female friend. "Well?" he demanded.

This time Solveig did speak, saying, "It is all my fault, I asked him to wait in the marketplace while I tried to infiltrate the palace on my own, I saw you go into the palace, and I...I do not know, we got separated."

"You got separated, is that it?" Gunnar solicited.

"I looked back, I wanted to reassure Olpaz that he would be okay, that I knew what I was doing, it would be fine, but..."

"Gunnar, come on, this is neither the time nor the place to have this conversation, people are starting to stare!" declared Atli.

"No! This is precisely the time and place, should I be going back across the river...?"

"What use would that be, Gunnar, we all knew the risks when we volunteered to go there in the first place!" exhorted Solveig.

"So, you are saying he is dead?"

"No!"

"Then what exactly...?"

"I don't know, I looked back like I said, and then it hit me, Olpaz stood 6' 7" tall, with grey skin, no matter how we dressed him up, he stood out like a sore thumb."

"Standing still at the edge of a busy market should have been fine, but what more are you not telling us, Solveig?"

"I don't know, maybe he accidentally drew attention to himself, but when I looked back, he was surrounded by guards, he was looking at them, not at me, so I continued to follow you hoping that Olpaz would be fine."

"Do you think he was taken prisoner or did they kill him, what are you trying to say Solveig?"

"I was inside, I lost sight, I just don't know."

"Look, Gunnar's emotions are running high, we are all upset, but don't take it out on Solveig, okay?"

Solveig put her hands to her face in mock shock, but underneath those hands was concealed a smile, a smile of satisfaction gained only when a secret plan was coming to fruition.

"While I was in the palace, there was an incident that I have no more knowledge of than what I was told," recalled Gunnar, "someone had been murdered in the marketplace, and the guards were talking about what had happened. Unfortunately, I was worse for wear having spent the night drinking heavily with the prince, and it was late the following morning, one of the idiot captains thought that I was a spy and that perhaps I had killed the man, obviously they didn't know who he was and so didn't give a name or description, then it all seemed to get sorted out, but my head was so muddled I still don't know who it was, but it sort of makes sense that it was Olpaz, so perhaps it was my fault Solveig, I'm sorry?"

"Don't worry, Gunnar I understand, I do, you two were close, now, we can stay here and attribute blame, it won't change a thing, we have a mission to complete, Rogan will be waiting for any news we bring him, urgently." Said Solveig tartly.

"But what if Olpaz isn't dead surely one of us could go back and check if there is a chance we could help him, perhaps even to escape, who knows?" offered Sigrunn placatingly.

"No, we stay on mission, Rogan is depending on us!" Gunnar agreed reluctantly.

"Agreed, let us get moving." Said Atli.

"Agreed!" said Solveig.

"Aye," said Sigrunn who had remained quiet until now, but she never took her eyes off Solveig as she spoke.

Once the group was mounted, they turned their horses towards Kaldakinn and began the long journey home, but they were not alone, streams of people, mostly men, and boys, were either walking or riding along the road it appeared in the same direction as them, some in fine looking clothes, some in rags, others with old rusty weapons tucked into belts, some had no weapons of war but carried farming implements like iron-shod spades with a wooden blade and handle, iron picks and iron-shod hoes. Iron scythes, sickles, and even wooden pitchforks and rakes.

"Where are they all going do you think, Gunnar?" asked Atli.

"I don't know but either they are following us or we are following them, how strange is this all since we left this fair land."

"Gunnar you are our leader, go ask one of them!" Atli pressed.

So that is precisely what Gunnar did. Kicking his spurs into his horse's flank so that it would move a little faster, he came alongside a man who wore a tattered old uniform tunic, no discernible armour, and who carried a very old long-bladed sword at his side, that was ill-fitting with its scabbard on account of the blade is slightly bent out of shape.

The man paid no heed to Gunnar at first, he just kept his eyes fixed firmly on the road ahead, he knew that Gunnar was there, though he did not know who he was or why he had suddenly begun to ride alongside, in fact, he had no intention of engaging or being engaged with he just wanted to be left alone and so he did his best to ignore Gunnar, he even kicked his horse in its flanks to move away.

"What are you doing old man, you'll kill that old nag if you are not careful?" inquired Gunnar.

"What does it look like I'm doing, young fellow?"

"I don't know, that is why I am asking you!"

"I am trying to get this 'stupid old nag' of mine to move away from you. Look at you boy, as anyone ever told you that you look very menacing!"

"Oh! I am sorry old man, forgive me, but I did not mean to intimidate you."

"You are not intimidating me, I merely said that you look menacing!"

"What? There is a difference?"

"Yes, there is a difference, as you seem to be so simple, I will try to speak plainly, you look scary but you don't scare me, there, now do you understand me, boy?"

"I am only trying to be polite and start a conversation with you that's all."

"No, you are not!"

"Er, yes I am!"

"Not!"

"I just wanted to ask a question, that's all!"

"Are you with the sheriff's men?"

"No, I am not with the sheriff's men, why would you ask that?"

"Because you accosted me and then started asking questions, it's what one of the sheriff's men would do!"

"Look stop this, I just wanted to know where it is that everyone is going."

"Do I look like I am leading these people, they are all in front of me, so how should I know, anyway mind your own business and kindly move away from me!"

"All right, old man, I am sorry I was just…oh, never mind, good day to you."

Gunnar looked back towards the others and they were all making silly faces and urging Gunnar to carry on, so he shook his head cleared his throat, and continued outpacing the rag-tag column of people until he set his eyes upon a carriage of sorts.

It was shaped like a box with curtained windows and it was painted with religious symbols around the outside, Gunnar was relieved, if it were priests then they might know what was going on or at least be a bit more fourth coming, so off he galloped to catch up with whom shall ever be inside.

To Gunnar's surprise, the enclosed wagon was being drawn by a team of six oxen and it was struggling to make very much headway on the thick muddy surface of the road, and it was then that it occurred to Gunnar that many, hundreds of people, horses, and wagons must have come this way in a short space of time to cause this much destruction to the road, in what has been hot and dry conditions.

"Hello, good day to you, good sir!" Gunnar hailed the Wagoneer who was sitting high up on a hard wooden bench about halfway up the front part of the box-shaped vehicle.

"Good day to you too, lord," the man said with his eyes transfixed on Gunnar's sword, even though it was sheathed, he knew a true warrior when he saw one and it made him a little nervous.

"My name is Gunnar Helgisson and I am travelling to a little fishing village called Kaldakinn, that is where I am from, and I am amazed to see so many people, people of all sorts travelling the same way that I am today, and I wondered if you knew why?"

"Sorry mister Helgisson but I was hired to drive this carriage, that's all I know…"

Suddenly one of the window blinds was rolled up on the side of the vehicle, leaving the inside of it open.

"We are all travelling to Kaldakinn, Rogan Ragisson has called us, perhaps if you are from there you might have heard of him!"

"What? Rogan Ragisson has called you, did you just say that, lord priest?"

The portly man in the vehicle was well dressed like a bishop or at least someone eminent in the cloth.

"I said…oh don't bother, if you think that I am a lowly priest then you are obviously too stupid, and therefore a waste of my time trying to explain!"

"That is the second time somebody has called me stupid for trying to ask a perfectly good and simple question, in the last few minutes, what is it with people and trying to get a straight answer, has the world gone mad?"

"Ah, perhaps you are not so stupid as you look, the whole world has indeed gone mad and we are going to save it from itself before it is too late, now do you, see?"

"It's getting clearer, yes I think I am beginning to understand." Gunnar lied.

"'Armageddon' that is where we are going, Armageddon, and we must get there as soon as we can to save all these brave souls, and you too, if you like, for only a small remittance?"

"I am going to Kaldakinn priest, not Armageddon, I don't even know where that place is, I mean is it far from here?"

"You poor simpleton, my name is Bishop Hugue d'Athenous, surely even an imbecilic like you has heard of me, and I am trying to explain that we are both going to the same place, Kaldakinn, however, it will be Armageddon, if we don't get there in time!"

"Kaldakinn is a very small fishing village and I don't know why you think it is also Armageddon, it makes no sense to me, that is what I am saying."

"Rogan Ragisson has called to arms every available fighter in the world of men, to defend Kaldakinn from the devil, the devil in the form of the Orsk is going to lay waste to all in their path, and we have to get there before it happens so that we can bless every valiant fighter."

"Why do we do that, I hear you ask?"

"I didn't but please continue…"

"Harumph! We do that so their souls can go to heaven when they die, otherwise, they will go in the other direction and who knows, they may even come back as Orsk, now do you see the importance of the matter?"

"Well now that you have put it like that, it explains everything, I am grateful, and I will fetch my companions and tie our horses to the front of your wagon so that you may make haste, you truly are very kind to take on such important work and at an expense to yourself like that."

"What are you babbling about now, I charge one silver shilling for every baptism and there must be thousands of folks going there, so you see I actually hope to make myself rich, and still have enough coin left over to build a cathedral, God does love a generous giver, and he does so richly reward his humble servants."

Gunnar thanked the bishop for his helpfulness and dropped back a little for his companions to catch up.

"What did you learn Gunnar?" said Atli.

"Everyone is going to Kaldakinn, apart from those who die without getting baptized, they are going to hell and shall be returned as Orsk, anyway, apparently Rogan has put out a call to arms to fight the Orsk."

"All of the dead come back as Orsk!" balked Sigrunn.

"Only the ones who aren't baptized!" replied Gunnar.

"Wait, what? No, never mind that, we are supposed to be on a secret mission, nobody but the king should know our business, this is terrible news, Gunnar, what are we to do?" pleaded Atli.

"There is nothing we can do except help these poor fools to get there safely," noted Gunnar.

"Rogan would not have put out a call to arms surely not," Sigrunn remarked.

"No, he would not, so it appears someone has been telling tales, these people have been coming for days, even it appears before, it appears we crossed the river and I spoke with the prince."

There was nothing that could be done to change what was happening, ordinarily, Gunnar would have just tried to outrun the column, but he realised people must already be at the village, so he remained true to his word and he hitched his and his companions' horses to the two lead oxen and helped them pull the heavy wagon that bit faster, at least until they got to firmer ground.

When it was time to bid the bishop 'farewell', the four unhitched their horses and spurred them on to get a little way ahead of the steady stream of humanity heading to Kaldakinn. "We still have some time ahead of us, and many of these people are on foot, how on earth will they manage to get there?" Sigrunn asked rhetorically.

"How will we feed them all or find them shelter, if I didn't know better, I would say that our mystery someone is looking to overwhelm Rogan's resources and those of the village, which means, whoever they are they are not friendly!" pronounced Gunnar.

"Atli, can I ask you something?" whispered Sigrunn.

"Ask away, my lovely!"

"Shh, you fool, keep your voice down, it's about Solveig!"

"What about her?"

"Don't you think that she has been acting rather strangely since we all joined up again?"

"Her partner was taken or killed, that can make a person reticent at least…"

"You know why we waited for her to fetch the horses, just before Gunnar got off the ferry. I happened to notice she was standing for a moment talking with someone."

"Is that a crime now, who was it, did you see?"

"No, and that's why it made me a little uneasy, the person was standing at the side of the toll house, so he was hidden by a dark shadow."

35

"So, he probably said 'hello gorgeous' and she brushed him off!"

"Atli can't you be serious for one minute here?"

"Sorry, my love, you know that I am enthralled by your beauty and nothing else matters to me but you!"

"Hmm, too busy looking at my…"

"Sigrunn!"

"Everything all right back there?" Gunnar asked in response to Atli's outburst.

"Oh, we are fine, it was just Sigrunn telling me what she wanted to do once we returned to Kaldakinn."

Sigrunn whipped her beau with her reins across the back of his left hand. "I'm telling you, Atli, it's a women thing I think there is something wrong."

"I have to be honest I've never seen her with a man before, and saying that every one of us who escaped those caves together has stuck together, like us, except for poor Solveig."

"Atli, take your mind out of your breaches for one minute will you, I would even go as far as to say she hates any form of male attention."

"You think she likes women?"

"God grief, you are such a boy at times, not everything is about sex!"

"I never mentioned the word…"

"You were thinking it though, I know that look!"

"All right, I get it you want me to be serious for a moment, well here it is then, and don't say I didn't warn you…"

"…okay?"

"All of you girls were raped, repeatedly by those monsters and none us men could do a darn thing about it, am I surprised that Solveig despises men, no, not at all so when of those grey-skins befalls some mishap, would I expect her to show any sort of concern, probably not!"

Sigrunn did not speak, instead, she looked daggers at her man.

"See, that right there is why I don't speak my mind."

Sigrunn kicked her horse forward so she overtook both Solveig and Gunnar.

"Hey, guys, is everything all right?" Gunnar called back to his friend.

"It's that time of the month, Gunnar, just let it go…"

"Oh gawd, sorry."

Atli watched how intently Solveig listened although she pretended not to, but he noticed that she relaxed when he mentioned the 'woman thing'.

36

Eventually, the party approached the main gates into Kaldakinn and as they did, they noticed that a wide track veered off to the right, of the drywall leading up to the gatehouse. Two deep ruts had been worn in the ground and it was exactly like the track where they had met and helped the bishop, the nauseating smell hit their nostrils well before they asked the guards a question, and a slight tilting of the head revealed the new shanty town that had sprung up further down towards the sea.

"Guard, what is this all about?" inquired Gunnar.

"Who are you? State your business and residence, then in through the gates, everyone else follows the track right, come now hurry up they are starting to bunch up behind you."

"I am Gunnar Helgisson, who are you, foolish man!"

"Is that supposed to mean something to me, I have met over a hundred 'Gunnar's' this week alone, and none of them were residents of the village, so move to the right!"

"I mean I am one of Rogan Ragisson's trusted housecarl."

Gunnar turned to his friends. "You see, I said the whole world has gone mad, what are we to do, should I draw my sword and cut off this man's head?"

"Guard, fetch Brother Cuthbald, his hall is nearer to this gate than sending someone to the village hall. Bryn will vouch for us, go now and be quick about it, we have travelled a long way this day and are tired and hungry!"

The guard shouted up to one of the sentries on the rampart between the two gate towers.

While Gunnar and his companions moved over to the left to let others speak to the guard.

They waited and they waited and Gunnar had counted hundreds more people being sent off to the right, and it made him ask the other three in his group; "where were they all going?"

While they were still waiting, who should appear but the bishop and his ox-driven enclosed vehicle?

"Open the gates!" called the guard. "Let them through, everybody else stay back!"

As the gate guard spoke several other guards came out from the village and formed an ad-hoc guard of honour for the bishop's vehicle.

Gunnar's mouth opened, his lips moved, he turned to his companions but no words would form and as he looked at them, each in turn and they looked at him, and as if to add insult to injury, the heavens opened and it began to pour down with rain.

Eventually, Brother Cuthbald came to the gate and of course, he did vouch for Gunnar and his party, Gunnar glared at the gate guard who had held him up as he walked past him soaked through to the skin.

Bryn invited them all back to the hall with him with the promise of hot food and warm mead if they wished. "Come, come, one and all and let my housekeeper spoil you as she does me, usually!"

Gunnar was not a happy man, the mission was a thankless one at best, it is part of the job, however, but losing a close friend and ally is not, and it made Gunnar feel like he had somehow let everyone down, including himself. "I'm sorry Brother Cuthbald, but I am in no mood to fraternise especially if that pompous ass, the bishop, is also going to be there!"

"Bishop, what bishop, we don't have bishops in our organisation, only elders and brothers, oh and sisters as well, pardon me, ladies!"

"Find out from the guards, Bryn, I have had enough of priests and their ilk to last me a lifetime!"

"No, no, no, Gunnar, all of you, come with me, I insist, and please let me explain."

Solveig Arnulfrid was the next to bow out of the invitation, "I have things to attend to, I cannot just up and leave and have someone there to fill in for me, I must go!" and with that, Solveig walked away briskly.

Bryn was about to say something aimed at Solveig, when Atli grabbed his arm and began shaking his head. "Let her go preacher."

"Yeah, I'm out too, sorry Bryn…" Gunnar said, but then Atli switch his grip from the preacher to his friend, "Please stay, Gunnar, we have things to discuss."

"Without Solveig?"

"About Solveig, but before you say another word, let Sigrunn have her say."

"Okay, there is something wrong so please as I said, follow me, and we can discuss it over a warm meal." Instructed the preacher.

Atli began the story and Sigrunn interjected as and when with details that she thought were pertinent, Gunnar was the one who was more taken aback by the things that were said than the preacher. "I am afraid that I have not had much contact with her since you all came to our village, what I have noticed is that she is always missing when you get together as a group."

"I will talk to Rogan when I get to see him next, anyway, preacher you mentioned hot food…"

"First let's have those wet clothes before you all catch your death of cold!"

"Er, should we just strip here…?" asked an embarrassed Gunnar.

"What? Heavens no go off into my private room over there, ladies first of course!" Bryn said as he pointed over to a small room to the left of the large fireplace.

Sigrunn poked her head around the door after being in there for a few minutes. "Erm, Bryn what am I to wear now that I have removed my clothes?"

"There are robes, my dear, pick anyone you see, my housekeeper keeps everything clean and lice-free!"

"Lice-free!" Sigrunn's face was a picture, which made Atli laugh.

"Do you need any help my love?" inquired Atli.

"Tell me Atli, when are you going to make an honest woman of Sigrunn, I've seen enough of you both to know that you are made for each other."

"I do not know, Bryn, I would say yes, today, now even, but Sigrunn is a shield maiden. Are they even allowed to get married?"

"Don't be ridiculous my dear, wonderful friend of course they are, I will talk with her when you take a turn trying on my robes!"

Atli smiled weakly, marriage was not something that was on his mind, especially with the impending war, there would be widows enough if Rogan got his army, without Atli adding to their number.

"So, tell me, Gunnar, while our two love birds switch places, how was your meeting with, Waegstan Godhelm?"

"How are you so well informed for a preacher?"

"Do you know that God sees everything, Gunnar?"

"In that case, you already know that I did not get to see the king, it was his son who agreed to send troops to join our alliance and he said that they would be ready and waiting for a sign at the end of the winter months."

"I heard that he pledged over three hundred soldiers and twice as many untrained men?"

"You know Bryn, for someone who protested not get involved in the things of this world, you are mighty well informed I would say that whatever organisation you use they are better than anything I have ever seen."

"Rogan will be pleased, he had wanted a spring campaign and this will give him plenty of time to have the army trained how he wants them to be, in accordance to his orders of battle. Ah, our two love birds have finished putting the robes on, now it is your turn and then I have something to show you, okay?"

Gunnar did not take long to get out of his wet clothes and put on one of Bryn's long robes. "Well would you look at the three of you, my servant will now take all of your clothes and get them dried out, in the meanwhile you must follow me!"

"Why do I feel like you are taking us to perform some half-baked ritual which will end with one of us being sacrificed, Bryn."

"Don't be such an…"

"Don't call me an idiot, I am fed up with people calling me that today!"

"Then don't act like one, now pick up a torch each and follow me."

Down the narrow stairs, they descended and into the undercroft of the hall, with the four of them holding torches the whole place lit up very quickly and it wasn't long before they spotted the long green cloak and wondered who it was that was sitting down here in this Godforsaken place it wasn't until they heard words being exchanged and began to think that a prisoner of high value was being questioned.

Bryn called ahead to the figure in the cloak. "Henri, I have some friends for you to meet but first can you tell Tukor that they mean him no harm?"

"Who is Henri and Tukor?" Gunnar inquired as he took a moment for his eye to adjust to the flickering light.

Henri reached around 5' 8" in height once he had stood up, which was hard because the ceiling could not have been much over six feet, Gunnar recognised the uniform as being that of a royal guard from Hamund Arnbjorg, King of Råvenniå's bodyguard. Whoever was hunched over in the cage was harder to see as they were bathed in shadow.

Henri finished speaking to Tukor in some unknown language before turning to face Gunnar, and the others, each in turn he clasped his right hand firmly on their left arm and greeted them formally. "I am Captain Henri Damours of His Majesty, King Arnbjorg of Råvenniå's royal guard."

Gunnar likewise introduced Atli and Sigrunn as personal housecarl to Rogan Ragisson before the captain stepped to one side and allowed them all to see just who it was that he had been talking with, their eyes took a moment to focus and then their expressions turn to shock and horror.

"Brother Cuthbald, I don't understand, what manner of creature is this and why is it in your cellar?"

"Tukor, we think his name is Tukor or Tokka, and from my limited knowledge we believe he is a Troglodyte, a cave dweller if you like, and he has fallen into our laps rather fortuitously ahead of Rogan's forthcoming campaign, and don't worry he is perfectly harmless, aren't you Tukor?"

"Esss!" was all the forlorn creature could say in reply.

Aethelric the Bard was the next to return home to Kaldakinn, bringing yet more welcome news of the alliance, with Lornica came the promise of an army in the spring to join in with the invasion of Obreā. However, he did return alone. Brenn and Willem Wigheard wanted to stay with their families in Lornica, whom they have not seen since they were taken prisoner by Rogan almost two years ago. and spend some time back in their own country, Zaryi and Nariako wanted to stay with the boys since their time together had drawn them close.

The Headman of Kaldakinn, Renwick Heldursson was in the main hall, at the centre of the village talking with both Bryn Cuthbald and Gunnar Helgisson, all the royal guard were out teaching various battle technics to the large body of mercenaries and militia who had already swelled the ranks of the townsfolk considerably.

Aethelric walked in alone asking about the sea of tents and other awnings that had sprung up outside the southern wall, and he asked if anyone knew the actual number of people there. "Always the pragmatist Aethelric, wanting to know what is happening before explaining what has happened to the people who are under your command!" observed Gunnar.

"Under my command, Gunnar, you know that I consider myself a lover, not a fighter, and strangely enough that is what happened on my mission, the boys and the girls got together to make sweet music, so I left them behind to enjoy what was left of this year together before they were called to fight."

"I see, well to answer your question, we have had the wall guards keep a rough tally of newcomers and as of this morning the number had risen to three thousand souls."

"How on earth can we possibly feed and clothe that many people especially over winter, the whole countryside will be bereft of wildlife and edible plants, please tell me you have a plan?" stated Aethelric.

The three went very quiet for a time and Aethelric was forced to speak again, "Tell me that you have a contingency plan to deal with this problem?"

"To tell you the truth, Aethelric, we have no idea what to do about all these people, they just keep coming and we do know not from where, but here they are and we simply can't just send them all away, we don't have the men ourselves to mount such an operation, and we have not heard from Rogan…" Gunnar was saying before Atli interrupted.

"Every time we shut the northern gates they start a fight, they are already raiding the fish factory and stealing everything in sight, we drill them every day, to fight, and they return to the shanty town, and guess what, they fight each other!"

"People are being killed already." Advised Renwick.

"Renwick, do you have any maps of this area, possibly covering the north right up to the sea?" Bryn said, suddenly having thought of an idea on what to do with the growing number of people.

"Go on Brother Cuthbald, please enlighten us," Renwick advised.

"We go to Jarl Sigfusson in Ingolfsfell and offer to buy an area of land in the northernmost part of Råvenniå, in the mouth of the river Tawa, to relocate all of those outsiders to that plot of land."

"And what if they don't want to go that far north this late into the year, and what supplies will they have to survive up there any more than they have now?" Gunnar chipped in.

"There is no shelter that far north, no trees or anything, and the ground will be frozen solid so they will be unable to plant even a late crop," Atli added.

"So, we buy them wood from Gufi, look on the map, following the road to Hundsnes, it is six hours by horse."

"Six hours, that has to be around seventy-five miles away, that's still quite a hike, Bryn."

"How far away is it by road from Gufi?"

"Less than fifty miles, so the journey would take a little over three hours by horse."

"Have you any idea of the cost of such an undertaking?" asked Aethelric.

"We have no choice either way because the cost to do nothing will be far more than any of us are willing to pay, we have reached the tipping point!" Renwick interjected.

"Okay, say we start the undertaking tomorrow, how will you get that self-appointed speaker of the 'uninvited', that Father Oswald Dansson to agree to it, there's just no way, and he is their 'unofficial spokesman'," Gunnar offered, shaking his head at the very thought of it all.

"So, we appeal to a higher calling!" said Brother Cuthbald.

"I think it is beyond the power of prayer Brother, with all due respect." Atli retorted.

"You miss understand, what I mean is we approach this new bishop, Hugue d'Athenous, he has made it very clear that he wants to build a cathedral, and I know for a fact he has coin enough, but he wants to make his fortune for himself first, so we give him a little nudge."

"Yes, he certainly has made a lot of coin from those baptisms he keeps performing at a shilling a time, so what is this little nudge, Bryn?"

"Once we have purchased the land, he can build whatever he wants on it, we'll allow him that much, on provision he takes that little pipsqueak, Oswald Dansson, with him."

"Did you hear that Dansson was calling himself Headman outside the village?"

"He can Headman alongside his bishop once he is out of our hair!"

"What about the loss of all those men we have trained up?"

"They won't be a loss they will be nearer to Obrea and they will have land with which to invest a future, it's a win, win situation."

"You think that he would gamble on its success this late in the year, Bryn?"

"Yes, I do, especially if we make a large enough donation and appeal to his ego, tell him he will be God's line in the sand against the Orsk, a beacon of hope to humanity and all that, he will be so busy planning his inauguration speech, he'll have it built before winters end."

"It might work, I don't think it can do much harm trying, but where is the extra funding going to come from, we have already used up the last donation you gave us Bryn." Said Renwick Heldursson.

"The Lord our God will provide, as he always does…"

"Excellent, now we just need to work out who goes where and to whom they speak, Aethelric you should go to the jarl, Gunnar to Hundsnes to get Gufi on our side because he is going to lose a lot of trees, Renwick, you approach Oswald the priest in your capacity as one village Alderman to another, and I shall make a great flowery speech to tickle the ears of the bishop." Said Cuthbald.

"Just a couple more items of business to attend to and then I think we are done, so who wants to speak next?"

"I would like to say something on behalf of the fishermen whose catch is stolen by the mob every time they put to shore."

"Atli, go back and pay them compensation for their losses and then hire all of their boats to transport all of those people and their possessions north, that should compensate them enough."

All right then, the final order of business. "Can any of you who have returned be added to the roster for patrolling the village, Captain Faucon and his men are being run ragged at the moment as they are working double shifts?" disclosed the Headman.

"Yes, Sigrunn and I will add our names, but don't ask me what happened to Solveig, she supposedly went after she went to visit her family and friends but nobody has seen her since, anywhere in the village."

"So, if that is everything, then I shall bring this meeting to a close, and tomorrow we can invite all the local parties to a banquet here in the great hall and set our plans in motion, agreed?"

Everyone said "Aye."

The following morning Aethelric arrived at the Hall of worship just as Bryn had asked him to do so, and Bryn was waiting with a saddle bag full of coins, there should be more than enough there, lad, and I have taken the liberty of hiring six guards from our mercenary army to accompany you, and keep you safe!

Gunnar arrived just as Aethelric placed the saddlebags over his mount. "Excellent timing Gunnar, here are your saddlebags, with more than enough coin to pay for all the wood that will be required to build a new town, and as with Aethelric, six mercenary guards to get you to Hundsnes and Gufi, it will be safer if you both travel together."

After they had left the village, Bryn returned to the village hall to check on preparations for this evening's feast. Three large tables had been placed end-to-end and Brother Cuthbald made sure that everyone would be sat opposite the person they needed to talk to and in-between each of them would be one of Captain Faucon's royal guards.

Renwick Heldursson was given the task of talking to the bishop, as it was thought that if it were Bryn, the bishop might take offence given their differences in scriptural interpretation. If any of them were nervous about just how the evening would play out, they would soon find out, each recipient from beyond the village wall had gracefully accepted their invitation and were already arriving up to an hour before the event.

"So, Bishop Hugue d'Athenous what brings you to our humble village?" began the Headman.

"To be honest, humble it most certainly is, however, mysterious are the ways of our lord, he has brought me to your village and I am here until I receive further instruction, in the meanwhile I baptise."

"We are so privileged to have a man of your eminence among us, I am only sorry that our erstwhile leader, Rogan Ragisson was not here to greet you in person."

"It would perhaps have been more fitting if he had, but with a war to plan for I can accept that he is quite busy, as for his people, that is why I came here, to save the wretched souls of these deviants and misfits in their hour of need, and at great cost to myself, both personally and professionally I might add."

"Won't you be missed at your old cathedral your eminence?"

"Oh, no need to call me that, not yet anyway, we are both men of the cloth and all that, I like to think of myself as a simple man, from a simple old place in the capital and I erm, well let's say there are a lot of bishops in the capitol, and not enough ecumenical work to go around."

"What's the saying among the well-educated, many hands spoil the broth?"

"My point precisely, so here I am with only the clothes on my back and a rather shabby roof over my head!"

Renwick Heldursson then lowered his voice and leant in towards the bishop, "I hear that you have come to our humble dwelling to build us a fine cathedral, is there any truth in that rumour?"

The bishop coughed to clear his throat before continuing, "The thing is, I did rather hope that this place was, well, of better standing, and that your fine council would prove me with all the funds that I would require, but honestly look at the place, and please do not take offence when I say this…"

"No offence, please your eminence speaks freely, you are among friends."

"All right then, this village is too small and an absolute shambles, it simply wouldn't do for me to have constructed, a large monument to our Lord in such a filthy run-down backwater, do you see my point?"

"I do so agree with you, lord bishop, and if the coin were to be made available because Rogan is not without means, how would you go about building this magnificent building?"

"I would level this place that's for sure and start again, the streets would be laid out in a pattern of squares, everything in order and with a purpose, and at its centre, the masterpiece, the cathedral, but where would all of the people go if I were able to carry out such an enterprise, Headman?"

"You said yourself, on many occasions I'm sure, 'the Lord moves in mysterious ways' and by bringing you here to this awful place he has also risen you up to the place you rightfully belong, bishop!"

"He has, how so because from where I am seated, I see only mud, filth, deprivation, and dereliction!"

"Do you believe in visitations lord bishop?"

"From above, from angels is that what you are asking me?"

"Yes, precisely!"

"Well, I must admit that I have seen some heavenly sights in my time, and I have been moved at those times by those sights, but they are all too fleeting and never last."

"Well, last night, good sir, I not only had a visitation but I was also given a vision of a shining city with your cathedral at its very centre, and you, Bishop Hugue d'Athenous, sat on a throne watched over by the most holy that's what he called you here on earth, his most holy!"

"His most holy, do you mean like the Pope?" The bishops' eyes lit up with the very thought, that would certainly show all those cretins he left behind in the capital.

"Yes, what a truly magnificent thought to see you finally seated in your rightful place, and you will have your kingdom, your diocese, and think about it this way. You will be the focus of God and all the angels when in the spring the battle takes place in full view of the cathedral, God will be sat on his throne next to you as the Armies of Råvenniå smite the last army of the devil here on earth!"

"What? Wait a minute, I was rather hoping that I was invited to discuss building my cathedral here, in Kaldakinn!"

"You see it is worse than I thought!"

"It is, er, what is?"

"You have too long been just another man of God in an ocean of men of God in the capitol, you who have sacrificed everything you had and owned, and for what, to be chased out of the capitol because of the word of a Hoare!"

"Yes, my thoughts exactly, eh? What? how did you…no never mind, continue telling me about my cathedral?"

"Kaldakinn is a fishing village, and it already stinks like an open sewer, do you think that the king is going to want to make a personal pilgrimage to this filthy place each year?"

"The king you say, a pilgrimage?"

"Why yes of course, he will want to be here in the spring to wave his beloved soldiers off to war, this is a holy war after all, a crusade if you like, the very first of its kind in our history, and then every year after such a famous victory, and with God and the angels looking down, he will want to return every year thereafter to pay his respects. Along with everyone else in Råvenniå, think of the money, literal waterfalls of silver and gold coin if nothing else, your eminence!"

"Well, when you put it like that, how can I refuse God his seat in his own house with which to view the destruction of the devil and his minions, Pope Hugue d'Athenous, does have a ring about it, you have to admit?"

"Just one last thing bishop, where is Athenous, I am a student of Cartography but alas I can find it on none of my maps?"

"It's, well, its, oh all right then, may I be as frank and honest as you have been with me?"

"Please do, I believe your God loves a sinner and a confessor of sin more!"

That raised the bishop's eyebrow, and he wondered if the Headman did have a revelation of just how much the good Lord had revealed, "since you have taken me into your confidence, I will be honest, I made it up, the name Athenous, there I am a sinner, and I just wanted a name that sounded so much better than my parent's name, Uglubathrsson!"

"We are all given new names when we are baptized in the name of the Father, and his Son and the holy spirit, and I know this that your new city shall be called Athenous, it is a reverent sounding name, Pious and Godly and I can already see the Almighty and all of his angels rejoicing!"

"What have I done to deserve a friend such as you, Renwick Heldursson, it brings tears to my eyes just to think how a humble servant such as I could have fallen on such luck."

"Luck, no sir, you have dedicated your life to doing nothing but the lords work, and this is your reward."

"So, I shall have my cathedral then?"

"You are to be given funds to build a new city, to the north, to raise it from the ground in whatever way you see fit, and at its centre shall in deed be your cathedral, and your workforce awaits beyond the village walls, all that is required from you now is to speak to them and show them the coin."

"Where is the coin, may I at least look for myself?"

"Pull back the cloth on the edge of the table."

The bishop looked down at his lap to where the rich green tablecloth was folded over itself, and with a nervous hand, he lifted the edge slightly. The bishop's face shone with the reflection of all that gold and silver that sat in a large barrel but a few inches away. "Praise the Lord!" the bishop shouted.

Everyone else stopped what they were doing when they heard the bishop shout, and he was at first embarrassed by his outburst until Renwick Heldursson stood up and began clapping furiously.

Bryn Cuthbald then stood and raised a toast, "To our good friend Bishop Hugue d'Athenous and to all who follow in his footsteps, may you all be blessed every step of the way."

Oswald Dansson leant to his left to speak more quietly to Bryn once he had sat himself back down again, "What was that all about, and whatever do you know about it?"

"I don't know anything for sure, I only heard a rumour of course, but I thought nothing of it until now."

"A rumour, what rumour, tell me Bryn, what is going on, if you know, and if it affects my people then I should know!"

"I have heard that the king has given the Jarl of Ingolfsfell the task of building a new town to the north of here, it is to be a staging post for the invasion of Obreā, and he wants God to bless his armies before they march. If the bishop should agree to relocate to that new place, think how many people it will take to build, possibly hundreds if not thousands, so that it is ready before the spring, they would need to be trained in warcraft as well so that they could defend against outsiders."

"Hmm, go on, I'm listening…"

"Well, you can imagine a town or city that size would need far more than a wooden church, and I also hear that whoever is chosen to be its city administrator would hold the title of Jarl, now who would be the best person to fulfil that role, surely not a peasant upstart like Rogan Ragisson."

"Bryn, I always liked you; you know that right, you are not like all these others and you seem like a reasonable man, who knows what is what!"

"Ah. well, I thank you for your kind words, did I ever tell you what a magnificent job you have done with the people beyond the wall, just know that you have my support already."

3

Shadow and Bone

King Arnbjorg stood as his wife breezed into the room without waiting to be formally invited. "Please, yes, do come in, my dearest wife, I think you already know Captain Brecott and Sister Wenyid, but I don't think you know, Chief Rogan Ragisson, Ongar, Halla Greilanda and of course Ingrid Hallgerd, now please let's all be seated once more."

"Hmm, a noble savage eh, I have heard your name mentioned before today, Rogan." She said as she walked around the table so that she should pass by Rogan.

Rogan found himself having to crane his neck to keep eye contact with the queen and he wondered what game she was playing by referring to him as a savage, he probably would not have minded if Ongar had called him that or even Ingrid, but the for the queen to do so, and when he was a guest in the royal palace, then it was obvious she was trying to get a rise out of him.

"Do you mind me calling you a savage Rogan Ragisson?" the queen purred in his ear as she put her hands softly about his head.

"I do believe in the presents of such beauty my lady, then everything should seem savage to one's eye."

"Ah, I think I like you already, savage!" she almost bit off his right ear when she snapped those last words out.

"Come, my queen, sit down and behave yourself, look you are making our guest blush!"

"We were just discussing the problem of the Orsk, in the north and what if anything can be done about them."

"Hmm, how interesting." Said the queen, changing her gaze from Rogan to Ongar.

"And what do you think about the problem of the Orsk in the north Ongar?" she asked pointedly.

"Honestly I have no personal opinion on them one way or the other, but I think that there must be another solution to the way my people are brought into this world."

"You think, did you say, a savage and his noble beast, how quaint."

Aatu awoke and barked twice.

"Oh, how vulgar! To whom does the wild dog belong?"

"That would be me, my lady."

"Yes of course it would, I see you have two pets one that talks and one that barks, how very thrilling, tell me do they both sleep at your feet or perhaps you all share a bed?"

"Helga! That is quite enough of that these are our guests."

"You dine with dogs! Husband, and I will not, but don't let me ruin your supper, I will be in my chambers, if you can tear yourself away that is. Goodnight." And with that, the queen left the room and slammed the door on her way out.

There was an awkward silence.

"Rogan, you have my pledge of, one thousand, of my finest soldiers as well as six hundred mounted Horse Guards and I will begin the order to prepare for war as soon as you leave, now when do you want them and where do you want them." That was when Rogan explained his plan to build a staging post in the far north by the mouth of the river Tawa, at this time he had no idea what his comrades in Kaldakinn were planning except they knew that he wanted to land and permission from the king to build the wharf and a military base there.

"There is one other problem that we have, we don't know how or where the Orsk is getting so many women from as know where that we have inquired in the kingdom as reported that many women missing."

"Your Highness, the only reports of missing women we ever get are from relatives of women they believe have been wrongly locked up in the county goal." Said the captain.

"How big is this county goal," asked Ingrid.

"I don't know I have never been there but I know it is big."

"Big enough to lose several women who don't have a family to inquire after them?"

"The Gods be blessed, yes, every drunk, whore, or ne'er-do-well and homeless woman is sent there, but wouldn't the warden know if his prisoners were going missing?"

"Good question, I think it is worth us paying a little visit there tomorrow, with your permission, Your Majesty."

Queen Helga was in her bedchamber brushing her hair and was about to get herself underdressed and ready for bed, her servants had been dismissed when she heard lightly creaking hinges, somebody was slowly and carefully trying to enter her room. She immediately looked on her dressing table for something sharp to protect herself with, then came the feeling that she was being watched and the hair standing up on the back of her neck, that sinking feeling in the pit of her stomach, and then the footsteps.

Queen Helga Arnbjorg was herself a shield maiden, many years ago now admittedly, but she was sure that her reflexes were still there, one never forgets one's military training.

Then a hand came about the soft part of her neck and she immediately grabbed the hand with her left hand, holding it tight just away from her neck, and she spun around with the sharp end of her comb exposed in her right hand, ready to stab.

"My darling queen, I do like a bit of foreplay but honestly you look like you are going to stab me!"

"Skuld! What are you doing here and at this time of night, I could have killed you?"

He embraced her in his arms spinning her round so that she now faced him, pulling her svelte body towards him, close enough to smell the musk she had just put on around the exposed parts of her neck. "I had to see you, things are moving so fast now, and there is so much to talk about."

Skuld gently moved the queen towards the end of her bed, she intern began to pull the hem of her dress towards her waist. "What is it that we need to discuss so urgently?"

Now she was falling onto the end of her bed as Skuld took the weight of her and then he gently allowed himself to fall on top of her. "Rogan is well ahead with his plans to gather a large army, and he wants to invade Obreā in the spring, by my reckoning he will have raised nearly five thousand men."

Helga put her hands lightly on each side of Skuld's fresh young face and kissed his lips, before pulling back to take a breath. "Since my men put the word out that he was raising an army mercenaries and glory hunters have poured into the village, even now threatening to swamp it completely."

"And what if they don't?" she said in-between kisses.

"Then Oswald Dansson will lead a rebellion, he has support from the bishop, d'Athenous, he is an ambitious man who craves power and coin, and I have bought and paid for both of them."

"Rogan Ragisson is no fool, what if he sees through our plan, they are here for a reason and my husband is even now entertaining him, what if they can connect me with the disappearance of all those girls?"

"I am sure they are too distracted by the impending war, that they will never have, Kaldakinn is at boiling point and anyway, I still have Prince Tostig as my plan 'B'."

"How so?"

"He has promised to send soldiers, as well as Lōrnicā and Råvenniå as part of a three-pronged attack, but the prince's forces will hand back a little and once the black guard swarm down off the mountain, they will take care of anyone the black guard miss."

"How many black guards are still on the mountain?"

Skuld laughed. "About twenty thousand, I almost feel sorry for Rogan and his joint army of five thousand, they will be annihilated!"

"All of those who conspire against and try to stand in our way will be crushed in one fell swoop!"

"Yes, they will, now enough talk I am getting tired."

"What! Too tired to…"

"Pull the covers over us, the fire is low in the hearth, and I must be warm."

Rogan and Ingrid shared a room at the palace and they were both embarrassed and surprised the following morning when a procession of servants came into their room, the first two brought a large copper bath and the others brought buckets full of hot water.

"What is the meaning of this intrusion?" barked Rogan, unaccustomed to this sort of thing.

The servant girls began to giggle and smile at Rogan, who had forgotten that he was on top of the covers and completely naked. Then as the last of the servants brought the hot water in and poured it into the copper tub they said, "Would you like us to stay and wash you?"

"No, thank you, but why do you think we needed all this?"

"His Majesty's orders!" was all they would say and then they left.

Ingrid strolled over to the tub first and wiped her hand across the surface of the water. "It is really hot, come on it can't hurt can it, it might even be fun," she said with a wicked grin on her face.

"I wonder if Ongar and Halla are having the same thing delivered to their room?" Rogan said shaking his head as he walked over to the tub, now that Ingrid was stepping in the water.

A shout, followed by some choice words in black speak indicated that perhaps Ongar and Halla were being invited to take a bath, Ingrid and Rogan burst out laughing.

About an hour later the servants return, one of them was holding a fresh clean set of clothes one for Ingrid and one for Rogan, then they began emptying the bathtub.

There was a silk curtain between where the bathtub had been placed and where the bed was situated and Ingrid pulled it across to give them both some privacy while the servants went about their business. "Look at these clothes Rogan, they are beautiful and so soft, here feel them."

"Where are my normal clothes, Ingrid?"

"I think they got up and left in the night!" she laughed.

"Ha ah, very funny, I will look like a…"

"Real gentleman, and a handsome one at that, come on get ready the day is getting on and we want to visit this prison for women, it is important."

Ongar and Halla had indeed had to give in and bath on instruction from the king, he said that they would be travelling with him today in his carriage so they needed to look the part.

The lady's prison was about half an hour's drive by carriage through the cobbled streets of the capital. The building was three stories high and dominated the landscape, it was surrounded by a high whitewashed wall and there was only one way in and out and that was manned by many guards.

The carriage was halted at the gate while one of the guards looked it over, and while another went to fetch the governor. The king and everyone else were asked to leave the carriage once it had cleared the first set of gates, then it was parked up in In front of a second set of gates, and that is where the governor was waiting as everybody alighted the carriage.

"Your Majesty, may I say what a wonderful privilege it is to have you finally visit our establishment, and may I also say a big thank you to your good wife for her continued patronage, I dread to think where any of us would be without her love and generosity."

"Thank you, governor I will be sure, to pass your remarks along to my wife when I see her next, but in the meantime, we have come to ask you a few questions."

"Of course, Your Majesty, what is it that you would like to know?"

"Forgive me first of all, but my wife does not tell me everything that she does, especially if it is to do with spending my money!"

"Ah, well I wouldn't want to get anyone in trouble, Majesty."

"No, no, of course not, whatever she is doing I am sure it is wonderful, now tell me all about it, please."

"Very well, your wife, the queen sponsors a program of repentance, to help all of the women of child baring age to clean themselves up and start their lives over new, and may I say to date she has saved over six hundred of the poor wretches, from just this establishment alone, praise be to God and your wonderful wife, she is a living saint, Your Majesty."

"How does this program work exactly governor, and can we speak to these women who have been helped?"

"Well, let me see, so as you know, any women who fall on hard times or who fall foul of the law are brought here while they await their sentencing, but before they go to court they are offered, through the generosity of your wife, to take part in a special program of repentance."

"Repentance, how?"

"If they are agreeable, then they are taken by boat upriver to a convent farm where the nuns are dedicated to helping them stay sober, regain their dignity from prostitution, and general reform from a life of crime, once they are cured, they are allowed to go freely back into the community."

"So, we can meet some of them, the ones who have been returned to the community?"

"No, no, no, it doesn't work like that, they are given a new name and identity so that nobody knows who they are, you see, they could be anyone and you wouldn't know."

"You said that they were taken to the river, to the docks I presume?"

"Yes, that is correct, once a week they are taken down to a warehouse and kept there until the boat comes to take them to their new life."

"What is the name of the convent?" inquired Sister Wenyid.

"How should I know, I keep the women here until the transport arrives, why don't you ask your wife, Your Majesty?"

"She is away visiting, er, family and she won't be back anytime soon."

"Ah, then you should try down at the docks, they took another wagon load first thing this morning, seven girls, they should still be at the warehouse."

The king's carriage was quickly turned around and the first set of gates opened to let them out, the docks were about another hour away.

"Which warehouse they're so many, how will we find them in time?"

"We will just be patient, and I think I know just the place, come follow me." Said Rogan.

The darkly lit rickety-looking business had a sign hanging over its doorway, it hung from a single wooden arm that stuck out from the wall and it swung gently in the breeze, the wooden sign read, the Swan Alehouse.

As the royal entourage entered through the front door the whole place fell silent, the stench and the smoke almost had the king convulsing and the dimness of the torch lights made it hard to see every nook and cranny. "Welcome to all you fine ladies and gentlemen!" shouted a voice from over at the bar. "Come in now don't be shy, what'll you have, find a seat and I will bring it over."

"Ingrid, take everyone over to that far corner and I will order the drinks. A jug each of your finest ale and a round of drinks for anyone who can help me with a small problem?"

Everyone erupted into laughter. "A small problem?" one person quipped. "Go see Rani, upstairs and the second door on the left, she's usually the best with small problems!"

The barmaid brought over a tray containing a jug of ale for each who was present when Aatu began to whine. "Can you also bring a jug for my dog and pour it in a bowl, he isn't too clever picking up these jugs on account of his paws."

Raucous laughter could be heard in the background, but from men winning games of dare or dice.

"Oh, and one more thing, please get everyone a drink of whatever they like," and with that, Rogan nodded to the king and he produced a leather pouch which he began taking coins, five silver shillings before Rogan nodded once more to say that was more than enough.

As the royal party sat and began to drink, a tall man with fair hair came over to the table. "What'll it be that you fine gentlemen are looking for?"

"Women of course, what else, but not the kind that is found here, we are looking for a group of them who usually spend the night in a warehouse around here."

"Give me a coin or two and wait here, I will ask around."

"I will give you a silver shilling now and another shilling if you really can find them for me."

The king nearly puked after the first jug of ale. "My God Rogan what on earth was that I just drank?"

"It's called ale, Your Highness."

"It tastes like horse pee!"

"So, it does, but horse pee doesn't give you that warm fuzzy glow after several jugs."

Shortly after the man had left, he returned holding a much smaller man by his collar.

"Good you are still 'ere!" he said through broken teeth. "This scoundrel has quite a tale to tell and it does include those women you are inquiring about, but first where's my money?"

"Here, how much is in it for me if he gets paid and I am the one with the story?"

The king opened his leather money pouch and pulled out a silver shilling for the tall man. "Here is the closure of our business, and go with our thanks."

Once the tall man had bitten the coin and was satisfied that it was real, he left them in peace.

Now the king reached into his leather pouch once more and this time he produced a gold coin, and the small man's face lit up. "Is that for me your lordships?" he asked greedily sizing the coin up.

"Only if the story you have to tell entertains us."

"Oh, it will I can assure you!"

The man never once took his eyes off the coin throughout the whole telling of his tale.

"Every week they bring those girls down to Pier three, there is a warehouse there called 'Bjorn's' or something like that, I cannot see so well so I think it's called that, anyway, at the dead of night when nobodies about a ship come in to dock, a ghost ship it is, as black as the night its self, black sails too."

"How do you know it is a ghost ship?"

"I was just getting to that part because when the crew appears as if from nowhere, they are skeletons!"

"Skeleton's, this man has had more to drink than all of us put together!"

"No, dear sweat ladies and gentlemen I have not had nearly enough to drink to witness that ship and then all those ladies they have taken to God only knows where." As he finished his tale, he crossed himself several times before falling silent.

"So, if you can just take us to this warehouse and leave us there and promise not to tell a single soul, this coin is yours, agreed?"

"Agreed!" and so the small man took the group to the warehouse and sure enough the girls that had been transported earlier that day were still there awaiting the events of this evening.

The king turned to the rest of the group and apologised to everyone for demanding they get dressed up instead of letting them bring their weapons and armour, if there were to be a fight they may have been served better in armour.

"We have a few hours until nightfall so I suggest a couple of us stay here on guard while the rest go back and retrieve the weapons and armour." Said the captain.

It was decided that the king, Ingrid, and Sister Wenyid go back and the rest would stay on stand guard. The king insisted on returning with the two women and would not take no for an answer, he wanted to know exactly what was going on and just how deep his wife was into all this.

The group pulled their chain mail shirts over the clothes they were wearing and put their weapons belts on around their wastes and then agreed to split into three groups of two, Aatu would always follow Rogan and then wait until the dead of night.

At some point in the darkness, Ongar signalled to Rogan, but Rogan had no idea what he was signalling about and so he decided to take the chance to sneak over to him to see what had got him so spooked.

"What is wrong Ongar?"

"Remain perfectly as you are Rogan, we are not alone."

"Not alone?"

"I caught movement out of the corner of my eye, on the rooftops, but when I stay as still as I can, I cannot see anything, but they are there I am sure of it, just be careful Rogan that we are not caught in a trap."

Rogan made his way back to Ingrid and Aatu, and he explained what Ongar had just said.

Aatu whined a low-key whining sound almost like a whistle, and he looked up at the rooftops just as though he not only understood what was just said, but like he could see what the others could not, Ingrid shivered visibly and Rogan put his arm around her gently and cuddled her. "Everything will be fine!" he said before taking his arm away and feeling the pommel of his sword.

The moon was high in the night sky and apart from the noise of wild animals scrapping about, nothing stirred, all of the women inside the warehouse must have long been asleep.

Then came the gentle sound of oars lightly being drawn back in the water and the occasional splash as they lifted and then dropped back down again, nothing could be seen on the water but every sense now said that something was. Then came the rustle of wind on canvas and the sudden bump as though something wooden had banged against the docking wharf.

As if like magic, out of nowhere they came, dancing and weaving about each other, but without making a single sound, skeletons and lots of them, Rogan counted over twenty, possibly less but they kept up this routine of dancing in and out of one another so it was hard to keep track. They slowly weaved their way over to the warehouse and went inside. Whatever they were doing, they made no sound doing it, nor did the women inside all was deadly silent.

The first of the girls came outside with a brown sack over her head and two ghosts guided her to their transport, then another, and another until all the women were out of the warehouse.

It was now or never and so Rogan raised himself from his hiding place and leaped out to face the ghosts, and Aatu bounded towards the first one who had stopped and realised what was happening, Aatu barged the ghost to the floor and sank his teeth into it, Rogan began a sword fight with another, then the others revealed themselves and some of the ghosts began to turn back to help their ghostly comrades.

One after the other they came out of nowhere five, ten, fifteen, twenty, twenty-five, ghosts encircled the group of six and Aatu. This was suddenly a fight that Rogan and his friends would not win, Captain Brecott took a cut to his right arm, Ingrid a cut to her left leg all the time the circle of ghosts began to tighten around them. Aatu brought the first ghost down and took him out of the fight with aplomb, Ongar caught another who had defended himself against a sword slash but Ongar then smashed him with a left hook knocking it straight down, and then from out of the shadows and high up in the night sky came the first of a volley of arrows, each arrow finding its target and taking it down, a second volley took out another group of ghosts and finally Rogan and his group took care of the rest. "don't kill them all keep one or two alive we need information!" cried Rogan.

Two of the ghosts were kept alive each with a blade held against their throat, and out of the shadows came yet more figures, these held bows in their hands, intricately carved bows, and each wore a cape of green that when stood still it made them as though they were invisible. One of the green-cloaked figures stepped forward and pulled back the cowl from her face, a radiant face that somehow managed to glow in the darkness. "Hello Rogan Ragisson, my name is Aylild and I am an elven ranger from a realm known to man as Avanore, I, we are here to offer our services to you in your fight against the Orsk, and we are privileged to have already begun our quest."

On closer inspection, the ghosts turned out to be men, men with white painted heads and hands, wearing black robes with bones arranged on the fronts taken presumably from corpses. The boat was indeed painted black, everything was black and they had rigged a sail cloth which was also black up the side of the boat so that anyone walking behind it would appear to disappear completely. The two men said that they were paid to sail upriver with the girls to a place in Fōrren, where the girls would be taken away in closed wagons and the sailors would all be paid handsomely.

Rogan needed to be on the boat and time was now against them if they wanted to arrive on time where the girls were offloaded, and so he bade the king farewell. He then turned to his most trusted companions and asked them to stay behind with the king and make sure he gets back to the palace safely, he asked the company of elves if they would come with him on the boat and help see his plan through to the end, and they agreed.

"As soon as you can be on the road to Kaldakinn, we are long overdue and they will all be wondering what has happened to us, tell them, and do not worry I will see you all shortly, with that the two prisoners were cajoled into casting off."

The members of the crew who manned the boat oars were oblivious to what was going on until Rogan came aboard with the elves, there was nothing they could have done, each one had an elven archer with an arrow pointing at them, so they sat impassively for the time being.

Rogan stood on the side of the boat near the stern as that was how the oarsmen were facing. "As I see it, you men have two choices work for me or die now and be thrown overboard, which is it to be?"

Nobody spoke for the moment but they all looked towards the two prisoners who were dressed in the skeleton attire. "How does one gold coin apiece sound to buy your services?"

Suddenly all the eight-man crew wanted to pledge his allegiance, and they began to row as was requested. Aylild approached Rogan with another elf at her side. "This is the leader of our expedition to find you, Rogan, may I introduce Ranger Wyrran Neribrlla." Wyrran bowed slightly and held out his hand, Rogan thrust his hand forward and gripped the young elves' forearm as was his custom, the elf was a little taken aback but after looking at Aylild for understanding they both laughed.

Aylild was fascinated by Rogan and stayed by his side while the boat was rowed upriver towards its, as yet, unknown destination. Rogan was by this time feeling the electric atmosphere of being in Aylild's company, they seemed to be drawn together inextricably.

Aylild moved closer to Rogan and asked if she could touch his face, Rogan's head began to spin at this point and his heart was thumping in his chest like it wanted to burst out, but he was being driven by a mixture of want and desire, he could not refuse the request and so the elf reached up to his left temple, placing her hand so gently that he wasn't even sure if she was touching him or this was part of some crazy dream.

That is when he heard Aylild speak, she said "it is all right Rogan, just let yourself drift with the current," but Rogan was looking wide-eyed at the elf and although he could hear her voice, soft like the rays of the sun, he could quite clearly see that her mouth was closed and she most definitely was not speaking.

"I think I know what the problem is."

"Problem, what do you mean, problem?"

"How can you be true to yourself when you don't even know who you are?"

"I am Rogan Ragisson! Of course, I know who I am."

"You are not Rogan or Ro-Gan, but your real name is Arathorn and Ragisson, well that is a stupid name, which was made up for you!"

"Arathorn? Where did you get that from?"

"It is the name given to you at birth, that is who you are in the eyes of Aru, and that is why when I use this other false name nothing is happening, either that or you are just to…"

"Do not even think it! I have had quite enough of people presuming that I am not all there."

"Okay, we try again, Arathorn…"

Did he just blink or were his eyelids just too heavy that they closed by themselves?

"Open up your mind, Arathorn, let yourself bathe in the glow of Aru."

Her voice was so hypnotic, Rogan/Arathorn, began to let his mind go…and feelings, strange and wonderous feelings, began to flow through his body and his mind, the sensation of standing in a windstorm with his arms outstretched and feeling the rain beating down on your face, but at the same time feeling warm and safe and secure.

Then the images in his mind, at first confusing but after a while reassuring and then they were intoxicating, the warmth became passion and heat, his heart began to race and his head to spin, he imagined himself entwined with Aylild, he could smell cardamom, olive oil, and cinnamon, but it was the same perfume that Ingrid wore, it was strong, spicy, and faintly musky, and then the image of Atylid and he together.

Whirling around and around, both were naked and he saw that Aylild was stunningly beautiful he could feel every nerve, every muscle, every sinew, in his body suddenly blazed into life, it was the most incredible feeling, and he felt right there and then, that he did not ever want this feeling to stop, love and lust laid bare, becoming raw emotion mixing into a myriad of different coloured lights, feelings, and sensations.

Aylild's words began to drift back into Arathorn/Rogan's mind again and the image of them wrapped in the warmth of each other's bodies was beginning to change, and Rogan felt that they were tumbling downwards and it made him hold on to Aylild that much tighter. Suddenly there was a huge splash, it felt like they had both fallen into deep water, and Arathorn/Rogan was very aware of the dangers if they kept on sinking, his lips met hers and they kissed passionately almost as though they were desperately trying to steal each other's breath to stay alive.

"Arathorn," it was Aylild's wispy voice again, "Arathorn, let yourself breathe." But Arathorn/Rogan didn't want to breathe he just wanted to stay connected, his lips on hers, but she began to sound louder in his head, "Breathe, Arathorn, you must let go, and breathe." And so, he finally pulled a little way from her, and as quickly as he did, he felt like the water had just whooshed away and they were back on the deck of the boat and it was the early hours of the morning and they were stood staring at each other.

"Arathorn, I want you to slowly open your eyes," she said.

"But my eyes are open, open so I can still see you standing there in front of me!"

"Arathorn you are speaking to me through your mind, your eyes are tightly shut."

"Eh?"

"It is called 'Emyfa Ancalen' it is something an elven mother does with her newborn baby, a bonding of the minds, that way I think some of the images are easier to deal with the first time, just think if it were Wyrran who first did this with you and not I!"

"Okay, that is an image I never want to see, no disrespect intended!"

"You are funny Arathorn, do you understand now, that from birth and sometimes even before birth elves can connect minds, to be able to sense and speak over great distances."

"Oh god did I see you naked, I am so sorry, I just don't know why I would do that, I mean, oh…!"

Aylild laughed. "It is perfectly normal, we each see what we want to see but there is no hiding place in Ělyāh, before Ělyāh we are all naked, and I do not think that I have anything other girls don't have, look! We are all Ělyāh's little children, and you just don't know how to control that 'sight' yet."

Then she spoke with her mind once more, "There are many different types of love, for us it is 'Nhamashal' or Familiar Love, however, Ělyāh reveals in you Tarathiel or Selfless Love, it is an unconditional love, so much bigger than ourselves, a boundless compassion, an infinite empathy. It is the purest form of love that is free from desires and expectations and loves regardless of the flaws and shortcomings of others."

"Getting back to something you said earlier, 'Emyfa Ancalen', as you call it?"

"Yes, the ability to tap into Ělyāh's spirit force."

"Surely then aren't I supposed to be an elf, I mean not just anybody can do this, right?"

"Your mother was an elf but your father was human, so you have the ability, you just did not know until now. Have you ever had dreams that seem so real at the time, but when you reach out to them, they disappear?"

"I do, yes, but over the years I have just taught myself to let them go, they are just dreams and therefore not real, you mentioned my mother, how could you possibly know anything about her or my father, if you had not met me before, that is?"

"I have never met your father, I have, however, met your mother, many times, and I knew who you were because I was sent to meet you, to offer our help, the elves of Avanore, Arathorn, and my hope now is that you to will get to meet your mother to be able to bond and to get to know your people, but all of that is for the future."

"But I thought for sure she must be dead, I remember being left as a foundling with the church, I just assumed she had died and my father too?"

"We elves do not conform to the natural lore like other races, even in death we are born again into the light of Your Ĕlyāh, in the land of the undying, which some of your kind call heaven, and we keep our memories, unlike humans and other races who when they fall asleep in death and pass into the memory of Ĕlyāh, until the day of the great re-awakening here on earth, until then just be content that, yes, you have a mother and a father and that they are both, although not together, alive."

"Oh boy this is so much to take in, before today my life was that much simpler, now I have a mother and, a father too, and they are both alive, and I have a different name, and I have Ingrid, whom I think I have always loved since the first time I met her, and now you whom I feel such love for, this is so, so complicated!"

"You love Ingrid, and me differently, it is hard at first especially when you have not been taught our ways, but that is what I am here to do, that is what family is for, for when life gets complicated."

"Wait, what, did you just call us family?"

"Yes, I am your sister, well half-sister!"

"How can that be for a start off you are like thirteen years old, I am sixteen, urgh! This is making my head hurt, honestly."

"Our mother is the same mother, but you and I have different fathers, yours is human and mine is elven."

"Well, I am just glad that you at least got to grow up in a beautiful environment with parents who loved and cherished you, and you look so delicate, like a blossom that has just opened."

"Hmm, I can see why this Ingrid loves you, do you talk this way with all the girls?"

"Now you are teasing me, I...I can sense a shift in "You can detect now when I am telling the truth and when I play, this is good, so soon."

"Why don't I have memories from all those years then, all I have are broken fragments."

"That is easy to explain, they were changed, your memories, your true memories were altered so that you would literary wake up one morning and 'poof'!—all your memories of the life you should have had, are gone."

"Who would do such a terrible thing, and why?"

"The why is much easier to explain, why? Because you were the product of a forbidden union, a coupling of an Elven princess and a human prince, and it was out of wedlock which is a very grave sin in the eyes of Ělyāh, just like when you coupled with Ingrid for the first time, last night, was it."

"What! How do you know about Ingrid and myself, were you spying on me?"

"No silly, you revealed it to me when we engaged in Emyfa Ancalen, together, you saw me naked because you were looking into my mind, but when I was looking inside of yours, I saw Ingrid."

"All right, I will buy what you say if you promise never to mention the naked thing again, and that thing we did, Emyfa Ancalen!"

Aylild laughed again and again. "No but seriously, you and Ingrid must now be as one in the eyes of Ělyāh, he does not approve of fornication, be warned, or be cut off!"

"Cut off, from what?"

"From his spirit force, his blessing, and trust me, when I say that the path you have chosen for yourself, you will need all the blessings you can get, now enough of this talk we are nearly there, I can feel it amongst the men, they are getting apprehensive."

"Okay, but just one more thing Aylild, you mustn't call me Arathorn, my people do not even know about the half-elf thing, they might not understand, so please, from now on, my name has to be Rogan."

Men began shouting from the left bank of the river Tawa, "Brinleaf, is that you?"

One of the men in the boat shouted back that Brinleaf was not here but all the new girls were aboard as they should be. Brinleaf was one of the men who were killed on the dockside.

Rogan had all the elves hidden around the inside of the boat, their elven clothes rendered them practically invisible provided they stayed still, because the boat was made from natural material.

A couple of men got up from where they were sat on the rowing seats and through mooring lines over to the men on the river bank, they pulled the boat in and then secured the ropes with large wooden pegs, then some more men came aboard to take raise the women from their seats, each still had the sack covering their heads, Rogan had decided to leave them covered as he didn't want any further complications, and it also had the effect of keeping those who were aiding and abetting their abduction more compliant if the women could not later identify them.

Once the women were taken from the boat they were guided into another covered wagon, and once they were safely locked inside a man came forward to ask if Brinleaf wasn't onboard then who should he give the coin to in payment for the women.

Rogan recognised the man from Ingolfsfell but he was not sure about how or why, so he motioned from the concealment of the stern for one of the other men to take the payment.

Soon the mooring ropes were being thrown back aboard the boat and it was attempting to turn around on the river to head back the way it had come; Rogan watched the wagon pull away and the men who he had seen disappear back into the shadows.

After the boat had gone a little way back down river, Rogan called for it to pull into the side of the river that the women had been taken from, within moments of the side of the boat touching the right bank, every elf, Aatu, and Rogan was over the side on back on dry land. Rogan waved to the crew and told them to go back to where they had come from, one of them asked what they should do with all the money they had just been paid, it was enough for thirty men and now there were less than ten aboard, Rogan waived his hand at the man and said, "Keep it! Share it out equally, and do something right with it," then he waived them to leave.

Now it was very well known that Orsk could run for long periods at a greater speed than man, but if Rogan was impressed by their stamina he was in for a pleasant surprise because these elven rangers could run and track far, far greater, so much so that even he had trouble keeping up with them all, and he was not helped by the shimmering cloaks that they wore, as they kept making them visible, then in visible every few seconds apart.

Once the lead ranger, Wyrran Neribrlla had picked up the scent of the human traffickers he quickened the pace, and before the sun was up to signal the start of a new day, they had them firmly in their sights. "How do want to play this, Rogan?" asked Aylild.

"Let's see where they take the women, I don't want them to take them as far as the orsk but I do want to find out who is involved, and that man over there the one who looks like he is in charge, I know him from somewhere but where I just can't remember."

"He is very well dressed; his clothing looks like the same material as you are wearing under your mail shirt."

"That is, it! I did not recognise him because he met our group on the road to Ingolfsfell and he was wearing clothes like a common traveller when I saw him again, he was in a side room at the palace waiting to see the jarl, it did not click because he was dressed in fine clothes by that time too, and I only caught a fleeting glimpse of him, Tostig, that's his name, but who is he?"

"Someone with money to dress that finely out here in the middle of nowhere."

"They look like they are camping here for the night, perhaps we should post guards and get some sleep too, Aylild."

Just before dawn, a cold misty fog was laying across the sunken embankment Rogan had chosen as their camp, and it had caused his clothes to be damp. "what would I give for a nice warm fire right now, perhaps with a slow roasting bird and a jug of warm mead."

"Rogan," somebody whispered, from the heart of the concealing fog.

"Ahshala, what is it?" Aylild asked in a low voice.

"Somebody new has arrived at the enemy's camp."

"What happened after they arrived?"

"They approached the man that you say you recognised and called him Prince Saeweard, after which they went inside his tent to talk about a meeting tonight with the 'half-bloods'."

"So, Tostig is the King of Fōrren's son, and I have recently sent men to Fōrren to ask for an alliance, I have asked that he can support our attack on the last Orsk realm in the Shattered Kingdoms, and I don't know what answer he gave, yet, but if he is part of this whole set up then he cannot be trusted, if he was at the court of Jarl Sigfusson, then can I even trust him, either?"

"Do you know where we are Rogan?"

"We are somewhere near the top of Fōrren at the side of the river Tawa, why do you ask?"

"Perhaps it is time to take the women back and then make our way back to your village and your men."

"This is the last stop before the women are traded with the Orsk, then so be it these men have sealed their fate, let us surround the camp and take them all out as quietly as we can."

The fog made it very difficult to see more than a few feet in front of your face, but Aylild said that by projecting himself, or imagining what was in front of him his mind's eye could tap into Aru's active force and see beyond what is actual eyes could, but every time he tried it he just got little glimpses and then a thump in his head that was unpleasant to say the least, Aylild said that it would be another thing to work on when they have time.

After about fifteen minutes, the elves came within striking distance of the camp, but they were too late to catch the prince, he was just leaving on horseback as they started to fan out and surround the camp.

Once in place, Aylild placed her right hand on the right side of her face and called out to each of the other elves, it was time to attack, so each elf picked a target and loosed an arrow, within seconds all the men lay dead and the elves and Rogan were up and running towards the wagon where the women were locked up.

Once the women were out of the wagon the elves took off their hoods so that they could see what was going on, Rogan said that it would be a shame to waste the campfire as the men had been cooking hot food, so Rogan told the women to feed themselves and then to collect whatever they could from the bodies, but especially to be sure to take all the weapons.

While they ate their food, Rogan explained everything to them and of course, they had no idea they were both shocked, but also very grateful to have been freed.

Rogan's plan now was to get them back to Kaldakinn before anyone came back to the camp, so after packing all that they could, Rogan and the twelve elves and thirty women began their trek across the river Tawa and into Råvenniå.

Around midday Rogan realised that they were to the west of the great forest, which meant that within a couple of hours, they could reach Hundsnes, and from there, Kaldakinn. The elves spread themselves out wide in the shape of an arrowhead, just ahead of the group, this part of the country was relatively flat and open and they kept their keen senses of sight and sound alert until they reached the outer edge of the forest.

Another hour passed and they could hear the distant voices of everyday life in Hundsnes and a further half of an hour saw them being waved through the gates of the village.

Shortly thereafter Gufi was striding towards his old friend and embracing him tightly. "My dear friend and ally, Rogan Ragisson, welcome, welcome, welcome, you are a sight for sore eyes, come to the great hall and bring your friends, not more refugees I hope?"

"You know me, Gufi, I can't go anywhere without bringing something back!"

At the great hall, Gufi began recalling all the events since Brother Cuthbald's last visit, and he told of the large shanty town that was growing bigger every day outside the southern walls of the village, but he also said that Rogan should start for Kaldakinn as soon as possible and make all Gods haste to get there as things were as dire as they had ever been, looking at the state of the thirsty women he even offered them a haven here in his village so they wouldn't slow Rogan down.

Gufi offered to furnish Rogan and each of the elves with fast horses and they agreed that after the long run they had taken to reach this point that it might make more sense if they travelled the rest of the way on horseback.

Later that night Rogan and the elves arrived at the gates of Kaldakinn and Rogan sighed a little and said that it was good to be back home. Once inside they made their way to the great hall and once there set about sending out servants to call all those in his confidence to an emergency meeting of the council.

Ingrid was the first to arrive, she had arrived the previous morning along with Ongar, Halla, Sister Wenyid, and Captain Brecott, they had stayed in the manor house to discuss what to do next, but knowing that Rogan was back it became a moot point at least for the time being.

Next through the door was Renwick, followed by Gunnar, Atli, Sigrunn and Aethelric, and finally Brother Cuthbald. Both parties took most of the night to tell their stories and it was almost dawn before everything that needed to be said was, Rogan asked if the bishop was leading the outsiders up to the northern place where they were to build a new town, and Brother Cuthbald delightedly said that he was and he had taken, 'Jarl' Oswald with them, in fact barely anyone was left outside the southern gate, even the women and children joined the procession, all with bulging purses from Kaldakinn's coffers.

As Brother Cuthbald eagerly stated the only road in or out of the new town is being constructed out from Kaldakinn, so any supplies they will need they will come back here to buy using the money they were paid to clear off in the first place, Brother Cuthbald said finally what goes around comes around, and he laughed at his joke, and he was the only one, as none of the others quite understood it.

"Everyone, get some sleep, for tomorrow we have a war to plan," Rogan said wearily.

That night Rogan had a vivid dream, he saw a figure dressed in black with a white-grey beard and hair to match, he saw lightning strikes and an elf of great age, whose face was lined with worry, a beautiful elven princess, and a young prince who loved her and he saw a great battle, a battle to end all battles.

Then a voice interrupted his dreams, it was the old elf, and a name that sounded alongside him as a whisper, Ascarli, and then as though a hand had touched his brow he woke up, and Ingrid was telling him he had a fever and was talking in his sleep, but he did not have a fever, it was the manic nature of the dream that had made him this way.

The following morning the servants were up early setting the hearth fires and the servants were preparing the food for the start of the day when a guard came knocking vigorously on the door of the manor house.

"Who calls at this ungodly hour, make known yourself, immediately," the head servant demanded.

"I am Karri from the northern gate, a messenger arrived from the new town moments ago with urgent news for the chieftain."

Rogan was taken over to the great hall by Karri and there scoffing food like he had not eaten in days was a man who looked like a vagabond. "I was told that you had come through the night from the new town and that you had important news for me, well here I am, so tell me!"

"Lord, lord, we found a boat drifting in the mouth of the River Tawa, it was the boat that was stolen from Kaldakinn weeks ago by those men who went to attack the Orsk and who hoped to steal their treasure, well four of them survived and we picked them up and brought them back to the town, Bishop d'Athenous dispatched me instantly with a very important message lord, the Orsk have built defences, massive defences right across the base of the mountain, as far as the eye could see and beyond, they have a high wall and a tar-filled ditch making it impassable for an army."

"Stay and eat and get refreshed, here take these coins for your trouble and then go back to the bishop and tell him that in the spring we will have assembled the biggest army the world has ever seen, and we will have our victory if we have to take that whole mountain down one stone at a time!"

The news came as a blow to Rogan who had not given thought to the Orsk being that clever or coordinated, and he thought to himself that human involvement was the only reason, so information was still getting through but where there is a will there is a way, he thought before heading off over to see Brother Cuthbald, who had asked him over early to meet a new friend.

After first meeting, the two captains Henri Damours and Bernardin Faucon, Rogan was taken down the stone steps and into the church's undercroft, and it was there that he set eyes on his first ever Troglodyte, who was called Tukor.

Tukor had learned a basic greeting in Ingolandic and Rogan was impressed but spoke in return in the language of the orsk, not because he particularly wanted to have a private conversation, but so that whatever was about to be said would be heard and understood clearly.

As it transpired, Tukor was the son of the old Orsk shaman, Berba-Shin, his father was a human who was once a captive in the tunnels, she had taken advantage of him, many times until she became pregnant, when the other Orsk heard about what she had done they killed the human and they held Berba-Shin down and forced her cruelly to drink poisons to kill the baby.

However, she took remedies to counter the things she had been forced to drink, eventually, Tukor was born and raised in secret. He was discovered eventually and banished, and that is when he found Rogan's group one night and tried to follow them across Obreā, but his tale does not end here, for he looked Rogan in the eye and smiled. "There are so many tunnels under the mountain outside of the Orsk defences and I know every one of them I have the map in my head," he said.

4

A Woman Scorned

Queen Helga Arnbjorg was up earlier than her husband, they lived separate lives, having separate bedrooms but she knew that he would look in on her at some point, so had told her servants that she was going to the city's cathedral for her weekly confession and that she would be back sometime later that morning.

The queen was wrapped up warm in a fine fox-skin coat and underneath wore one of her favourite gowns; today, she told herself, was going to be a good day, despite her husband's meddling and the appearance of that rabble, he still had not had her arrested, not that she believed she should have been, she was misunderstood, that was all.

Her work was of benefit to the kingdom, think of all those unfortunate wretches who once sullied the streets, offering their bodies for a single coin, had they no shame! The queen thought to herself. *I am providing a public service.* She declared to her reflection as she stood admiring what she saw, and as time went on, she felt for sure her husband, the king, would see things her way, he always did in the end, oh, he would find some little way to punish her to make his point but it would not amount to much, and that gave her cause to smile. "There, how is one expected to improve on perfection?"

The cathedral at the heart of Østergård, the capital of Råvenniå, was the most magnificent building in all the kingdom, on the inside it was nothing more than an oblong with many stained-glass windows, and painted vaulted ceilings depicting the creation of humankind and the fall from grace of the angels who disobeyed God's word and tried to create humanoids in their image.

On the outside, the cathedral had ten brilliant white chiselled columns out front that went as high as the first floor, then on the second floor, there were only eight windows and a single door that came out onto a balcony.

Down each side, there were another twelve columns and around the rear, there were yet ten more. In the centre of the building was a single huge dome with a much small dome on top of that, then in each of its four corners there were four smaller domes, and the whole building was carved from white marble blocks.

Queen Helga glided through the main entrance, dismissing her guard as she passed through the ornate oak doors. The building was empty but for a couple of people who were busying themselves with the work of keeping the huge place clean and tidy.

The queen glided her way over to the confessional booths which were situated down the left-hand side of the inside wall, she waved to her audience of well-wishers who existed at this precise moment, only in her imagination.

Inside the building in one of its many sectioned-off areas out of the view of the public, there was singing and in others, there was just the squeak of sandals on highly waxed floors, Helga nodded to one minister after another until she had reached her destination, and as she gripped the mahogany door handle, she felt a knot inside her stomach, and she hesitated. A crisis of confidence, or a voice from above, was this the last roll of the dice for her, her biggest gamble?

She swallowed hard, patted down her gown, fussing over bits of lint before turning the handle of the door to the little booth, it protested at being opened and gave out a squeak in mock resistance to her action. The priest was already sitting in the other booth behind a patterned screen. "Forgive me Father for I have sinned."

"Oh, my dear child, tell me how have you sinned?" said the familiar voice, barely able to contain his smile.

"I have fornicated with another man, and I have plotted with that man against my lawful husband, and together my lover and I have converted his crown, his palace, his land, and his whole country, what do you have to say to me, Father?"

"Well, you have been a busy girl, that is for sure, but tell me did you enjoy the pleasures of the flesh or have you come here to denounce your lover?"

"No, I have not come here to denounce my lover, I have come to say I want more!"

"Then what are you waiting for, I am here in the next booth!" It was the mercenary Skuld Stormshield.

After a length of time had gone past and the two lovers had, had their fill, there was a knock on the booth's door from the outside.

"Go away I'm in confession!" shouted the queen.

"My lady, it is I, Archbishop Honorius and I am here with your bodyguard, members of the king's royal army, and I must inform you of your discretion, madame!"

"Discretion! You dare to talk to the queen in that way?"

"I dare my lady because I fear your 'confession' is so loud that the whole of the interior of this fine building can hear you."

The queen laughed at first and Skuld just frowned, he was in a pickle of that there was no denying it.

The archbishop demanded that both the queen and her confessor come outside immediately.

"I shall emerge once I have finished my good man, now run along and do whatever it is that Arch-bishops do!"

"I cannot my lady because it has been brought to my attention that your confessor was seen leaving his booth to join you in yours, which is highly irregular."

"It may well be highly irregular, but I can tell you it is very satisfying!" the queen exulted churlishly.

"My lady, I will not ask again, present yourself and your co-conspirator for arrest on the charge of adultery and fornication in the sacred house of God and against His Majesty, Hamund Arnbjorg, the king."

The queen put her forefinger to her lips and smiled at Skuld.

The archbishop did not wait for a reply or the sound of movement from within, he instead continued with his diatribe. "You will be taken from this holy house of God, and stripped of your clothes and tied to a stake in the square outside, so that everyone may look on your shame!"

Skuld could take no more. "Hey! Hey! Out there I do not want anything to do with this, okay, I didn't know she was the queen, I'm going to ease the door open now…"

As Skuld placed the palm of his left hand on the inside of the door and reach for the lock with his right, Queen Helga screamed at the top of her voice and kicked the door open. Everyone was caught by surprise and paralysed with shock. Helga used that moment of sheer confusion to lung at the archbishop.

Through gritted teeth she propelled herself forward hands outstretched, stopping only when her outstretched fingers reached the man of God's face. "What are you doing, Your Highness?" the archbishop blurted out in astonishment. However, that moment turned into searing pain as the queen raked her fingernails down either side of his rotund face.

Tears mixed with blood as he recoiled in horror squealing like a wild bird caught in a trap. Skuld slouched back inside the small box, dumbfounded while he watched this drama play out before his eyes, he wanted to laugh but it was not funny not anymore, and if he feared getting caught before might end with a flogging, the queen by her actions had now signed both their death warrants.

After the queen was restrained by the king's royal guard, and the archbishop had regained his composure, Skuld looked at him, head bowed with his eyes upwards in a manner not unlike a man possessed, what had he got to lose right now? He thought to himself before speaking slowly and deliberately; *who would like to be the first to meet their maker this day?*

The guards looked at each other and then at the archbishop and then at each other again.

"Do not just stand there gaping! Get him, there are four of you!" The others just watched while holding tightly onto the queen.

Skuld had drawn his short sword, called; a gladius, and now he too flew out of the stall and rammed his sword into the nearest of the guards, causing his guts to spill out as he withdrew it twisting and turning his hand as he did.

The second guard fell with a violent blow to the right side of his neck, almost severing his head from his shoulders, the mercenary was in full swing swinging and lashing with his blade much to the delight of the queen who stood transfixed with his magnificence.

The royal guards had not been trained to repel such a feral hand-to-hand combatant in such close quarters and the presence of royalty and the archbishop they simply crumbled in fear. Skuld sliced the third guard through his throat and the fourth down across his head from scalp to chin, after which the other four guards simply let go of the queen and looked to the archbishop for orders.

The archbishop was cemented to the spot with shock, he could not move a muscle, and between his legs flowed a yellowy liquid that caused his garment to steam as the wet patch spread across the stone-cut floor of his cathedral.

The queen scooped up one of the fallen guards' swords and slashed the archbishop this way and that across his face until it was just a bloody mass of torn flesh, exposed teeth, and bones, but still he did not move a muscle, it was if he had been petrified and turned to stone, even after one eye fell from his exposed skull.

Skuld had to kick him hard in the stomach to bring him down, and blood spilled out from his body in a great wide pool of crimson to mix with the yellow liquid, leaving the archbishop to gurgle and his blood bubble in his throat where words once formed.

The queen leaped upon his stricken corpse and continued to hack him into little pieces, covering herself from head to toe in his blood, the other guards now themselves in full flight for the main doors.

Outside, and unbeknown to them, a whole company of guards stood and waited, the king was running towards them now and so they waited for his arrival. That was when the cathedral doors were flung open and the four guards came flying out like the devil himself was chasing them.

The king arrived at the head of the guards standing outside and not knowing anything thing about what had happened inside he called to his soldiers; "Follow me!" he shouted and they came through the cathedral door four bodies wide, with swords in hand and shields raised out front to support one another.

That was when the queen played her final hand, reacting to this unfolding blood-soaked nightmare, she dropped her weapon and ran over to her husband sobbing her heart out, and threw herself down at his feet. "Mercy! Husband, I came here to repent in the eyes of God and was attacked by Skuld Stormshield, and he has slain all these people in the sacred house of God who sacrificed their own lives that I might live!"

In this moment of utter chaos and a sight beyond any comprehension, Skuld took hold of a wall-hanging torch, turned, and ran towards the back door of the Cathedral, slamming the torch through the looped handle on the outside in order to prevent anyone else from coming through that door.

The king seemed to take pity on his wife and appeared to shield her while he shouted at his guards to accost the outlaw who was fleeing through the rear of the cathedral, in all his days the king had never seen or heard anything like this, but his wife was covered from head to toe in blood and gruesomeness.

"Where is my guard husband?" she asked timidly.

"They are back at the palace my dear, you must have dismissed them when you arrived, do you not remember?"

"Send for them, I do not feel safe without them being here." The queen said meekly.

"One of you, fetch the queen's guard and be quick about it!"

The queen raised her eyes towards her husband. "Thank you, my husband, I love you, but I am so confused, did you catch my attacker?"

The king sent the rest of his guard around to the rear of the cathedral leaving only the four guards who had run from the building standing alongside both the king and queen. "What happened in there, do you know who the assassin was?" the king asked the four. They all looked at the queen who was still huddled at her husbands' feet, but now she was looking at them with an icy glare and smiling, it was a smile that dripped with malice.

"Er, no, Your Highness, I don't think any of us recognised him." Said one of them.

The awkwardness continued until a unit of the queens feared black guard arrived, twenty soldiers covered from head to toe in black leather undergarments, augmented by plate armour layered over the top, every one of them standing no less than six feet tall.

The queen's demeanour changed the moment the unit formed up behind the king and herself.

"Nonsense, didn't I hear your sergeant shout the mercenary's name?" the queen offered.

"Please my lady if you heard his name, it might remind us…" one of the king's guards offered feebly.

"Skuld Stormshield, that was the name I heard!" announced the queen seeming to have perked up enough to raise herself to stand alongside her husband.

"Skuld Stormshield! Why do I know that name?"

Cough…"We er…we arrested him a few weeks ago robbing the queen's bedchamber, he…he escaped jail the following morning your Highness, he has a bounty out on his head, one hundred silver coins!"

"Make it one thousand!" decried the king.

The following day a message arrived from the cathedral, bishop Kenelm had been appointed acting archbishop, and he wanted a public display of repentance for the queen's involvement in the debacle that took place the day before. "Why though, husband, I've told you that I wasn't involved, that mercenary lay in wait and surprised all of us."

"Yes, my dear I know, and I believe you, truly I do, but you know the church, and yesterday they had a lot of blood to clean up, so they want the people to see someone suffer as a consequence, it's just the way it is."

"Then you do it!" the queen petulantly scolded her husband.

"You know that if I could, I would, but it doesn't work like that…"

"It doesn't work like that!" the queen mimicked her husband in a child's voice. "Well, it should it should work whichever way you want it to, you are the king, not the church!"

"Word has got out…"

"You mean those four guards have blabbed in the taverns?"

"I don't know…"

"Your precious royal guard, whose loyalty is to the bottom of an empty flagon, I hope you have all four of them up on a charge!"

Later that same morning the queen dressed only in a simple white sackcloth gown, with her hair hanging unbrushed and without any makeup or jewellery was forced to crawl on her hands and knees, before the whole of the capital in front of hundreds who turned out to witness her act of absolution, it was only a couple of hundred yards from the palace to the cathedral but the streets were packed.

The king was cheered loudly when first he arrived on the steps of the royal palace, but when his wife arrived at his side the cheers soon turned to gears. People shouted abuse at her and scoffed, scorned, and even cursed her, others had brought rotten fruit and vegetables and threw them at her as she crawled, without let up, without mercy.

By the end of her slow and painful journey, her body was blooded, battered, and bruised but she had endured, survived, and from her prone position on all fours she looked up at the crowd through her one open eye, the other having closed over through being bruised and swollen, she vowed revenge, secretly and to herself through gritted teeth, *they would all pay, from the king right down to the poorest peasant, they would pay.*

The king ignored the belligerent crowd and all of the cat-calling for the queen to endure still more hardships and punishments, she had been absolved in his eyes. However, the surviving clergy, in the form of the new Arch-bishoped demanded that the queen be banished to the cathedral to live out the rest of her days away from the public's glare, as she crawled up to his feet and was supposed to kiss them both.

Archbishop Kenelm called for her to be made mother superior of the cathedral, where she would be locked away in a part of the building reserved for nuns who service the needs of the male clergy until they are deemed unfit to serve any longer and are then farmed out to distant nunneries never to be heard from again.

In the days that followed the queen being taken into the cathedral's custardy, the king demanded that the queen's bodyguard, the five hundred-strong black guard were to march out of the capital city, and back to where ever they had come from, and the queen, at the tip of a sword, swore that they would do just so.

However, as the people gathered once more to watch this final act of atonement from the queen, they realise the true nature of her treachery. The black guards marched first into the centre of the city outside of the cathedral, in column formation, there they halted.

The units of soldiers still loyal to the king and all the hundreds of other onlookers gasped to witness such a precision military operation, once they had deployed in formation, they stood to attention silently. The queen was wheeled outside for what was to have been one last public appearance, and she took the opportunity to shout what was a command.

The command was spoken in a language that no one present recognised, except for the black guard. Suddenly those soldiers split into hundreds of sections, leaving perfect rows, north to south, east to west, between them all.

The queen shouted another single word in the same tongue as before and the sections now turned to face four different directions, north, south, east, and west. Then a second solitary command and the sections marched in perfect timing, one to the north gate of the city, one to the south gate, one to the east gate, and finally one to the west gate, one hundred and twenty-five of the most highly trainer soldiers in each section then attacked the king's men at each of the gates and within minutes they had taken control of the city, closing the gates to the outside world.

The kings' men attacked, wave after wave but they could not dislodge the black guard from the gate towers or the surrounding walls, the city was fast succumbing to a vice-like lockdown, and the bodies of the fallen littered the streets. One final order was given by the queen, to the black guard, they were to send a dispatch rider to each of the other black guard units spread around the country, they were to repeat what has happened in the capital until the whole country had been brought to heel.

Some days later Skuld turned up in Ingolfsfell, there he ran straight into the waiting arms of his dear mother, Matilda Steinolf. Matilda ever the schemer could not believe her luck, if she could somehow engineer her son to take control of the thousands of people who were gathering outside of Kaldakinn, then she could destroy Rogan Ragisson once and for all.

Matilda did not even want to hear any of her son's tales of woe, she was already sure that whatever this was, it was all a giant misunderstanding and that it could all be sorted out in the fullness of time, she was after all close friends of the queen, Helga Arnbjorg.

Neither Matilda nor her husband the sheriff, knew that the three thousand inhabitants outside the northern gate at Kaldakinn, whom the queen and her had worked tirelessly to put there through their misinformation, lies, and with their vast fortune spent, were no longer there.

The thousands had been bought and paid for by Rogan's gold and a dream of something so magnificent their names would be written in the Book of Life, a new scroll that was being written in heaven at this very moment, but for a few old men and women, either too elderly and infirm to move again, there was nothing left of the camp outside Kaldakinn it had been abandoned.

Skuld bought into his mother's plan and went out into the city to round up some of her most trusted men along with Scoppi, Arnvid, and Guthorm, and later that day they rode out of the town of Ingolfsfell heading for Kaldakinn.

Skuld, feeling like a new man, the sun was nowhere to be seen in the sky it looked gloomy and overcast as though all it promised was rain, however, the rain if it ever was there, never actually fell, it made him feel like a God. Maybe, he thought he had somehow taken the soul of the murdered archbishop.

Skuld from now on would look out for the small things in life as pointers from above, that this was his mission, that the war against the Orsk would never take place. He did not think it was too arrogant of him to demand success either, for if this war was to take place, then, all the Orsk that would be killed, an entire race, and that did not figure in the queen's grand design or his mothers.

The Orsk, was a creation of God, or else why were they even allowed to live in the first place, it was his God-given duty to help them survive, and he had supplied them with all the information that they needed to build the fortifications, he had supplied them with countless thousands of women and children over the last few years to build the most impregnable army, women who were the scum of the earth, whose worthless presence only added to the burden of others, and their screaming, squaring brats whom themselves were destined to become the burdens of the future.

Skuld, after preventing the war would, of course, return to the capital as a conquering hero, who, through his wisdom, saved so much sorrow and heartache, think of the mothers whose sons then would not after being sacrificed to the Gods of war, who were the ones provoking a fight, it was not the Orsk, they were completely happy with the arrangement, no, it was Rogan Ragisson and his merry band of muckrakers.

Everywhere that cretinous man went, his talk was of war, and to what end, was it because he truly loved the people and wanted to rescue those poor filthy louse-ridden bitches, no Rogan just wanted the glory, and the power that came with such things. Strangely enough, Skuld supposed he could understand Rogan, power can be a seductive mistress.

The journey took a full twelve hours before Skuld and his mercenary band arrived on the outskirts of Kaldakinn, where the ground they were on rose above the land around them, Scoppi noticed something that made him look twice. "Lord Skuld, look over yonder, the fields with which we are to find our army are empty!"

Skuld was not pleased with the interruption to his daydream. "Scoppi what are you whining about you are like an old hag sometimes?"

Arnvid raised himself a little in his saddle and craned his neck. "Lord, look he is telling the truth, they are not there!"

"Not there! Do not be ridiculous, bishop d'Athenous is firmly in my pocket, and that of the queen, we have promised him all the coin he would need to build a cathedral, Oswald Dansson is my sworn oath man, who has been paid handsomely, what do you mean, they are no longer there?"

"Well, if that's the case, then I think you had better be asking for a refund, Lord Skuld!" both Arnvid and Guthorm laughed, even Scoppi was struggling to keep a straight face, as he spoke.

"We must return to your mother, Skuld, she will know what to do, look around there is nothing here for us."

"No, no, no, no, no! We need to know exactly what happened before we go back."

"All right then Skuld, let's ask the gate guards and then get out of here."

The gate guards at first were not at all interested in conversing with the newcomers, but after a small financial incentive their tongues began to loosen, and they told them that the outsiders had all either been transported up north or were taken on carts and wagon to a place where they were to build a new town.

"Why?" asked Skuld.

"I don't know other than it has something to do with the impending war and that the place had to be constructed before the winter set in."

"I bet if it is in the far north, it is to be used as a staging post for Råvenniå's attack on the Orsk, and they need it to be finished before the offensive begins in the spring!" deliberated Scoppi Hranfast.

"I can tell you that everybody was paid for their work in advance, for a whole week the village was awash with coin, and there was the promise of more where that came from!" elaborated the guard.

"I heard tell that timber was paid for from Hundsnes, and stone from Langaholt, to build houses and a road that connects to the main road between here and Hundsnes." Added a second guard.

"Was it all Rogan Ragisson's idea, or did he have to put pressure on them to go?"

"Rogan wasn't even back then, it was more the Christian brother, Bryn Cuthbald, and the Headman, Renwick Heldursson."

"Are you saying that they went willingly?"

"Everybody wanted to be part of it, especially after the bishop, Hugue d'Athenous, said that all those involved would be immortalised in God's name, and he was going to build his cathedral there and everyone would come to know the name, Athenous."

"Athenous, why would anyone come to know his name?"

"No, not his name, it's the name of the new town, they even have a signed scroll from the jarl, which bares the king's seal."

"Oh yeah, I saw that when the bishop stood in the village centre and unrolled it!"

Skuld was beside himself with rage, but now was not the time to show it, though he imagined lucidly, drawing his sword right now and cutting these gate guards down where they stood, every one of them, he knew that he must return to his mother first, then perhaps she would know exactly what to do, and no doubt she had agents working for her within this new camp.

A whole day had been lost with all this toing and froing, but it had to be done, and when Skuld arrived back at his mother's house she was deep in conversation with her husband, the sheriff. Their townhouse, as they called it, was situated alongside the main jail. Skuld watched as a dishevelled-looking man dismounted his horse and limped into the sheriff's house.

Sinhadd Ketilborn was one of the sheriff's men, whom he had sent to the capital city on business, and he had returned far too soon. Skuld and his gang followed inside the house shortly after tying their horses up outside, just in time to catch the gist of the conversation.

"Sinhadd, why are you back so soon, I wasn't expecting you until early next week, and tell me, why are you limping, were you attacked on the road?"

"Pardon me, my lord, for I am the only survivor, and I took an arrow to the knee, all of the others are dead, and our goods are lost."

"Dead? Why, how, speak up man you are not making any sense!"

"It was not bandits, my lord, we made it to the city gates and they were shut tight, in the middle of the day, and when sent Guthrie to bang on them to demand entry in your name, Sheriff, they opened fire on us, huge men wearing black clothes and plate armour, they didn't even say a single word, they just turned their composite bows on us and fired!"

"The gates to the capital were closed in the middle of the day, why would that be?"

"Lord, in the time that it took me to bring my horse about all of the men were lying dead or dying about me, so I kicked my heels and ran."

"The soldiers you described, tall and dressed head to toe in black, leather, and armour over the top?"

"Yes, Lord."

"But why, I don't understand?"

"This was not supposed to happen yet!" Matilda blurted out.

"Wife, what are you talking about, what do you know about what is going on, tell me!"

"I can't tell you husband for you will go and get yourself killed, for you are a fool!"

"Speak, or by God, I will have you all thrown into jail!"

"It was only supposed to happen if Rogan got his way and there is war, between Råvenniå and Obrea, then the queen's black guard would seize control of each of the towns and cities they were in, across Råvenniå to prevent more soldiers from joining Rogan's cause. Something has happened, maybe something has changed, Skuld, why were you running from the capital, what do you know of these matters?"

"When was Skuld in the capital, and why, I don't understand, what is going on here?" said the sheriff completely in the dark.

"Not what, but who, our son has been coupling with the queen, and he got caught a few days ago, there was a scuffle and that is why he came back so suddenly."

"A scuffle, Son, this sounds a lot more like a rebellion, the queen's black guard was not supposed to be anything other than her bodyguard, her plaything…"

"Look we don't know what is happening in the capital and it doesn't look like we will for the seeable future so let us concern ourselves with matters we can control, now Son, how are things in Kaldakinn, or more precisely, the settlement outside the walls, husband we, the queen and I, have been paying for people to stir up trouble there for Rogan and his companions."

Skuld was about to speak when his father held up a hand to silence him. "Why would you do that Matilda, I don't see how anything like that can benefit our family?"

"Our family, you are nothing more than a tax-collecting lackey of that pathetic moron the jarl, neither of you could see beyond that which is put on a plate and placed right in front of you!"

"Matilda!"

"Oh, do be quiet you know I speak the truth, anyway, I am building something for the future of this family, and that is why we need to stop the war from ever happening because we are the ones who are creating the black guard, the queen and I, we instruct the Orsk on whom to target and they attack those people, then we lease those targeted people the black guard, on the premise they will keep them safe, and it was working perfectly until that stinking mud-skipper, Rogan Ragisson stuck his nose in!"

"Are you trying to tell me that the queen is also involved in this, wife, without the king's knowledge?"

"Oh please, husband, all you menfolk are the same, everything neatly wrapped up with little bows on, yes, our glorious queen is the one who approached us to become involved in this in the first place."

"Skuld, is any of this true?"

"It is all true, Father, and I was sent to be with the queen to keep her on track for Mother."

"So, our son was sleeping with the queen, committing adultery with his mother's blessing, and to what end, to stop her from killing the king?"

"Much more than killing the king, my dear husband, she wants to use her black guard to seize the whole country from the king, but why stop there?"

"You are all mad! And I do not want any part of this, do you hear me, no part!"

"Then leave go visit your family in the hills, they still run that small holding up there don't they, I'm sure they would love to have their precious little boy back to help muck out the pigs!"

"Matilda…"

"Oh, do shut up husband, look my son is eager to tell me something, isn't my lovely boy?"

Skuld backed up by Scoppi, Arnvid, and Guthorm told what they found during their trip to Kaldakinn. "Mother, they have all gone, the place was deserted."

Matilda said that they must go to the jarl straight away, and without delay, Magnus the sheriff was already walking away shaking his head and looking for a servant to fetch him his horse.

Matilda, Skuld, Scoppi, Arnvid, and Guthorm all waited for the sheriff to leave then they too fetched their horses and set out to the jarl's palace. All was not how it should have been and when at first, they arrived they were unable to gain entry, the guards had been instructed to let no one in the palace under any circumstances.

Matilda was not a woman who would be prevented by any mere gate guard, and so as they walked back towards their horses, she instructed Scoppi, the assassin, to visit them after she had caused a diversion.

Matilda walked over to her horse and dug a small concealed blade into the beast's flank causing it to rear up and slip the reigns from her hands, she screamed and shouted for the guards to come to her aid.

Scoppi slipped in behind them and trust a thin stiletto knife, first into the back of the one nearest to him, and then to the other, their dead bodies were then dragged to a nearby flower bed to be hidden.

Once inside, Matilda searched all the public rooms of the palace for the whereabouts of the jarl. It was not until she caught sight of his servant that she located his whereabouts. Jarl Sigfusson was taking a bath in his private chambers when Matilda stormed in with the others. "There you are Gudrod!" she said as though she was greeting an old friend. "Oh, no need to get up, we won't be here long!"

The jarl did think about standing when he realised that he was naked, and so he thought better of the idea and hoped that someone would come to his aid "What is the meaning of this Matilda?" he cried.

"I am here to ask you a small favour."

The jarl was looking at each of the other men who stood around his bath, hands on sword hilts. "And what would that be exactly?" asked the jarl nervously.

"The camp outside of Kaldakinn has disappeared, and as it transpires that you gave Rogan Ragisson the deeds to land in the far north for those very people to build a town and staging post, for the attack on the Orsk next spring." She said pointedly.

"Yes, that is correct, they had a signed letter from the king, intermating that was his wish, the letter bore his official seal, what else could I do, I just gave them what they asked for, is that so wrong?"

"Yes, it was, very wrong, you should have sent word to me, first, and then thought up ways to tie them up in ways that would have made it impossible to start building anything until we could come up with a better plan!"

"What would you have had me do? question if the document was real, this was Rogan Ragisson after all, a friend of the king and God himself for all I know, do you think me fool enough to mess with this fellow, what with his reputation?"

"No, you fool, but surely even you could have found some way to have slowed them down, anything that would have stopped their planned invasion in the spring."

"You can add two more names to that list of vermin if we are taking names, Bishop d'Athenous and his treacherous lackey, Oswald Dansson." Offered Skuld.

"Forgive me, but have you not heard the news coming out of Østergård, the whole capital is in lockdown, and rumour is rife that every city and town with a garrison of that black guard will be in the same predicament before the week is out, make no mistake, the queen has revealed her hand and far too soon for my liking," interrupted Jarl Sigfusson.

"How does that affect us directly though, are we not among the queen's most loyal subjects, isn't this why you encouraged our liaison, Mother?" proposed Skuld.

"Let me ask you Skuld, where do you think those guards loyal to the queen will be coming next, once she has taken the rest of the country, she will be coming for this tiny corner of the north?" said the jarl bitterly.

"Why would you make it sound like they would come through here like it is a bad thing, we are allies, do you not think her precious black guard would have instructions not to harm us?"

"As you said, I granted those deeds, and she will surely find out that little fact, and when she does Ingolfsfell will be wiped off the map, my guard wouldn't stand a chance, and anyway, most of them have already heard the news and have run off, if you haven't noticed the whole town is in panic."

"Enjoy your bath, Jarl, maybe when that black guard does arrive, they can scrub your back, good day to you, and goodbye!"

Once outside Matilda said that as far as things stood it was over. "whatever has happened in the capital has happened without the queen informing us, and there is but one road into the town from the south and that is the way the black guard would come. If she has given those pets of hers an order, it would be to kill everyone and destroy the town so that it cannot be used by any rebels."

"Why would she turn her back on us now?" Skuld whimpered.

"Pull yourself together boy, or scamper off with your father, do you believe the queen has had time to draw portraits of us all and hand them to her soldiers?"

Scoppi offered his opinion; "We should make like everyone else and pack our belongings."

Skuld asked where they should go, especially if, like it was now thought, the black guard would roll through Ingolfsfell killing everyone on sight. Matilda said that there was only one place left to go, they must make all haste to reach the realm of Fōrren.

Prince Tostig was their fall-back plan if the war was to proceed as Rogan wanted, then the prince would now be the critical piece on the board, he had already agreed to send over three hundred soldiers to Rogan's cause. "What Rogan doesn't know is that the prince intends to betray him so Deliciously When the prince places those warriors loyal to him in Rogan's reserve he will have the shock of his life when they turn on him late into the battle instead of coming to his aid, I only wish I could be there to see the look on Ragisson's face!" declared Matilda.

"So, we must go to the prince and let him know what has happened and what he can do to help next, and we, might yet win this inevitable war," Skuld sounded almost excited when he spoke.

"Come we must hurry before the roads and the ferries get blocked." Advised Matilda.

"Mother, what about Æstrid?"

"Oh, don't worry about your sister, she is the apple of your father's eye, and I dare say Rogan's as well, they will see to it that she come s to no harm, now speak no more of either of them!"

Aylild came to see Arathorn/Rogan. "You seem, troubled Brother, what is it?"

"I don't know Aylild it is just a funny feeling."

"Then act upon it if it troubles you so much, it could just be 'Faejyre' or far sight."

"Farsight?"

"Yes, for every person you have ever touched, you now have a connection, and with some, that connection is stronger than others, and if they are feeling strong emotion for whatever reason, you too will get an inkling of it."

Rogan was not entirely convinced, all these new and weird elvish senses and things that have been stirred up are causing him to question or second guess everything, the timing of such things could not be worse, however, a feeling in the gut is also a human quality that shouldn't be ignored, so the first thing to do would be to gather news from any visiting trader or priest, they usually had all the gossip from everywhere else.

Later that day a trader was brought before Rogan with very distressing news, the trader told of the fall of Råvenniå, and the impending march of the black guard on Ingolfsfell, and its near-deserted streets. Rogan had called all his close friends and advisors to the meeting to discuss what they should do next.

Captain Brecott advised that they pay a visit to the jarl and see what stories are true and what are just the mutterings of fools. Gunner said that they should reach out to Gufi and Arn and at least see what forces they now would have if they had lost the king's royal army and possibly that of Ingolfsfell. Aethelric said that they should also talk to Oswald and the bishop, after all, they may now be building a town for nothing. Ingrid turned to Aylild and asked if the elves could send support sooner than the spring.

There was even talk of sending delegations back to Fōrren and Lōrnicā to see if they could help in this most severe time of need. But Rogan wanted to be more cautious regarding those two countries, the alliance could crumble to nothing if they thought Råvenniå was unable to field an army in the spring after all Råvenniå was more than twice the size of those two countries put together.

First things first, Rogan wanted to visit the jarl and see what the state of play in Ingolfsfell was and then they would take it from there. If they decided to draw a line in the sand across the top northeast of the country, then Ingolfsfell would be the lynchpin to everything.

So, it was decided, Rogan, Ongar, Ingrid, Halla, Aylild, and all her rangers would go to Ingolfsfell, everybody else would stay in Kaldakinn and make sure that the village was well stocked with winter grain and other supplies, the fortifications were all in good repair and most of all, quell any rumours of impending doom, life for the moment must go on as normal. Secretly Rogan was beginning to see the cracks appearing, and Aylild tapped into his concerns and tried her best to soothe him and show him her full support.

The road leading to Ingolfsfell was choked with traffic coming out of the town, families on wagons and pushing hand carts, and people with bundles so big on their backs that one fall would crush the life out of them, at first, they came in dribs and drabs but the closer Rogan's party got to the town, the higher the number of people, all grim-faced and without hope, it was the most pitiful experience of Rogan's life, even more so than when he was a captive of the Orsk.

The gates to Ingolfsfell were left wide open and still people were leaving unchecked as not one guard remained at his post, the streets of this busheling market town were all but deserted, and now only the hardy, or foolhardy were left behind, Rogan indicated that he did not want to go straight to the palace but instead took a left instead of a right, heading towards the sheriff's house.

Quite what, or whom Rogan had expected to see was anyone's guest as he had remained tight-lipped for this part of the journey, and every time any of the others tried to close the gap with him, he spurred his horse forward a bit more, indicating he wanted to be alone, Aylild detected that he was incredibly worried about the safety of someone, but just who she could not see he was shielding his thoughts and so Aylild respected that and stopped trying.

When Rogan did next speak, it was as he rode up to the sheriff's house and dismounted to tie up his horse on the wooden rail outside. "Ongar, Halla, check the lock up I have a feeling there are prisoners who have been left in haste," he had been correct, there were two, and they were pleading to be let out from the moment they set eyes on Ongar and Halla.

Rogan still had his back to the house when somebody came strolling out, sword in hand, it was Magnus the sheriff. "I can honestly say, I did not expect it to be you who I next saw this day, Rogan Ragisson!"

Rogan turned slowly and purposefully. "I am not here to check on your well-being, Sheriff, merely curious as to if you and your family had already fled."

Æstrid followed her father out of the house, more cautiously at first but on seeing Rogan, her heart leaped and she found herself running towards him with sudden abandonment. "Rogan! Oh, Rogan how my heart is glad to see you!"

Magnus tried to put an arm out to stop his daughter but she brushed it aside and ran straight to Rogan, throwing all caution to the wind and as her body slammed into his, her arms wrapped tightly around his torso. "Well at least one of them is pleased to see you lord, perhaps I should do the same with the sheriff!" Ingrid said sourly.

Rogan did not reciprocate the affection that he was being shown, instead, he gently pulled Æstrid away from him. "I am pleased that you are unarmed, but tell me this, where is the rest of your family, and by that, I mean Skuld?" Rogan said stoically.

"He is long gone, he and my mother, they fled to where we do not know!" Æstrid, spoke as tears began to well in her eyes.

"Is this the truth, Sheriff?"

"What do you care if what my daughter says is true?"

"Why did you not go with them?" Rogan asked pointedly as his right hand instinctively cupped the pommel of his sword.

Æstrid placed her hand tightly over Rogan's right hand and she whispered into his ear, "No! please you do not need to draw your sword my father is just upset."

Magnus watch his daughter's actions and answered all the same time, "We, Æstrid, were not invited to leave with the rest of our family as it happens instead, we like the rest of the town have been abandoned."

"What about the jarl?"

"What about him, he was another of my wife's friends with whom I was not acquainted, perhaps you had better ask my daughter once more!"

"Æstrid?"

"It's true Rogan my mother and the jarl were very close, however, I have not noticed any coaches leaving the palace quarter, so unless he fled on foot or by some other means, he must still be there, one would have thought."

"Sheriff, do you think we should at least try and save the town?"

5

Defenders of the Realm

Magnus and Æstrid tagged along with Rogan and his party, as they now headed over to the palace Æstrid did not leave Rogan's side, and she chatted nervously to him in hushed tones the whole way there, several times their horses touched as she leant over towards him. Ingrid complained the whole way there but as it amused Ongar, it saddened Halla, she had found happiness, and a measure of contentment in her life and she could see that two people who were meant to be together keep pulling apart through fear of getting hurt.

Æstrid was, without doubt, one of the most beautiful women in Råvenniå, and when the sun caught her golden locks and she turned to face you with one of her fabulous smiles it was as though you had been approached by an angel, however, when Rogan did catch her gaze, he saw her as delicate, demure, far too refined for the likes of him, and yet somehow empty like something caught on the breeze.

Rogan was a rugged warrior, as rough as a mountain crag, as course as the salt drawn from the sea, and when he looked into Ingrid's eyes he saw fire, and passion, and not just a will to live but a fighter so fierce he could barely keep up, Ingrid if anyone, was his soulmate, he knew it, she knew it, but neither could let their defences down for long enough to explore that fact, much to the annoyance of Halla, another who knew these things to be true.

As the group approached the deserted palace they saw no guards, and no servants the place was completely open and unguarded, but not like everyone had just left for the day and they would return later, there were upturned and broken furniture, and rugs, large and small strewn everywhere, along with broken pots and half-opened boxes and many other things besides. Sheer unadulterated panic had swept through this place.

Rogan was able to continue his horse right through to within a hair's breadth of the jarl's courtyard, right outside of his great hall, and that was where they dismounted and tied up their horses.

The jarl, Gudrod Sigfusson, was alone and slouched on his throne, his right hand supporting his head while he snored loudly. Rogan was suddenly incensed and Aylild had to put a calming hand on his right forearm. "Jarl Sigfusson, wake up, you, odious slug!" cried Rogan.

The jarl jolted slightly at the noise and murmured a single word to match his ability to half open one eye. "What?"

Rogan stepped forward and kicked the Jarl's booted left leg. "Wake up, you, drunken sap!"

Slowly, the jarl managed to open both eyes, first widely and then after blinking several times, more normally. "Oh it's you and him!" He pointed to Ongar. "I suppose you have come to accept my surrender?" He slurred still looking at Ongar.

"We have come here to save this town and this wretched realm, and we wondered if it were not too much trouble if you, my lord, would care to help us?"

"Why?"

"Why, what?"

"Why do you want to help?"

"Because you are clearly in no fit state to do so yourself, now where are all of your men?"

"Don't know!"

"Fetch me a bucket of cold water someone, please!"

Halla and Aylild went off together, while Ingrid just stood staring at Æstrid, who in turn graced Ingrid with one of her sweetest smiles, a smile that would melt the snow on top of the mountains if they were male.

"Magnus, where are the warriors, and wasn't there a detachment of black guard here at one time?"

"The black guard went some days ago, without a word, they just up and left, out of the southern gate, and the militia, which forms the biggest part of the jarl's army, around seven hundred fighters, they have mostly just fled with their families."

"My God, how can this be…?"

"You probably passed most of them on the road north, since the rumours coming out of the capital are that anyone attempting to go south is just being summarily executed nobody is running in that direction."

"But the trained men then, surely some of them have stayed even out of duty if nothing else?"

"Again, around five hundred foot soldiers and two hundred mounted, but you have seen yourself, there are no horses left in the town save our own, so the soldiers are all on foot or they too are gone."

Aylild returned with a wooden pale filled with cold water which she handed to Rogan; in turn, he threw the whole contents over the jarl. The jarl opened his eyes wide and gave out a loud cry.

"Welcome back lord, we feared that we had lost you there!"

"Rogan, by the Gods, I should have your head for that!"

"Where are all of your men, your guards, those who swore an oath to you?" Rogan continued, ignoring the jarl's protestations.

"I don't know, I think, they are in their barracks over the other side of the palace, last night we had such a feast…"

"Magnus, you go, take Æstrid, and tell them to assemble in the courtyard outside, Æstrid, when your father speaks, I want you to hold on to his arm as your life depended on it, do you understand?"

"No! but I will do as you say." Rogan believed that the sight of her in distress would be like a beacon to the soldiers and their sense of honour.

Two hundred and thirty-two men returned with Magnus and about half as many women, all worse for wear and looking incapable of standing up straight never mind anything else.

Four captains came inside with Magnus. "These men are the only ones who stayed behind, they are all oath men, and when they sober up a very capable force."

"Lord Jarl, what have you to say to us, or to the men and women outside who have stayed because you have stayed?" demanded an irate Rogan.

"They are yours to command!" waved the jarl as if it were merely a slice of buttered bread that he was giving away.

"What?" remonstrated Rogan.

"I no longer want to be the jarl, I resign, I am a confirmed coward and I will get everyone who stays with me, killed, that is why everyone else left, there I said it, so go play soldiers or do whatever it is you think you should I shall make my way to the wine cellar and lock myself in down there!"

Not for the first time in Rogan's recent past had a few words spoken silenced an entire room.

The jarl realised that nobody was speaking nor were they moving, so he reiterated his stance, "I give them all to you Rogan Ragisson!"

"You can't Gudrod, it doesn't work like that."

The jarl then looked around the room until his eyes settled upon Magnus Steinolf. "Sheriff, I can resign, can't I?"

"Yes, my lord, you can, but it has to be done properly and in front of witnesses."

"Then you do it properly, you are the sheriff, isn't your rank high enough, and the four captains, they are the witnesses, right?"

The sheriff bowed his head slightly not wanting to make eye contact, I guess in the absence of..."

"In the absence of anyone else!" Gudrod interrupted, before belching loudly.

"Yes, then, if you put it like that." Magnus' eyes now met with Rogan's and he nodded to him.

"Good! Good, Rogan Ragisson I am making you the new jarl and placing the safety of this town and anyone stupid enough to stay in it under your protection, there, have you got that, Sheriff?"

"Yes, my lord."

Gudrod then lurched into a standing position and wobbled away towards the courtyard outside, just before he disappeared through the doorway for the last time, he turned to face Rogan. "Sit down then, it won't bite you know, or don't you have seats like that where you come from." And then he began laughing and he almost fell over. "Somebody, fetch me the key, or better still, I will go and look for it myself!" after walking straight into the doorway that led back into the main part of his palatial home two of the captains ran over to the jarl to help steady him.

"Help me find the key will you, please, I always keep the wine cellar locked, you know, you can't trust anyone these days, not anyone!" the jarl continued.

"Magnus, as sheriff, you are now in charge of these soldiers and your first duty is to secure this town!" Rogan barked.

"What am I supposed to do against such formidable odds?" the sheriff asked.

94

"Round up every man, woman, and child, fetch tools, dig a ditch in front of the southern gates and fill it with wooden spikes, then get inside and bar the gates, brace them or fill the gap behind them with anything heavy you can put your hands on, mount a guard to keep watch to the south."

"What shall I say to the women and children who stand by and watch?"

"To the women say, be ready to form a line up each set of steps either side of the two guard towers, as for the children give them buckets, and tell them to fill them with oil, then they are to give the buckets to the women who in turn will pass them up the stairs to the men. When the enemy attacks the gate, throw the oil onto them and lite them up, is that clear enough."

"Yes!" said Magnus.

"Good, Aylild you and your elves, must return to your homeland and raise as many volunteers as you can to come here and fight, we simply cannot let this town be taken."

"What of you lord, what will you do?" asked Aylild.

"I will go with the rest back to Kaldakinn and raise our army and return as soon as we can."

"I can contact Ascarli right now, and ask him to come to our aid, that way I can meet him near the coast, and then together we can return here, probably before the end of the week."

"Fantastic, thank you Aylild, too should return before the end of the week, and I will bring one hundred warriors but I will leave the Militia in Kaldakinn, Magnus can I count on you?"

"Of course, my lord jarl, but only if you take Æstrid with you, I need to know that my daughter is safe; take her with you to Kaldakinn."

Æstrid did not need to hear her father's wishes twice, she looped her arm around Rogan's and said, "I feel safer already, Father."

Aylild and her rangers left Ingolfsfell by the eastern gate and as they left, she turned to her brother and said, "Be careful, and I will see you soon."

Rogan shouted back for her and the other wood elves to do the same.

Sheriff Magnus Steinolf also said his farewells and he hugged his daughter and kissed her lightly on the forehead. "Right, we have much to do here and not much time to do it in, so if you don't mind, Lord Jarl, I will take my leave and see you soon also."

Rogan was deep in conversation most of the journey back to Kaldakinn and so Æstrid found herself having to try to make conversation with Ingrid and Halla, neither of which were too enamoured with making conversation back, although after a while Ingrid did break the ice by asking Æstrid where she got her clothes from, Ingrid was looking at the expensive material to say how impractical it was, but Æstrid was so delighted that she ignored any sarcasm in Ingrid's voice.

Halla just kept on making gestures like she wanted to throw up, but every time Æstrid caught her gaze she would smile so serenely.

Kaldakinn was looking more like the place it had become over the last twelve months, with fishermen repairing nets, others scraping the bottom of their boats, the smell of whale oil hanging over the eastern part of the town, women walking around the market stalls and the smell of horse dung hanging in the air around the stables. The only difference Rogan could detect was the occasional sideways glances some people, who should know better, would give Ongar Half-blood.

The first thing Halla did when she had alighted her horse, was wrap her arms around Ongar, from behind, and tell him that she could not wait to get back home and just forget about the rest of the world for a few hours. Ingrid wanted to do something similar with Rogan but she was no longer sure about where she stood with him, not just because of Æstrid, and there was no denying she bore a type of beauty that could penetrate a man's soul. Rogan appeared to have the weight of the world on his shoulders and she did not want to add to his burdens.

Renwick was the first to show up as they left the stables. "Lord Rogan! it is so good to have you back, do you bring any good news, for days now we hear nothing but doom and gloom?"

"That will be Jarl Rogan from now on Renwick!" Ongar said as he slapped Rogan on the back and then said, "I need some proper rest, see you in the morning."

Renwick looked perplexed.

Halla told the Headman what had happened in Ingolfsfell and Renwick's cheeks flushed with colour. "I am sorry, my lord, I meant you no disrespect!"

"It's fine Renwick I will have someone chop off your head in the morning if it makes you feel better, but until then, I have a special favour to ask?"

"Yes, my lord...jarl?" Renwick replied stutteringly.

"Take this girl into your home and treat her as your own, I will give you an allowance for her to spend but only if she is put to work with your wife, is that understood?"

"Yes, my lord jarl."

"Oh, and Renwick, if you keep on calling me, lord jarl, I will personally chop off your head before tomorrow!"

"Yes, my lord jarl, very well, my lord…!"

Smiling to himself, Rogan turned to Ingrid. "Come my lady I require a hot bath and then perhaps some, entertainment!"

Ingrid deliberately looked at Æstrid before she smiled most curiously and said, "Good night Æstrid." Aatu dutifully followed his master everywhere he went and as usual, these days, was as quiet as a church mouse.

At the meeting that Rogan had called with the village council and his military advisors, he went through the events of the last few days and asked for any input, from those seated around the large oak tables.

"As far as anyone is concerned the war with the Orsk is set to go ahead in the spring, right?" It was Captain Brecott who answered first. "But Rogan is our main objective still to rescue the women prisoners and then any of the human and half-bloods who, want to come with us?"

"I am going to say yes, because that was what we had all agreed to in the first place, however, I am aware that things have changed and it isn't going to be that simple anymore," replied Rogan.

"Especially if those new defences are anything to go by, but do we know that we can trust the words of a boat full of drunken mercenaries?"

"I have spoken with them at length, they admit there originally foley but once they had sobered up they came here first to say what they had seen." Offered Renwick.

"Did they ask for payment for their revelation, Headman?" asked Ongar.

"I threatened to throw them all in jail for stealing the fishing boat, and that loosened their tongues, and yes I renumerated them for their precious words…"

"Precious words, Rogan do you believe this story or do you think it is sent to strike fear in our hearts before we even cross the great channel?"

"Ongar, Renwick believes it to be true and I believe him, okay, and besides we still have our secret weapon, don't we Bryn?"

"You put your faith in God, Rogan Ragisson, is that what you are saying?" demanded Arn Sigewulfesson. Arn was a brute of a man who stood 6' 2" tall with broad shoulders and who represented the outsiders who had been absorbed into Kaldakinn forces.

"No, Arn I am counting on the word and deed of an avenging angel, sent by the one true God, who shall walk us right through those Orsk defences like they are not even there!"

"Rogan are you sure you still want to try and negotiate with the humans and half-bloods who might man the defences, for one would not be wanting to try to talk to them while they are throwing spears at me, it could be considered detrimental to my health!"

"Gunnar, it's a fair point, and that is where our new friend comes in."

"You mean the creature, can we trust it, I mean trust it, not to lead us into a trap?"

Rogan wanted to assure everyone that he had used his newfound elvish abilities to read the creature's heart, but in fact, even Aylild had said that ability only belonged to Ĕlyāh, but she did say that the next best thing for an elf, or half-elf was their intuition, and Rogan's intuition said that Tukor's offer of help was genuine. "We can trust, Tukor." That was all he said.

"How bad was the situation in Ingolfsfell?" asked Sister Wenyid, desperate to change the subject amid fraying tempers.

"Bad enough that two-thirds of the population has run off, to God knows where, and the people left behind are terrified of the thought that the black guard is coming for them, but some positive news, I was wrong about Sheriff Steinolf, it turns out he is one of the good guys."

"Let's hope you are not wrong about anything else, Rogan!" Arn Sigewulfesson mumbled.

"Rogan you promised the sheriff warriors to fight alongside his, won't that make us critically short ourselves?" concluded Renwick.

"Not at all, by the time we reach Ingolfsfell we will be bolstered by the return of Aylild and an army of elves." Voiced Rogan matter-of-factly.

"Honestly, we should not worry about, Ingolfsfell, with or without the elves, there is just the one road in or out of that whole region, and it is blocked solid, those walls are solid stone and won't be breached easily, if the black guard attack they will be forced to funnel their attack into a narrow corridor, it will make the defence that much easier," Ongar explained.

"Look, the worst possible scenario is that the sheriff calls for help, and we oblige by sending what's left of our garrison, even then and I am convinced that we would overwhelm the black guard, by hitting them from the high ground." Rogan declared.

"Do we know how far along the new town is, and will they now form the biggest part of the offensive in the spring?" Sigrunn inquired.

"They should be our next port of call, they deserve to know what's going on, and what we have planned if things don't go our way at Ingolfsfell." The captain retorted.

"They will form the brunt of the offensive because even after everything, they should number at least three thousand fighting men and women, if we have any more warriors like the elves then it will be a bonus, Fōrren will sit in reserve with a further three hundred trained soldiers and Lōrnicā believe they can field an army of three hundred and add another five hundred militia."

Depending on the situation at Ingolfsfell, we should be able to put at least one hundred and fifty, very well-trained warriors into the field, then there will be three hundred from Gufi and another three hundred from Arn, all in all, a good solid number."

"Do we know how many Orsk and other fighters they have in the kingdom under the mountain?"

"Best estimate, around a thousand warband warriors, and let's say another thousand black guard, the Orsk themselves are so old I doubt they could even fight."

"Is that based on what the creature says?"

"No, he, said he had no idea what their strength is at all, he was chased away from the settlement years ago."

"Don't forget, if we can get inside with Tukor's help we may just cause an insurrection, in which case we might not even need an army, the humans and half-bloods could turn on the Orsk and the black guard, and kill them for us."

"If we return victorious and we can liberate our brothers and sisters, are we still going to offer them land here in Kaldakinn?" Ongar inquired.

"No, I have since had a better idea, but make no mistake, I expect everyone here will treat them all as equals, for now, I will keep my council and we can discuss those thoughts nearer the time."

"Should we make any plans to re-take the rest of Råvenniå?" Solicited Captain Brecott.

"That I honestly don't know, by the time we meet with the Orsk, this army will be the largest ever assembled on a field of battle in the Shattered Realms, afterwards I am sure many men will be blood sick, and not want to even talk about fighting again, despite what the bards sing about, war by its very nature is brutal and barbaric, and when it is over, you never want to see another one again in this life or any other."

"Amen to that Rogan!" said Brother Bryn Cuthbald.

"The new road is looking really good, I like the feel of the cobblestones, it makes it sturdy all year round so that even in the deepest winter we can still trade with Athenous." The Elderman of Ailgin was telling Aethelric the Bard, and Sister Wenyid, who had been dispatched north to visit bishop d'Athenous and to see for themselves how the building work in the new town was progressing.

Ailgin sat on the apex of the great west/north-west road that straddled the top of Råvenniå between Kaldakinn and Hundsnes. It had a population of just over two hundred and fifty of the hardiest souls who managed to make a living mostly off the services they provided to travellers who passed their way. However, since the advent of the new town, Ailgin was becoming something of a hub for everything coming into or going out of Athenous, as the new town was named.

Athenous lay six miles due north of Ailgin and its people were a perfect example of what to build, where to build it, and every other detail on how to thrive in the harshest of conditions. Unlike any other place in the country, this connecting road was to be built of cobblestones, in the manner of the old Kristosiãns who conquered these lands so many hundreds of years before.

Aethelric and the sister had decided that they would leave Kaldakinn early and arrive late and then find accommodation once they arrived and so had packed accordingly, along the sixty-nine-mile route, they periodically crossed paths with other people on the road and the journey was straightforward and it gave the two travelling companions time to get to know each other better.

Aethelric was nicknamed, 'the bard' because he carried a lute everywhere he went, and at every opportunity, he would sing songs while strumming his instrument. Admittedly most of his songs were just a collection of silly things sung to garner amusement, however, he was able to change track to suit most occasions. Rogan thought of him as a wise counsellor and friend.

Sister Wenyid Tanner was formerly a nun at a nunnery that was attacked, and where most of the nuns were raped before being executed or carried off to God only knows where, Wenyid survived the ordeal and set out on her quest to find those other sisters and to right the many injustices carried out, particularly by men, in the world at large. That all stopped when she met Rogan, she was entranced by his charisma and she saw him as her gift, and friend from God, ever since she has followed wherever he has led.

Having stopped off briefly in Ailgin, for food and respite, the two were soon on their way up the newly constructed section of the road, and they saw for themselves the incredible endeavour of the people who had also pitched their colours to that of Rogan Ragisson.

First, large bonfires were made at each side of the road and they were being fed by large lumps of coal, once the coal was red hot it was shovelled over to the frozen ground where others were digging what looked like a ditch on either side of where the road would be.

Next, they noticed a man with a very strange device and when they asked him what it was, they were none the wiser, he called it a gruma, an instrument that had two pieces of wood nailed together so that they formed a square cross with right-angles in all the corners. Each piece of wood had lead weights attached to the ends. When one lead weight from the same piece of wood lined up with the one in front of it, the man knew that he had a straight line.

Then, they watched as other men knocked wooden posts into the ground to mark out the straight line, for which the road itself would follow, the ditches were then dug on either side of the road, this was to allow for natural drainage. Any excess soil was carried away to the new town to be used on a raised defence ditch which was to be constructed all around its circumference.

Once all the preparations had been met it was time for various layers that made up the road to be laid on top. Aggregate from Langaholt made up the first level, then finer gravel, which was crushed on site, and finally, cobblestone, which again came from the quarries at Langaholt, was laid out on top of the gravel to form the road surface.

From the construction site, the two travellers made their way towards the new town of Athenous. Athenous rose like something out of a dream, everywhere you looked there was a light smattering of snow and as your eyes grew accustomed to the scene, tiny flecks of reddish-brown were interspersed where painted wood had been used to construct a building that had not yet been painted white, most of the other buildings seemed invisible at this point. As you got closer the wispy trials of smoke could be seen from hundreds of hearth fires, from the people who now called this bleak landscape, home.

It was long before the breathtaking beauty of the rolling mountains of Obreā came into view, a great wall of distant grey splashed across an otherwise white background where the snow-capped mountains met the cloud-filled sky. The air felt cleaner out here and there was a sense of serenity, of peace and calm, like the sort of place Brother Cuthbald was always talking about when he described what he called; 'the future paradise'.

Closer still and everything changed, the clinking and clanking of metal on stone, the audible hustle and bustle of a new town rising out of the dirt, and everywhere you now looked the ground was churned up, mud and ice mixed as hundreds upon hundreds of iron-shod, leather booted feet, had walked over the ground, repeatedly.

The smell was the next thing that hit the back of the nasal passages, it was burning fires, blacksmith forges, spit-roasted flesh, and human excrement, all mixed with the prevailing easterly wind. And everywhere your eyes now fixed, those hundreds of people beavered away like ants, carrying, fetching, hammering, and fixing things together, as the town rose from the ground.

The place that Rogan had chosen was perfect in every way, the land was flat down to the water's edge, where it ran into a curved open bay, the lower town was sprouting into life, then backing up there was a small incline that led to a large flat open area on top of a hill, this was the place the bishop had chosen to build his cathedral, and it would dominate the landscape all around when finished.

Wattle and daub appeared to be the composite building material used for making the building's walls, a method in which a woven lattice of wooden strips, called wattle, is daubed with a sticky material usually made of some combination of wet soil, clay, sand, animal dung, and straw, hence the smell.

Most of the buildings that housed livestock or other inanimate objects were simply made from timber roughly knocked together and all the roofs were being covered with the top layers of rough turf that was skimmed off before the diggers got to work on the ground beneath.

The first complete building that came into view was the alehouse, whose sign read, 'The Kings Arms' which was either incredibly optimistic or showed great foresight by the owner, especially if they believed the king would come this far north.

Inside the King's Arms was a roaring fire and a lonely barmaid, as the place was empty, Aethelric introduced his companion and then himself and the maid said that she was called, Ingulfrid. Then she offered them both a jug of warm mead and something to eat, Sister Wenyid asked, "What do you recommend for two weary travellers?"

Ingulfrid laughed and said, "That'll be the pottage, then!"

"Sounds yummy," said Aethelric while turning sideways to make faces at Wenyid.

"You aren't from round here then are you, deary!" remarked Ingulfrid as she fetched two steaming hot bowls of pottage.

This meal comprised gull meat, onions, carrots, and turnips with a sprinkling of cider and herbs and spices, from whatever type of such were available.

"What sort of meat is called 'gull meat'?" Sister Wenyid asked.

"Gulls! You know the birds that fly around this place, screeching and screaming!"

"I can't say that we noticed any on our way here," recalled Aethelric.

"Well not here, here, no, when we arrived though there were hundreds and hundreds, and hundreds, everywhere you stepped, gulls!"

"And now there are not so many?"

"Not so many, no, the bishop, a lovely man, by the way, very erm…Godley, anyway, said that they were manner from Evan, whomever Evan is, so we caught them, as many as we could, it was quite funny at first, chasing them with anything we could throw over them, then we stored them in cages while we built barns to keep them in, now we farm them, gulls, who'd have thought it, hundreds of the blessed things and the bishop thinks it's all Gods doing, makes us blessed, perhaps the sign above the door should be, 'the Blessed Gull'." Which made Ingulfrid laugh as she wiped the countertop down repeatedly.

Sister Wenyid was the braver of the two and placed a spoonful of the delightful-looking mixture into her mouth first. "Hmm, Aethelric, this is so good, you must try some," she said in-between chewing and then swallowing the pottage."

Aethelric after putting his first spoonful in his mouth nearly spat it out. "Oh is it not for you, young sir?" the barmaid said, looking as innocent as the driven snow.

"On. No, no, not at all it was just very hot! No, it is, really…tasty, you are an amazing cook, Ingulfrid." He lied.

"I guess I know where you will be rooming tonight Aethelric!" Sister Wenyid said disapprovingly but managed to smile at the same time.

Ingulfrid smiled too and continued to wipe the counter which apart from being pitted here and there was already spotless.

"Can I get you anything else?"

"Perhaps, we are looking for a roof over our heads, and then we would like to meet with the jarl, Oswald Dansson, and then perhaps we will take a look at the cathedral, it is starting to look spectacular up there on the hill." Replied Aethelric.

"Oh, but you can stay here, we have plenty of room, upstairs, may I ask if the two of you are together, or would you be wanting separate rooms?"

"Oh no, no, no, nothing like that we are separate, I mean single, not together at all, in fact, Sister…"

"Oh, silly me, she's your sister, well that explains everything, separate rooms, I'll sort those out later, they will be ready for your return." The barmaid said with a greedy look in her eye, and it was not for the want of coin that her look was directed at Aethelric.

"More pottage, anyone?"

Walking outside of the alehouse they noticed wooden walkways going off in every direction that seemed to connect to every building. "To keep us from trailing in the mud I suppose," said Sister Wenyid.

Aethelric nodded in agreement, before stopping a busy-looking man carrying a sack of something heavy, as he looked rather pleased to have been stopped just so he could unburden himself. "Where might we find the jarl, my good man?"

"At this late hour, he will be over by the docks finishing up his inspection for the night I imagine."

"The docks, would that be, that way or this?" Aethelric asked while pointing down at the wooden walkways that split on the corner by the cobbler's store.

The man pointed in the direction they needed to go and then once again heaved his heavy load back onto his broad shoulders. Oswald was not that hard to find, he was the one barking orders at different men who all seemed to be taking no notice as they began to pack their tools and things away for the evening.

"Jarl Oswald!" Aethelric called out and waved as he caught the attention of the man they had come to see.

Despite his new status as Jarl, Oswald still preferred the trappings of his church, he wore a single long brown robe that was tied at the waist with what looked like plain rope, and he wore a symbol around his neck that neither Sister Wenyid wore nor did Brother Cuthbald, which Aethelric found a little odd, but forgot the fact shortly thereafter.

"My lord, perhaps you remember me, Aethelric from Kaldakinn, and my companion, Sister Wenyid?"

"Of course, yes, the bard, if I remember correctly, but surely it has only been a few weeks, and my lady, Sister Wenyid, a living saint if ever I saw one, what brings you two all this way at the start of winter?"

"Sadly, we don't come bearing good news, but if there is somewhere we could talk, then perhaps we can offload some of our burdens and you can share your wise council, Jarl?"

"My Goodness, I bet he has the ladies eating out of his hands, Sister, what a silver tongue you have young man, and no wonder I suppose if you are a bard!"

Aethelric smiled impassively and bowed.

The walk to the jarl's mansion was not far but it was starting to get dark much quicker and the temperature was dropping considerably, men could be seen everywhere lighting braziers on street corners to light up the way and the flames blazed wildly as a cold easterly wind began to blow past.

Oswald's mansion was nowhere near as well built or palatial as the one Rogan had in Kaldakinn, however, and more importantly, it had a roaring open fire which the house servants had already set along with warm mead to drink and a Coldren full of broth.

Strangely Oswald took off his outerwear and then offered the two companions large bearskins to wrap themselves up with. "If you are planning on stopping more than an hour or so, you will be sorely glad of these, here take them!"

Aethelric and Sister Wenyid both took turns to tell the story that Rogan had wanted Oswald to hear and afterwards, Oswald thanked them both for their candour and honesty.

"So, do you want me to send men back with you or do you want us to carry on building here?"

"Carry on do! This whole place looks amazing and I cannot believe in just, what, five, six, weeks you have managed to achieve all of it!" Aethelric put in enthusiastically.

"Well, to be honest, Rogan never let us down, on anything, whatever we needed he supplied, and he continued to pay top coin to everyone who worked and so, work they did, and still do, never have I been part of such an exercise, especially in such challenging circumstances as these, yet the people work their fingers to the bone and never complain, it is truly miraculous."

It is indeed!" added the former nun.

"So, tell me about lord Rogan's war effort…"

"That is precisely why we are here, to assure you that the war will go ahead as soon as the spring is upon us, and there is no need to send us back with men-at-arms, Rogan believes the elves will come to our aid, and in good number."

"The elves, eh? That will put a few noses out of joint round here, half the reason they agreed to leave Kaldakinn was their hatred of the half-breeds, so quite how they will take to the elves, well I just do not know."

"Ah! Before I forget, have you seen or heard anything from across the river?"

"The Orsk and the half-breeds you mean, nope, not a hair nor hide."

"I do have some good news for you to take back with you, tell Rogan that we will be repaying a large amount of what he gave for all the wood and stone and foodstuff since we found the minke whales favour wintering in our bay, we just send out two or three boats and beat the waves vigorously and they beach themselves by the dozen, we already have hundreds of barrels of oil to send Rogan, and skins, whiskers, bone, bone implements, you name it we have it in surplus, soon with the money he sends we will be able to buy everything, instead of borrowing."

"I will convey that to him, I know he will be delighted to hear the news."

"So just one thing before you go, it's getting late, if you are staying at the alehouse, do you think Rogan will try to take Råvenniå back, after the spring campaign?"

"I think he will, but whether people will have had enough of fighting by then he doesn't know, but whatever transpires, it will be hard, long, and very, very bloody."

"Hmm, well he will certainly have our undying gratitude and support whatever he decides to do, and to think I wanted to kill the man shortly after I first met him, anyway you had both better be getting off before the temperature drops anymore or risk freezing before you can take two steps."

Back at the Kings Arms, Aethelric was greeted with a beaming smile by the barmaid. "There you are, my shift ended an hour ago and I was getting worried, I was just about to send out a search party, but look! Here you both are, you must be freezing, come, sit by the fire." The alehouse was just as empty as when they first went in and both wondered how the place stayed open.

"Thank you so much, Ingulfrid, you have been very kind to us both and we are very grateful."

"Oh, don't you worry, my dears, I have prepared your rooms and I have put a bed pan in them both to warm them up, and I have given you both an extra bearskin to throw over should you need them."

"Thank you again, I am sure we will both go up shortly, I for one am very tired," Sister Wenyid yawned as if to emphasise the point.

Aethelric you are first on the left as you go up the stairs and Sister, I have put you right down the corridor so that you get a peaceful night, I will bid you both a good evening." And off up the stairs, she went.

Neither took any notice of which bedroom Ingulfrid took as her own, so imagine Aethelric's surprise when he opened the first door at the top of the stairs and there in the bed that she had prepared for him, Aethelric found Ingulfrid. "My goodness, woman, you will catch your death of cold like that."

"Well you had better hurry up and keep me warm."

Aethelric smiled and said goodnight to Sister Wenyid and disappeared inside the room on the left at the top of the stairs.

Ingulfrid had been up an hour before Aethelric even noticed he was alone in bed, there were windows in his room like there were back in Kaldakinn, instead, there was a single square shutter that could be opened outwards, braving the cold morning air he opened the wooden shutter and looked out, there was no denying the view was breathtaking over the bay, and where there had been a smattering of snow yesterday, today there was some greenery pushing through as the sun was climbing in the eastern sky and the snow began to melt a little.

There was a knock on the door. "Enter!" shouted Aethelric, it was Sister Wenyid.

"I trust you got some sleep, Aethelric?" she said with deep amusement in her voice.

"I am sure I have no idea what you are alluding to, good sister."

"The space and turned-back furs on the other side of your bed tell a different tale, but don't worry I am only teasing you."

"Give me a minute and I will be down for breakfast, did you want to see the bishop early, or later?"

"Early if it is all the same to you, then the sooner we can get back the better, Rogan will need every sword he can get at his side if things go sideways."

The air seemed heavier as they stepped outside, and although the short walk up the hill to the cathedral looked inviting, they both decided to fetch their horses and ride there, altogether it took no more than fifteen minutes and they were there.

They sat atop their horses for a few moments looking at the vast enormity of the building, it was for all intent a palace fit for a bishop. The bottom half was completed every stone cut to precision and fitted so that the weight of it would help keep all those around and below it in place.

Bishop d'Athenous must have spotted the pair as he came out from the front door arms outstretched in a welcoming manner. "Sister Wenyid, and my dear friend Aethelric, how wonderful it is to see you both, please get down from there and come inside!"

Both dismounted and left their horse's reins under a heavy piece of discarded masonry so that they would not just wander away. Then they followed the bishop inside, still looking this way and that, drinking in the astonishing building even if it were only half finished.

Bishop d'Athenous insisted on showing them around, what each area would be called and why this room was where it was, and so forth. Sister Wenyid was transfixed with the conversation, and Aethelric was daydreaming about the girl with the long album hair, which incidentally ran down to her hips, she had an hourglass figure and her skin was pale and pure, and he longed to be in her company less than an hour since leaving her.

When the three of them finally got down to business, Aethelric was the one who told the story, and Sister Wenyid contributed when the bishop asked for more specific details, things like, why did Rogan believe that the creature, Tukor, would lead them through tunnels under the noses of his people.

Aethelric was better with the facts, and Sister Wenyid the conjecture and emotion. Satisfied with what they had spoken about, the bishop asked how he could be of assistance, and Sister Wenyid said, "By supporting Rogan and what he stood for, and by continuing to build the town and the boats that would carry the army across the river Tawa in the spring, and most of all, to hold tight to his faith, God was on their side."

Aethelric and Sister Wenyid took the bishop's blessings and assurances and just after midday they mounted their horses and turned them towards the unfinished road and home.

About a league into their journey and they met with a train of ox-drawn wagons transporting large barrels of whale oil and other items, Aethelric ailed the driver of the lead wagon to ask if Sister Wenyid and he could ride alongside them for a while.

Staying with the men from Athenous, gave Aethelric time to talk about what life was really like under Jarl Oswald and to ask what they thought about the bishop, each man, in turn, said how glad they were that they took up the offer to go to the new town and the opportunities it offered, and they had only good things to say about Rogan.

While Sister Wenyid was talking to the driver, Aethelric appeared to become somewhat distracted. "Aethelric, is there something bothering you, you are quiet?"

"I've just had an idea, could we put all this oil into amphorae?"

The wagon driver scratched his head and replied, "That'll be a lot of amphorae, about a hundred wagon loads if you want to swap contains with all that we carry!"

"Aethelric, why would you want to do that?"

"Sea Fire! I have just remembered a song I was taught when I travelled through Talamara a few years back, it was all about an ancient battle at sea between two warring nations and one of the nations used 'sea fire' to burn the other nations' boats."

"You mean the great Siege of Khalmondopolis, it took place about three hundred years ago, and was won by the Kristosian army, with the help of this fiery substance which they threw at enemy ships, but they didn't keep it in amphorae, it was something called a siphon." Sister Wenyid explained.

"How do you even know that, Sister!" Aethelric was mightily impressed.

"It was something I read about in the great library in Athephia, I studied early Kristosian literature while I was taking my vows, it was incredibly boring apart from the different battles and sieges, I loved reading about how 'we' thought up these ideas to defeat the infidels, of course, it was all by the hands of Aru the Almighty!"

"Infidels?"

"Never mind, what was it you wanted to know about sea fire?"

"I was wondering if we could use it against the black guard?"

"Yes, it would be a very useful weapon, except the recipe was kept secret, and the man who invented it, well, took that secret to the grave."

"Do you have any idea what the mixture was, I mean sure they used oil, it is highly flammable?"

"Let me see, sulphur, pine resin, oil, and quicklime were ingredients I think since it catches fire in the water, but have tried to recreate it but without the success of the original formula, Pfaff!"

"I want to try to recreate it, but I was thinking more in containers that we could hold and throw with our hands, what do you think?"

"It can't hurt, well hopefully it can't hurt us, but it could be the very thing that stops the black guard!"

When the convoy arrived in Kaldakinn later that evening, Aethelric spurred his horse off in the direction of the apothecary's house. "Where are you going in such a hurry?"

"To see a man about some fire!" and he disappeared into the direction of the old part of Kaldakinn, the place where the wooden houses are on stilts and have turf-covered roofs.

Jarl Rogan Ragisson was holding a council meeting at the great hall in Kaldakinn, it had been days and no information was coming in from anywhere outside the northern villages, there were no attempted attacks on Ingolfsfell, and no sightings of black guard the only real complaint at the meeting was about Aethelric, he had been making a nuisance out of himself with several potters and kiln owners.

Sister Wenyid said that he was working on a secret project and that she would look in on it from time to time, but she would not elaborate any further, other than to say it was his little surprise. Rogan brought the meeting to a close and everyone began filing out of the hall, there was nothing much anyone could do now but sit and wait.

When the alarm was finally raised in the days that followed Rogan rounded up over a hundred warriors, some were guards who had originally fled Ingolfsfell and who came to Kaldakinn to reform as a unit, and the rest were selected from the Kaldakinn guard, Rogan selected only those men and women who were single, added to that number were his housecarl of thirty-two mounted troopers.

In the past, a journey to the regional capital would have included a trip around the top of the country but there was a far quicker route south. Riders were dispatched to Hundsnes and Langaholt, however, this time the army would take the southern route, and the mounted units would ride ahead of the foot soldiers just to bolster the town's already depleted guard units.

By the time, Rogan and his thirty-two mounted men arrived at Ingolfsfell. Nine hours after leaving Kaldakinn, the battle was well and truly underway at the southern gate, the infantry would not arrive until the following day. There was no time at present to look for the sheriff as Rogan asked Ongar to get up one of the gate towers to give him some idea of what was happening.

Ongar wasted no time in shouting down to his commander, "Rogan, they have a large battering ram with a covered housing over it, and they are using humans to fill in the ditch in front of the gate."

Using humans meant that they were residents from the capital and human shields, Rogan had a tough choice to make as the ditch was central to slowing the black guard down.

"How much time have we got, Ongar before they cross the ditch?"

"We're out of time, the ditch is filled and the spikes have been hacked down, they have a clean run of the gates!"

The ditch and spikes had been circumnavigated by bringing the covering up but without the battering ram and using the human shields to fill the ditch with dirt, the spikes were then hacked down by black guard berserkers armed with large two-handed axes.

Now the contraption was being carried back by black guard soldiers, and suddenly Magnus the sheriff arrived with about twenty-five extra soldiers. "We have braced the inside of the gate with iron strips is there anything else you can think of Rogan?"

"Where is all the stuff we used to fill the gap in, can it be replaced?"

"The men used it to make fires, but we could pull beams from some of the houses, if need be, to use as brace bars!"

Black Guard warriors came forward in a testudo formation, they had interlinked all their shields together in such a way that the defenders' arrows and rocks could not find any purchase and so they were gradually having their ammunition eroded without any effect at all.

The first strike from the ram struck the gates in the centre of the two, shaking both gates almost out of their hinges. "Those gates aren't going to take much more punishment if they continue like that, we need a plan!" Rogan shouted, to no one in particular.

"Have you got any fire arrows or oil you can throw down?" Ongar directed this question at the sheriff.

"We might have one barrel of oil left, that's all, sergeant-at-arms, see if you can fetch it up here to the ramparts!"

"You men, start ripping up some cloth and get wrapping it around your remaining arrows, once the oil is brought up, dip them in and light them up," Ongar instructed.

"Gunnar, get everyone mounted back up, I have a plan to buy some time until the infantry arrives, tomorrow."

Aatu was the only one who seemed excited by the plan, once all of the thirty-two were remounted, including Ongar, Rogan called them to arms, and they followed his lead as he rode through the deserted streets towards the west gate of the town. There was a unit of fifty guards stationed there and when they heard the hoofbeats, they strained their necks to see who was riding there, Rogan shouted, "Open the gates!" and a group of the guards hurriedly pulled the wooden staves away that braced the gates, and pulled them open.

Once outside of the town walls Rogan pulled his horse to the right and lined himself up with the side of the black guard formation that was operating the ram. "Form a column behind me, and keep it tight!"

To their left was line upon line, row upon row of black guard soldiers standing like gigantic black monoliths, spears at the ready, shields in hand. "My God what is he doing?" yelled the sheriff, after seeing this small tight column of riders hurtling towards an army numbering five hundred or more.

"Is there anything we can do?" the sergeant-at-arms asked.

"Light up the fire arrows and aim high, it should buy them some time to make one attack against the ramming party, now send out the word!"

The black guard ramming party was some way forward of the rest of the enemy positions, and they might have looked up through the patchwork of thick leather hides protecting them from arrows, and thought that they were the lucky ones, missing out on the flight of burning arrows that only a split second later rained down on their kinfolk.

That was before they realised that it was, they who were the real target of the forlorn attack, Aatu was the first to strike as he easily outpaced all the horses and leaped up towards the top of the covered housing. His momentum, as he slammed into the leather hides, smashed a huge hole in the side of the housing and splintered an even larger part of the wooden framework that held the whole structure together.

The black guard soldiers cheered after realising that they had taken no casualties, and Aatu slid over the top of the housing and down the other side. Aatu was the second distraction, as he danced between their attempts to spear him, they left themselves wide open to Rogan and his housecarl and when they struct the open side of the frame, they tore it to shreds along with nearly every black guard soldier trapped inside when the housing collapsed.

Rogan was unable to see that the whole of the rest of the black guard army had changed formation and the sheriff was unable to make his warning shouts heard above the noise of the battle. The front ranks opened to allow black guard archers to move forward and take up positions across the whole of their front, the order was given for the archers to fire directly into the melee that was the ramming party.

"Shields up!" roared Rogan when he saw his housecarl begin to fall from their horses but it was too late as the arrows dropped out of the sky decimating his bodyguard along with any surviving member of the ramming party.

"Sheriff, should we try to open the gates at least?" begged the sergeant-at-arms.

"No, all we can do now is hope that some of them can make good their escape."

"But what if we throw ropes down in front of the gates, they could at least try to climb up?"

"Hurry, sergeant, your idea might just work, you two soldiers stay here and keep shouting to Rogan, get them to come to the gates."

Rogan watched helplessly as men and horses fell one after the other, never in his life had he recklessly squandered anyone's life, quite like he had done this day, but it was done, and it only remained for him to help extricate what was left, and so he looked around briefly for that exit. Ongar was the one who pointed to the soldiers above the gate. "Look Rogan, I think they want us to run that way!" Aatu turned to face the black guard baring his teeth and snarling in defiance.

"No boy, our job is done they cannot break the gates down without this ram." As Rogan spoke to his blood-covered warg he noticed that the whole of the black guard army was moving forward in formation.

"Everyone, hurry to the walls, put the wounded on the horses, and retreat!" barked Rogan, unaware that he had an arrow protruding from his chest, just below his left collar bone.

Suddenly and as if out of thin air a very excited Aethelric appeared at the head of a group of three wagons and horses, they were riding fast towards the sound of battle. The bard jumped clear of the first wagon just as it was coming to a halt at the bottom of the stairs leading to the right-hand tower.

"Sheriff Steinolf, where is my lord Rogan?"

The sheriff did not speak but instead pointed over the wall, and when Aethelric looked that way all he could see was a sea of black-clad soldiers converging on the gates below, then he saw the first of the housecarl being helped up over the top of the gate, it was Sigrunn Hallkatla, Atli Hælæifsson's partner, and she was badly injured, three separate arrows were lodged in her upper torso.

Aethelric ran back to the other side where it overlooked his Wagon's, and where Sister Wenyid was in a hurry to bring up the fire-pots!

"What are you going to do Aethelric?" asked a bemused-looking sheriff.

"Watch and see, my friend, watch and see…!"

Aethelric held the rather plump-looking clay pot up in one hand while he asked one of the soldiers to lite the wick that was protruding from the top. He turned towards the dark mass of heaving black guard who were now just about twenty paces away from where Rogan was and he hurled it up in the air and towards the black guard. By this time, eleven housecarls had managed to scramble over the gatehouse to safety.

The wall guards watched as the small clay pot arced through the air, Rogan watched from where he was crouched by the gates until the pot hit one of the black guards on the top of his helmet. The pot exploded and a thick black sticky liquid splashed out in every direction, In a split second the soldier was engulfed in a searing hot ball of flame and his screams were the stuff of nightmares.

Every warrior who had come with Aethelric was now on top of the wall, pot in hand waiting as another soldier ran down the line lighting the wicks. A couple of seconds ticked by in slow motion until the order to throw them rang out, this time thirty fire-pots hurtled threw the air smashing all over the front ranks of the black guard immolating twenty or thirty of them, the rear ranks began to step backwards and they did not wait for a second barrage or the order to retreat.

Some of the black guard tried to use their large gloved hands to try to pat the flame out, but the sticky burning liquid just stuck to their hands and they too began to howl with pain as their fingers began to melt.

The remaining black guard broke ranks and ran for their lives, many of them had been drilled and trained to withstand anything that a normal human could throw at them, but this was some kind of magic that was anything but normal. Rogan was free to climb up the ropes unchallenged and between them, the town guard and Aethelric managed to save over half of Rogan's housecarl.

6

The Feign Attack

After gulping down fresh cold water that was brought up from the wells at Ingolfsfell, near the southern gate, and snatching at pieces of bread with lard smeared over it, the fighters began that ritual of praying to the one true God, or the other Gods, for there were many lesser ones, or they asked their spirit ancestors, whichever method worked, they all called for the strength and fortitude to get through another night together.

Shortly before the sun sank completely in the western sky, some began to see little flickers of light appearing from the road that led south. Where this weary eye's playing tricks, or was it witchcraft, a secret weapon of the black guard, as those flickers came closer the defenders steeled themselves for their arrival.

Three hundred paces, two hundred and fifty paces, they were well within the range of archers but Rogan stayed his hand when asked whether they should let loose a volley of arrows, two hundred paces and tensions were running high, some now turned to Rogan for answers but he stood like a man suddenly turned to stone, his eyes clenched tightly shut, and nervousness began to fan out across the top of the battlements.

One hundred and fifty paces and still nothing more than the odd flicker, glimmers of light flashing momentarily in the last dying embers of the sun, one hundred paces and the flickers were extinguished, and every eye was searching, scouring the twilight for a sign, archers strained at their bowstrings, ligaments, and muscle straining, hands clenched around fire-pots and throwing arms held out and back were beginning to ache, the urge to release building.

"Stand down, everyone!" came the call from Rogan, but before befuddled minds could process the order, the eyes looked upon a sign so rare and so beautiful it brought tears to even the most hardened of warriors, for suddenly cloaks were tossed back and there standing in perfect rank order, gold overlaid on dark hardened leather, so intricately patterned and glistening in the moons first light, were the elves, hundreds of disciplined warriors and Aylild was standing proudly just a step or two ahead of them with an elegant looking older male elf at her side.

A single order was called out by the older elf, and suddenly every elven soldier was throwing something dark round, and metallic forward towards the walls. "We came across these just less than a league back and thought you might like to see them, I believe it is your custom, human, to hang them from your battlements?" it was the severed heads of hundreds of black guards.

"I don't want to sound ungrateful, but, yeah, not my thing, but I can ask around!"

"Looks like you had quite an encounter with these monstrosities, Brother, they were strong and very capable warriors, you did well to beat them."

"Let me give the order to clear the gates and let you enter, Aylild."

"No need, we are used to climbing as part of our training, give me a moment." Aylild gave the command and all of the elves began running towards the wall, the first to arrive held out cupped hands, and the second wave stepped into them and were then hoisted up, a third wave climbed up the two bodies and were over the wall in seconds, they, in turn, leant forward to grab the second waves hands and they the first, and each pulled the others up.

The battle for Ingolfsfell was over, but the war against the blackguard was only just beginning.

The stories and songs about this most valiant of days would reverberate around the whole of the north of Råvenniå and beyond, in the proceeding days and months more and more of those who fled the town and surrounding countryside began to trickle back, some would proclaim their new champion, Rogan Ragisson, the King of the North, and just as quickly he would quash any such talk immediately, he had no wish to claim such a title.

Rogan finally got to meet Ascarli, the commander of the elves of Avanore, for the second time, in his life, but for now, at this moment, he was a stranger to him, far too young was he the first time they met.

"You are a most welcome sight, my new friend!" Rogan commented as he walked towards Ascarli and Aylild.

"We came as soon as we could, but you should know that news from your capital is not good, we had to pass nearby and thought it would be fortuitous to pay the king a visit."

"Has the queen's black guard somehow escaped the city, Ascarli?"

"Far worse my friend, your capital is in lockdown, nothing in, nothing out. The black guard has taken the walls all around the city and locked the gates, they fire at anyone who comes too close to the walls and the bodies are left to fester and rot in the streets."

"Why haven't the king's guards fought back?"

"There was no way of knowing, Rogan, we tried to get near but all of the buildings within a hundred yards had been put to the torch, including each of the winter storehouses, I fear starvation and diseases are ravishing the people."

"This is worse than any of us could have imagined, is the king even still alive?"

"I don't know, there was one man who had escaped via the river, but he was badly wounded and died the following day."

"What was he able to tell you…anything?"

"The queen and her bodyguard, are all who have been seen around the palace, otherwise her guards have stripped the market of everything edible and they enter people's homes to take what they want, everyone who lives is terrified of her, and them."

Rogan said that they must make for Kaldakinn and tell the council there this terrible news. Ascarli asked if would be more prudent to wait until after the spring. Rogan struggled to think of how to reply at first, but he understood why Ascarli had offered his opinion. The council would without doubt demand that Rogan march his army down to Østergård and liberate the capital, it was what he was thinking of doing anyway.

"Ascarli, can I ask that you leave the bulk of your warriors here in Ingolfsfell while we travel to Kaldakinn?"

"Do you fear that more black guard may attack?"

"Yes, and no! it's just that what's left of the soldiers and people here are worn out and your elves sharing the load would help bolster their morale and give them some respite."

"What about the food situation here, Rogan?"

"As far as I am aware there is plenty for everyone, the inhabitants left rather abruptly and most have still not returned, so it would be less of a burden if they stayed until called upon."

"I understand, it makes perfect sense, I will give all of my captain's orders before we leave, now will it just be Aylild and myself who accompany you or would you prefer an escort?"

"I think a small show of support would not go unnoticed, say about twenty-five of your best warriors, but I did not notice any horses, do your warriors not ride?"

"We are not known for having Aru's creatures carry us into battle where they may get hurt or even killed, and besides, my daughter's wood elves could easily keep up with your horses at a trot."

The council at the great hall in Kaldakinn was horrified to hear what news Rogan and his guests had brought them, and just as was suspected, the council called for an assault on the capital, after all, Rogan had already shown that he could defeat the black guard in battle. Rogan shouted above the cacophony of noise and demanded silence.

"We simply cannot brake away now, at the end of the summer season, dropping all of our plans and preparations to assault the capital, there are for all we know many hundreds of black guards dug in behind fortified positions, it would cost the lives of too many of our warriors to take back, and then what would we do in the spring, attack the Orsk with a starving disease-ridden army of walking dead and cripples! Besides which, the soldiers are needed in their home villages, in a few days it will be, Oineis, the start of the autumn months." That statement brought much division within the council, but there was no escaping the fact that it was the truth.

Oineis, the tenth month of the year, brought the leaves down off the trees and the snowfall from the heavens that would finally stay on the ground for more than a day, the capital was closed and would most likely stay that way anyway, what it did not bring was another attack on any of its fronts from Rogan's enemies, and there was a general easing of tensions between all the people of all races in northern Råvenniå.

Weaving was one of the main ways of passing the time, when not soldiering, Twigs were woven together to make fences and house walls or baskets, lobster pots, and thread was woven into the material. Baskets were often woven out of willow. Willow rods known as 'withies' were harvested during Oineis when the leaves had dropped.

The sowing of seeds was another important job that had to be done during the month of Oineis. Once the fields had been ploughed, seeds had to be scattered into the earth. It was important to spread the seeds evenly so that there was a good crop and even though the ground was hard, the crops for spring had to be sown.

Finally, there was milling, the process where grain is turned into flour at the mill, in each of the village's towns there would be at least one mill, the cogs that turned the grindstones would have needed the horses that men might have fought upon.

"In Necysios, the first month of winter, we will need to start butchering the herds, cooking all the meat, and salting it in barrels, no there are too many practical things that we need those men for, or as Rogan said, we will not have a fit army for the spring, and look we now have hundreds more mouths to feed already from the displaced people!" Renwick relayed to the council.

"Aethelric, tomorrow I will be visiting Athenous, for one last look at the town and particularly the docks before the winter closes in and the roads become impassable, you will remain here and be in charge in my stead, is that clear to everyone?"

"Yes, lord!" they all shouted.

"Good, Ongar, you will be coming with me, as will Tukor, and Aatu."

Ascarli the elven leader told Rogan that he would be coming too, he wanted to see the mountain for himself and get a feel of what sort of terrain his people would be expected to navigate, Aylild wanted to come as well but Ascarli refused her request.

Brother Cuthbald had also wanted to accompany the others on their trek north, he had grown rather fond of Tukor and did not want to leave him with strangers especially since he would be returning to a land that was harsh and unforgiving even in the summer, never mind this time of year, but Rogan was able to speak to Tukor in his native tongue, and he assured him that he would be safe and treated as one of his own.

When the party left Kaldakinn towards the end of autumn the weather had already turned and it was freezing outside, the Great North Road, as it was now being called, was covered by a light smattering of snow. "Gunnar, I think we are going to need some more furs, please tell me we haven't given them all away to the refugees?" called Rogan.

Ascarli had agreed to ride with the group and Rogan could not help smiling as he watched the elf trying to master the human saddle and calm the nervous horse. Each rider took a spare horse as Rogan had insisted on speed, the weather was unpredictable at this time of the year, also each spare horse wore horse blankets made from furs, that covered them from head to tail, they even had socks specially made for them.

Aatu was the only one who wore nothing but his natural coat, but it did not seem to bother him.

Aatu was too big to ride across the front of Rogan's horse, as he once was able, so he ran alongside on all fours. The group arrived in Athenous six hours later, around mid-afternoon and they could barely see the town at all, it was as though every building was now painted white, even the cathedral which sat on the hill, but the nearer they got the more incredible the sight, like a crystal city rising out of the snow.

They headed for the tavern, the King's Arms, which came highly recommended by both Aethelric and Sister Wenyid, the group debussed from their mounts and tied them to the rail outside the alehouse and went inside, the large roaring fire was a most welcome sight. Rogan told Tukor to keep his hood up and face covered.

"Ah, good afternoon gentlemen, my name is Ingulfrid and I am the proprietor of this establishment, how can I be of service?"

Rogan looked around to see who was in the bar area, and he saw no one although he was aware that there were other people in the alehouse, they were huddled away in the corners and in the shadows out of the way of prying eyes. "Do you have someone who can fetch all of our things in from our horses and then take them to the stables, I can pay for the service."

"Just one moment, I have a boy, Trygg! Trygg, where are you when I need you?"

"Here I am Aunty, I was just out back fetching more logs."

"Ah, he is a sweetheart, he is my sister's boy, and he always wants to help, do anything for anyone, that one. Trygg, I need you to go out front and fetch these fine gentlemen's things in from their horses, and then can you walk them over to the stable and make sure they have forage and a stall each to stay in."

"Who shall I tell the stable man is paying?"

Rogan opened his leather pouch and pressed four silver shillings into the boy's hand, his eyes widened as he stared at them, and he thanked Rogan for them without even asking his name. Rogan said two were for the stable owner, one was for the horse's keep and the other was for Trygg to keep after he had brought their stuff in off the horses. Then he thanked them profusely and ran outside to begin his first task.

Rogan asked for rooms and said that his companions were tired and they would want to be resting very soon, Ingulfrid said she would make them some of her potage and bring it over to them by the fire, but Rogan insisted they sit somewhere else, he said they did not want to rob the others in here the warmth of the fire and as they were already well wrapped up it would be fine.

What Rogan had meant was that Aethelric had already warned them that the people of the new town did not suffer other races well, and so Rogan had insisted that Ascarli, Ongar, and Tukor all kept their coats on, hoods up, and kerchiefs covering their faces. Ingulfrid brought the food over first and then the warm mead, watching the three visitors lifting their face coverings slightly to eat, she did wonder why they did not just take them off, but she had already seen the amount of coin one of them had and she shrugged her shoulders and carried on serving them.

Aatu now found a place facing Rogan but still near enough to the fire and he settled himself down stretching his enormous paws out in front of his body. "Can I get your dog anything to eat?" With that Aatu pricked his ears up and whined slightly.

"Yes, thank you, my lady, he will have the same as us!"

Now Aatu buried his head in his front paws as though he might have liked something else entirely, which did amuse the barmaid, but not Rogan.

"You should be lucky I don't send you outside to find your supper, dog!"

Aatu whined some more and then rolled over on his stomach.

"Don't you worry, Ingulfrid will find you something in the kitchen!"

Aatu rolled back onto his front and barked once loudly. The noise did cause a stir in the alehouse and Rogan found himself talking to the 'dog' quietly, "That's right, draw as much attention to us as you possibly can!"

Ingulfrid did indeed find a treat for Aatu, when she emerged from the kitchen, she was holding a large bone that still had some scraps of meat on it. "There you are, you, handsome hound!" she said, and Aatu jumped up and licked her face all over until she begged him to stop, but not in a harsh way, but a playful one. Then she turned to Rogan. "I'll be upstairs warming all of your beds if that's alright, if you need anything before Trygg gets back just hollow, and I will be right down."

121

That night Rogan tossed and turned in his cot bed, he realised that for weeks now that there had not been a night that he had not been with Ingrid, and tonight it was cold and he felt alone, like when he recalled waking up in the Orsk caves.

Aatu must have sensed his master's unease because he jumped on the bed, his weight causing it to creek heavily in places, and he proceeded to snuggle up with Rogan. "I don't know which of us is the big softy here, Aatu, you or me, now get some sleep and try not to squash me in the night!" he said while ruffling Aatu's soft white coat.

The following morning as Ingulfrid was serving Rogan breakfast she asked if the others had slept alright as none of them had come downstairs. Rogan said that they were very tired this morning but that he would happily take them their food up to their rooms, Aatu started to roll over and over once more and the barmaid knelt to give his exposed stomach a rub. "Will you be staying long my Lord?"

"No, we are traders and have come in search of fishermen who can satisfy our need for minke whale oil, if you could recommend anyone, we would all be very grateful."

"I will get Trygg to take you, there is an old sailor who is looking for extra customers, yes, he will be very pleased I'm sure, now let me spoil this gorgeous hound of yours while you take your friends their food and drink."

Trygg was eager to be a guide for the day and he could not stop talking to Rogan as they waited for the others to get ready and come downstairs. Rogan said that they would not be taking their horses and he offered Trygg more silver to pay for their stay in the stables, Trygg was once more, wide-eyed, at the amount of silver coins, and he even said that the amount was way too much, in fact for this amount the horses could probably stay all year!

Just as the others were coming out of their rooms and Rogan was facing them, the door to the alehouse opened, and in walked a man who was equally wrapped up as Rogan and his group were. "Good morning to you, and how is my favourite barmaid today?"

Rogan recognised the voice immediately and tried as best he could to hide his face, it was Jarl Oswald, and Rogan did not want anyone to know that he was there, they would start asking questions that he would not have liked to answer, and so he decided to walk towards the stairs leading up to the others, patting his pockets as though he had left something in his room. "Good morning to you friend!" the jarl called to Rogan as he started to climb the stairs.

Rogan did not reply, instead, he merely waved his hand, then he became stricken with panic as he realised the jarl would recognise Aatu, but as he looked around Aatu was nowhere in sight, he had just vanished. Aatu had crawled under the stairs and hid himself in the shadows. Rogan gathered all the men in one room and they waited until the jarl had eaten and left the alehouse. "By the Gods, that was close!" announced Ongar.

Once back downstairs they all thanked Ingulfrid and made their way to the door, Aatu had re-joined them and Trygg was waiting outside to take them to see the old fisherman, each of them kept a watchful eye out for anyone who might have recognised them, or more specifically, Aatu.

There was little need to worry as Ascarli was able to conjure a spell of hiding on Aatu that because of his already white coat, against the snow-covered ground made him almost invisible. Trygg was still his over-enthusiastic self and could not help himself but keep on asking questions. He wanted to know who they were, traders do not carry so many weapons or armour, to which Rogan did his best to deflect what was being asked of him, undeterred the boy asked if they knew Rogan Ragisson.

They all shook their heads, which did not amount to much considering how many layers they were wearing even as head coverings. "I want to be just like him when I grow up", the boy said before asking once more if they were sure that they didn't know him.

Rogan asked if they were near to where the fisherman lived, and the boy said that they were one street away, and that was when Rogan slapped his hand down on the boy's right shoulder. "Did anyone ever tell you that you ask too many questions, boy?"

"No, lord," the boy answered, his voice quivering slightly.

"Look, the truth is, and I think you already guessed as much, we are here on a secret mission, and nobody is supposed to know that!"

"I knew it, all those swords and stuff, I won't tell I promise, is the mission for Rogan Ragisson, is it?"

"If I said, yes, would it stop you any?"

"I knew it, I did, you do know him don't you, I bet you are his most trusted men aren't you!"

"Something like that yes."

"I thought so, you have a dog and I heard that he has a wolf that he trained from birth and it is as big as a horse, you could ride on its back, is it true?"

"Perhaps, but a secret mission isn't very secret if I answered all of your questions, so for now you have to be quiet, do you understand?"

"If I said, yes, then does that mean I am on the secret mission with you?"

"But of course, yes you are now part of Rogan's secret mission." At this point, Rogan was about to find a large barrel of frozen water and tip the boy head first in it just to silence him for a minute, however, he checked himself and realised that allowing the boy to believe he was part of the mission was the better idea.

"Here we are my lord, the old fisherman's shack!"

"What's all the noise, I can't hear my self-think, who are you all?"

The fisherman was busy painting the outside of his wattle and daub home with slack lime, which was used to keep the weather from washing the daud mixture away.

"Old man, this is my lord…I don't know his name but he wants to hire your boat!"

"I did not tell you that boy, why do you say that?"

"What! What! You do not want to hire my boat, then why the blazes are you here wasting my time?"

"He does want to hire your boat, don't you mister, and he's got coin, lots of it!"

"Trygg! Stop, I do have a tongue of my own you know!"

"Well make your mind up, because the winter is coming and the bay is already icing up!"

"How much to sail us across to the other side, old man?"

"Other side of where exactly?"

"They want to go across to Obrea, to spy on the Orsk, you should offer to take them for free, they are friends with Rogan Ragisson!"

"Alright, Trygg, that's enough, here take this shilling and take yourself back to Ingulfrid and remember, not a word to anyone."

"Oh, alright, I will go, but I could have come with you, I'm nearly fourteen now and I could have helped." He sulked, before turning on his heels and disappearing back the way he had come.

"A, gold piece!" the old man stated.

"A, gold piece?"

"Ah, well at least you are not deaf deaf, but would you like to swim across the river?"

"Alright, one gold piece, but only on the condition that in one week, you will return to the spot where you drop us and bring us back across the river."

"Done!" and the old fisherman spat on his right palm and held his hand out for Rogan to do the same.

The journey across the bay was uneventful, there was a slight wind and the fisherman said that there would be no more snow for a while, in his opinion. Rogan was watching the coastline ahead and he asked the others to do the same, without thinking Tukor pulled his hood down to allow himself to see more clearly.

"The Gods! What manner of creature is that?" demanded the old fisherman, then Aatu began to bark and sniff at something under a canvas at the bow of the boat, Rogan told Aatu to quieten down and the old fisherman said that he did want any trouble, then the canvas moved and somebody under it started to cough.

Trygg was still coughing when Ongar reached down and pulled the canvas away, revealing the stow-a-way. Tukor did his best to cover his head once more and kept muttering how sorry he was, the fisherman said that for the gold coin, it was none of his business but the creature had frightened him, Trygg just thought things could not get any better.

Rogan told the fisherman that 'the creature' was the best way that they could win the war in the spring, and he must be kept secret, Trygg added that if the old man blabbed, he would slit his throat open! And that was when Rogan told him forcefully to be quiet and to the fisherman he said, please, it was that important, and he asked if for another silver coin could he take the boy back across the river, or just drop him overboard about halfway.

The fisherman did not need to be asked, or threatened, he was old enough to know that this trip was much more important, and besides, who would believe a story like this anyway, he would get laughed out of town. He assured Rogan that he had no intention of sharing what he knew with anyone, adding, I am a loyal friend and subject, with a wink of the eye.

Rogan hoped in his heart that his cover would not be blown so easily by the Orsk.

The fisherman ran his boat onto the soft sand below a rocky outcrop and the group alighted from his boat, and Trygg was told that he must help the old man by pushing the boat off the sand before Rogan turned away and began to walk.

Tukor recognised where they had landed quickly, after all, he had spent most of his life living rough out here, and he began to point excitedly towards a small clef in the rocks ahead. "This way, master Rogan, this way!" he chortled away, finding the very place he had promised would lead them right into the heart of the Kingdom under the mountain.

"Find some driftwood and wrap the hemp cloth we brought around it, Ongar, do you have the container with the birch pitch in it?"

Ongar swung his rucksack from his shoulder and after opening it up, he produced a pot that held about a pint of the sticky black tar, which he then proceeded to drip over each of the other's hemp cloth until it was time to do his own, once the pot was empty, he laid it on the ground and they moved towards the entrance to the cave.

It was a tighter fit than they had anticipated, when this mission was being planned nobody assumed that they would be wearing several layers of sheep's wool and bearskins.

At first, it was a squeeze through the small clef, the tunnel was roughly hewn from the rock but by the hand of any creature, it was a natural spillway for water running off the mountains further inland, the rock was immediately sandy and brushed off when touched, it reminded Rogan and Ongar of their time in captivity. The mouth of the tunnel opened, and once inside they discovered it was wide enough for at least three to stand side by side and just high enough to stand without having to stoop.

Aatu pushed his way forward and entered the cave proper, first, then Rogan lit the torches with his flint kit and they each climbed inside and all immediately felt the benefits from being out of the exposed beach area. "I think we can lose a few of our coats in here, it is not so bad as I thought it might be." Said Rogan.

Tukor did not like fire and he struggled to hold the torch for fear of burning himself but Ascarli took pity on the creature and showed him how best to grip it so that it would be safe.

The party had not walked far into the tunnel when Aatu began to act strangely, he kept on looking behind every few moments and whining. "What's up boy?" Rogan would ask, but it just seemed to agitate Aatu more. Ascarli said that he would have more success if he stopped to look back on the way they had come.

"This is a good time to test yourself," he said.

Rogan stared at him vacantly, as did the others, all except Aatu, who looked at him and licked his lips, and wagged his tail.

"What is going on here?" Rogan asked.

"Focus, Arathorn, on the entrance to the tunnel, close your eyes and see what is behind you!"

"Oh, this again!" was all Rogan would say, the others just whispered to each other, "Who is Arathorn?"

"Try! Just let yourself—"

"Yeah, I know the drill."

Rogan closed his eyes tightly and tried to focus his mind on the way that they had just come, his first thoughts were of Aylild, and he had a strange feeling that she suddenly knew what he was doing and he saw in his mind's eye, she was smiling, approvingly, and that seemed to calm him down for a moment. "Trygg!"

"Trygg?" Ongar said, wondering why Rogan was standing there looking down the tunnel with his eyes closed in such a way that he looked pained.

"Trygg has followed us, he is somewhere behind us, wait here!" announced Rogan.

Minutes later after Rogan had stormed down the tunnel, he reappeared holding Trygg by his left ear and almost hoisting him off the ground at the same time.

"I didn't mean to follow you, I promise, it's just that when I pushed the old man's boat back off the sand, I sort of forgot to climb aboard."

"You are a ruddy fool if you think that this is going to be a great adventure, like when you play with your friends, well it's not and everyone from here on in will have to pull his weight or else!"

"Yes, lord, and I am sorry honestly." The boy said with a smile so wide it almost touched both sides of the tunnel. Rogan just let him go and shuck his head, Ongar was about to say that he had been a fine warrior by the age of this boy, but checked his tongue, not wanting to exasperate Rogan any further.

So began the journey proper, a company of five and their faithful warg, what could go wrong?

The journey was long and arduous, and a little claustrophobic at times, every twist and turn in those tunnels looked exactly like every other, and it was soon apparent that some form of marking the tunnels was required if the party or the army in the spring was not to get lost down here. Ascarli began putting markings that his elven warriors would be able to read and understand because it was the elves who were given the task of entering the kingdom under the mountains by this route.

The group arrived at their first cross-section of the tunnel and Ascarli marked it, this would be a good place to stay the night, it will give us some idea of what to expect when we return with hundreds of elves and not just a party of five, Ascarli said.

"Are we able to light a fire, it will get pretty cold in here tonight, I am sure?"

Tukor said that they still had a way to go and the way ahead led to the Orsk waste pit, which would mast any smell a fire would make, or even cooking food for that matter, and a hot cooked meal always went a long way to making folk more settled.

The waste pit that Tukor refer to was an almost vertical shaft that ran from somewhere way above their heads right down to where they stood, and where they stood felt and smelt like the belly of the beast. Tons of excrement dripped down the walls and lay all around on the floor, the smell was so overwhelming that each member of the party had to put a cloth over their mouths so as not to continually retch. Even Tukor found it difficult not to cover his face. "We must climb this wall, the way we need to go is up there." He pointed.

They stood and stared in utter disbelief. "Up there were the walls covered in dung and God only knows what else?"

"Yes, we cannot stay here, this part of the cave network leads to the sea, and we are below that level." Explained Tukor.

"What does that mean," asked Ongar.

"I think he is trying to tell us that at some point the sea water will wash into this part of the tunnel and flush all of this away, and probably us with it." Said Trygg.

"The dung will mask our smell, so the orcs will never suspect that we are here, it is good, master, yes?" implored Tukor, ever eager to please.

Rogan had suddenly lost his tongue and just began to climb. He placed his left leg on an outcrop of rock and pushed his body upwards with his right leg, then he swung his arms above his head looking to make a purchase somewhere so that he could pull himself up, and to his horror, his right hand sank into a large piece of Orsk turd.

The others shrugged their shoulders and began to climb too, Aatu looked up and barked, but it was not long before he was climbing too, he had found what looked like a very narrow spiral staircase, and it wasn't long before the others were trying to climb their way over to the warg.

About halfway up the funnel, Tukor pointed to another tunnel leading away. "There!" he declared, pointing for them to go that way. Aatu, who resembled a normal warg due to his colour, now bolted ahead of the others, Rogan was becoming breathless, as were the others, but they dare not remove their face coverings, they were no longer in the tunnel but they were caked from head to toe in excrement, enough to send the most ardent of Orsk running in disgust.

Aatu could be heard whining just a little way from where they were, and as they walked around a slight bend they could see why, this tunnel had been blocked, not by a cave-in, but by an iron gate in an iron framework which was locked. Tukor grabbed two of the bars and began to rattle them. "Don't understand, no bars before!" he said.

"No worries," Rogan said, "I can open this, give me a minute."

Rogan then produced a small knife from his belt and asked if anyone had anything short and blunt. Ascarli produced an arrow which he snapped the head off. "Will this do?"

Rogan poked the knife into the lock, and then the broken arrow, he wiggled the arrow around for a few moments but nothing was happening.

"Ah!" he declared. "The lock is so rusty I doubt anyone could open it!"

"Erm, I could have a go, Rogan Ragisson," Trygg offered.

"Trygg, this is grown-up stuff now, so go and wait out of the way, we will think of something/"

"But I have these," he rummaged around in his rucksack and produced a small wooden box. "It was my pa's, he gave it to me before he died."

Trygg opened the box with such reverence the other thought it might contain his father's bones or maybe his ashes, but it did not, instead there was a set of lock-picking tools.

"Do you know how to use those, Trygg?" asked Ongar.

"Course I do, it's the first thing he taught me after I had learned to walk."

"Humans never cease to amaze me," Ascarli stated while shaking his head vigorously.

Trygg moved forward to the door and within minutes he had sprung the lock. "You were right Rogan it was very rusty!"

"Hang on just one minute, you have used my name twice now, how long have you known?"

Trygg just smiled and then swung the iron gate open.

The further they went, the louder the sounds of life ahead became. "Tukor who is likely to be up there?"

"Orsk!"

"Yes, I know Orsk, but will there be any black guard?"

"No, none of them, this tunnel goes to the high balcony, but we go this way now, a secret tunnel to Mother." And Tukor pointed to another clef in the rocks, it was even narrower than the one back at the main entrance.

Tukor lead them along the secret passage that led straight to the back of his mother's cave, he tapped lightly and called out to his mother, "Mama, mama, it is I, your son Tukor."

From somewhere behind the secret door came the sound of movement, clumsily at first, like someone had been awaking from a drunken state, but as Tukor whispered, his mother drew her senses together. "Tukor, is that you Son, after all these years you have returned to your mama?"

"Yes mama, Tukor has found his way home."

"Tell me that this is not treachery on your part, my son?"

"Mama, there is no treachery, why do you say such a hurtful thing?"

"Because I might be old and the magic week but I can sense that you are not alone!"

"Mama, I have friends and they take care of me, but they need to speak to you before it is too late."

"Too late, why would it be too late?"

"Mama, just speak with them, for Tukor."

The secret door began to slide open.

"Argh! You tricked me my boy, my flesh and blood and you tricked me in the foulest possible way!"

"No, mama you remember Rogan and Ongar, they helped me mama, they are my friends, they come talk with you now."

"I smell an elf, is he too your friend, or do you not know that we are sworn enemies?"

Ascarli moved into the light of the torch. "I am Ascarli Northstar, the leader of the elves of Avanore, and we are indeed the bitterest of enemies, but we come this day to seek your help to avert a terrible war and much bloodshed, today, I come in peace."

"Neither of us are the people we once were, both have suffered terribly since the days of long ago, yet why should I believe you now, elf?"

"Because I come with Rogan and Ongar and Aatu, and because magic is wasting away and with it our lives and the lives of our people, soon neither of us will be here, but what legacy will we leave behind, for our children?"

"Our children? Don't you mean the half-breeds and whatever you call your whelps?" spat the Orsk.

"Do you deny them their place in this world?" Ascarli exclaimed.

"Who am I to deny or allow, I am but a pawn of the Gods, and so I believe are you Ascarli Northstar." And with that, the old Orsk began to cackle.

"Then let the Gods speak for us!"

"Who here can speak for the Gods?"

"I think you already know the answer to that question and that is why you seek to talk in circles."

"Aatu! Come to me Aatu."

Aatu hesitated for a moment, first, he looked up at Rogan, who nodded that he should move forward and then he looked back at Ascarli and whined, and Ascarli waved his hands forward and said, "Go, boy, speak to Berba-Shin!"

At that, Aatu ran to the haggard old Orsk.

"Alright, alright, I accept that it is the will of the Gods that we talk, but I will give no guarantees, do you hear me?"

Rogan and Ongar both took it in turns to speak to the shaman, without giving away too much detail they told her that come the first thaw of spring a great army would cross the Tawa River and descend upon the kingdom under the mountains, to liberate all those who live in captivity, and to end the heinous practice of rape and exploitation, perpetrated by the Orsk.

"So, where is it exactly that you see me in all of this, are you offering me something, if you are then I am missing it." Berba-Shin mused.

"We want all of the half-bloods to have the opportunity to be free, to live outside, and to live among the other people of the world without being afraid."

"I am not sure you understand anything that is happening here, this, all of this has come about because of you Hu-mans, Ro-Gan, because your type thirst for power and privilege, and we are a factory for that one product that your kind lack, strength, strength in the form of the black guard."

"Damn it, Rogan, I knew this would be a waste of time, listen to her, she is one of them, how could we have hope for anything otherwise?"

"No, Mama, you must listen to my friends, they let me live freely among them and Ongar too, their God is a loving God who excepts all his children who repent."

"Repent, what do you my baby boy have to repent over, was it not I who conceived you, who carried you for nine months and then delivered you into this world, all by myself?"

"But my people hate me, they were cruel and chased me off into the wilds to fend for myself, and where were you mama, where were you when I cried myself to sleep under the stars, no mama the Orsk in this place must pay with their lives for what they are doing to their children, half-bloods deserve the opportunity to live in the light of the sun, and not the darkness that is all that is for them down here."

Berba-Shin moved to her son and clasped her arms around him and began to cry, "Oh what have we done to you, what have I done to you my precious baby boy, you are right, and I am wrong, and I do not know how to put things right."

"Then help us mama, help Rogan and Ongar and the elf."

There was a loud banging on the door to Berba-Shin's door. "What is all that noise coming from in here, hag?"

"Who dares disturb Berba-Shin when she is conversing with the Gods?"

"It is I, Xu-Gor, leader of the Nedrakah warband."

"Good! Come in why don't you, I have something to say to you."

"Now quickly, all of you go back into the tunnel and wait." Then the old Orsk closed the door to the secret passage just as the door to her chamber opened.

"Xu-Gor, tell me something if you will, how are the defensive preparations coming along?"

"Why do you ask?"

"Do not seek to provoke me half-breed, just answer the question, unless you would like me to put a nasty little spell on your warband, that is, and I can you know?"

"I am ready as are my warriors, ready to taste Hu-man flesh for the glory of the kingdom under the mountains."

"Ah, I see, do you like living in the kingdom under the mountains?"

"I…I don't understand the question?"

"Do you like living in a filthy rat-infested cave under the ground, it is quite simple really."

"I don't know any other way of life, so I don't know what to answer."

"Oh, but you do, you know exactly what it is to run freely in the light of day in the world outside, how does that feel?"

"When we go hunting, yes, it is far better than to be stuck in here, but to live out there, I have no idea."

"Would you at least like to have the chance?"

"You mean like Ro-Gan and his warband, they live still, we were told that the Hu-Mans had killed them all, even their womenfolk."

"And if I could show you, now, that, it is a lie, then how would you answer?"

"A Lie? Why would Chief Nedrakah lie to us?"

"He would lie because while he has you eating out of the palm of his hand, he is strong, and he is somebody special to his masters, while you do all his dirty work."

"Quickly, close my door and lock it tight."

Then Berba-Shin opened the secret panel at the back of her cave.

"Step into the light Ro-Gan, and you too On-Gar!"

"What in the name of the Gods, how can this be, Ro-Gan and On-Gar, we were told that the Hu-Mans had murdered you in your sleep."

Rogan turned to Trygg, come here my boy there is someone I would like you to meet."

Trygg nervously came through into the Orsk cave chamber.

"Trygg, tell Xu-Gor who I am?"

"This is Rogan Ragisson, the greatest hero of our time, and he rules the whole of northern Råvenniå, and his people love him!"

"Does this Hu-Man speak the truth Berba-Shin?"

"I can't answer that, but my son can, Tukor it is your turn to give testimony, come!"

"This is your son Berba-Shin, your son who we were also told was dead?"

"I am he, Xu-Gor, and everything they have said is the truth, and when my people threw me out to die, the Hu-Mans were the ones who took me in, it was not easy for me at first, but with the help of a few good people I have survived and returned, to tell the truth."

"Now do you understand Xu-Gor, or would you like to hear from the Gods themselves?"

"Now you are trying to trick me, even I am not able to stand in the presence of such ones."

"Aatu, come forward and look this fool in the eyes, if you turn away first from his stare then he will know that I lie, that we all lie, but if you turn his gaze then he will know it is all true."

Aatu walked casually forward and sat right in front of the half-bloods, his head almost up to Xu-Gor's waist. Aatu locked eyes with him and the contest began.

Nobody spoke, and nobody moved a muscle, several of Berba-Shin's candles began to burn low and flicker in the last throws of light before they fell into the wax pool and dosed themselves.

The light was growing ever dimmer but Aatu's eyes seemed to take on a light source of their own as they seemed to glow in the twilight of shadows, one bright blue and the other bright green, Xu-Gor's eyes began to tear up and he tightened his jaw muscles and twitched his face but all to no avail, he found himself blink involuntarily.

Aatu had won, the Gods had spoken, and Xu-Gor asked what was the will of the Gods.

Berba-Shin came over to him and put a hand on his forearm, there is no shame in bending to the will of the Gods if we are always true in our hearts.

"I need you to talk to all of the other half-bloods and human captives, in the spring, I will lead an army, the like the world has never seen, and never will again, an alliance of men, and elves and half-bloods too, if you can join us, just spread the word and come the day that you spy our camps set up on the horizon, for the battle ahead, then sneak out from behind your barricades and join with us."

"A mighty roar will sound from our warriors because their brother has come to join us, and at the battle end, I promise that you can live outside, as free people, for the rest of your days, I am warlord and jarl, Rogan Ragisson, and I will command thousands of warriors who will prevail, it is the will of the one true God, Aru."

"Now we must go Berba-Shin, Xu-Gor, and we will return in the spring for your reply, you have until then," Ongar said.

They all spat on their right hands and shuck to swear an oath, then the party left Berba-Shin and the half-blood to work on their plan to change the fate of the orcs.

The return journey was much smoother for all of them and although they were eager to speak, they were well aware of where they were and so they kept quiet, when they reached the iron gate Trygg showed them another trick that his father had taught him, he reached once more into his thieves' toolkit and this time produced a small strip of leather. "Watch this, as I place it into the receiving hole for the bolt, and then turn the key and lock the door, yes?"

They all agreed that he had indeed just locked the door, however, when Trygg pulled back the bolt without using the key, the door sprang open, and he closed it once more and then repeated his action. "So, we don't need to lock the gate, that is worth remembering if the time comes to find another escape route for the half-bloods and their human companions."

Once back out onto the beach, they wondered just how many days it had taken them since they started the mission, Ascarli said it was half a day short of the time they had told the fisherman to return, and so they spent the next hours jumping into the ice-cold water of the river and cleaning the layers of filth that they had become encrusted with, even Aatu seemed to enjoy all of the tom-foolery as they dunked each other under the water and shot back up again because of the conditions.

As the boat approached, they hailed the fisherman and went back into the clef to retrieve their clothes, it felt good to dry off with one of the sheepskins and to dress in the woollen undergarments and then the fur coats over the top, and they were glad to climber aboard the boat before it ran its self-aground.

The eleventh month, Nocrimis, brought a deluge of snow and what animals had survived the previous month's winter cull were all now indoors, some in their barns and stables and others in people's homes helping them to keep warm at night.

Most of the back roads were now impassable and even the main cobble-stoned roads were becoming difficult to navigate and so most traders were staying in the towns or villages where they lived, no more scouts were being sent out and any soldiers were already billeted in their designated towns, and space was becoming a premium.

Kaldakinn had been left with spare rooms because everybody who wanted to be part of the spring offensive was still heading for the fishing village. It was one such arrival that had an alarm ringing out from the gate guards. "Men approaching!" was the shout, as the gate guards took it in turns to be away from the warm braziers to peer out into the blanket white around Kaldakinn.

Captain Brecott gathered a group of eight of his men and headed for the village gates that he hoped were closed, and on arriving there he saw that they were. He ran up the stairs three at a time and when he got to the ramparts he was greeted by a wonderful sight.

Around ninety mounted men in gleaming plate armour, whose horses were even wearing armour, several held banners on long poles, and all wore maroon-coloured cloaks that rustled and flapped in the light breeze, at the head of the two-man wide column was a rider whose armour looked fit for a king, bedecked with gold trim, and when he removed his helmet, his chiselled good looks would sweep any unsuspecting lady off her feet.

He was the first man that Brecott had ever seen with a cut and trimmed beard, it was so well manicured that, with the healthy sway of dark brown hair, made this man almost picture perfect.

"Glad tidings to you, sir, and your men, I am Captain Brecott of the king's own royal guard, who may I inquire is you on this ruddy cold day?"

"My name is Leofstan Ealdwulf, and I am a knight of the court of King Eadweard se Ieldra of Marcadia, and my men and I heard that you might like a bit of company in the spring, I am sorry for my early arrival but we had nothing better to do so we thought we would just pop along and have a look how things were going, now may we come in I have at least one old friend I am dying to meet, and possibly another if all the rumours are true."

"Open the gates!"

Leofstan made his way to the great hall and he was greeted there first by his dear friend Sister Wenyid whose embrace was vice-like for her old sparring partner, for it was the knight who taught her all the fighting skills she knows.

Rogan watched as the two patted each other on the arms, then embraced some more and finished with a kiss on the cheek from Leofstan. "It is really good to meet you finally, Brother Cuthbald has told me all about you, but not your rank, how may I address you, my lord?"

"My title is Knight-General of His Majesty King Eadweard's Royal Bodyguard, but you may call me Leofstan, and may I say how humbling it is to meet one such as yourself, ever since Brother Cuthbald informed me of your existence I have been dying to meet you, we have so much to talk about, but alas, not now, I am greatly pained from such a long ride and I am sure my men would benefit from some warm hospitality."

"Rogan called to Renwick to sort the knights out," and he invited Leofstan over to his manner house to be his special guest. Æstrid Steinolf was in the kitchen helping the housekeeper prepare dinner when they walked in. Leofstan was captivated by her beauty. "My lady, what an absolute pleasure it is to meet you."

Æstrid blushed. "Where did you find this…gentleman Rogan?"

"I er…"

"It was I who found your lord, my lady, I have come from Mårcådiå to help in the spring, and I bring with me the finest knights in all the lands."

Just as they were about to sit down there was a loud, and enthusiastic knock on the door, but before anyone could get to the door to open it, Brother Cuthbald burst in, apologising most profusely before launching himself at the figure of his oldest and dearest friend.

"Rogan, may I talk candidly with you?" Leofstan asked. "Brother Cuthbald I think as guessed the other reason that brought me here so urgently."

"I am intrigued Leofstan, please continue." Offered Rogan.

"I have come here to tell you that your father is not in the best of health, and he might not see many more years, now whether you want to meet him or not is largely irrelevant, but what is of utmost importance is your claim to the throne of Marcadia."

Aatu, who was until now nicely snuggled up around Rogan's feet, suddenly stuck his head up and began to howl. Rogan Ragisson sat in stunned silence.

Brother Cuthbald looked around the room furtively as though he thought someone might be eavesdropping, but it was just that this revelation had taken Rogan's breath away completely.

Rogan did a double take. "You think I am a legitimate heir to the throne of the biggest, most powerful country in the whole of the Shattered Realms?"

"It may come as a surprise to you Rogan, and that is not your real name by the way, but I have been scouring the Shattered Realms looking for you for the past six years, ever since you were snatched from that place in Mårcådiå."

"Why don't I remember any of this, though?"

"You were raised by foster parents, who loved you dearly, but your past, from the day you were born, was erased from your memory by a very powerful sorcerer named Olórin Stórmcrów, he was the king's mage at the time of your grandfather, who was king, when you were conceived."

"You are not the first to tell me of such things, but it still does not explain why such a terrible thing was done to me."

"It was decided that you needed to go into hiding, your life was under threat from the moment you were born, and it might come as a surprise but if I had

137

dedicated my life to finding you, then think how many others would gladly see you dead are doing just the same."

"Well, be that as it may, please don't assume that I will just drop everything and return to a country I have very little knowledge about, king or no king, my mission is here!"

"Yes, of course, and I admire you more for your commitment, and I am truly hoping that we can spend time together over the next couple of months, discussing it all including telling you all about the Kingdom of Mårcådiå."

"I think you should meet my sister, Aylild, you two have a lot in common!"

"Aylild! She is here?"

"What? You know my sister as well?"

"Why yes, it was your mother and Aylild who put me on my lifelong quest!"

"Well, these are truly strange times, this is a lot to take in and I am not sure that I want to do anything about any of this until after the spring offensive."

"That, my lord Rogan, is perfectly understandable, and that is why I am here with my men, to support you with both."

Gēola, was the twelfth and last month of the year, when the Kristosians celebrate the birth of their God, and the pagans make many sacrifices to their many Gods and Goddesses and a time when Brother Cuthbald refuses to celebrate or commemorate anything, as he says it is not in his holy book! Rogan found himself drawn more to Brother Cuthbald than anyone else during that last month of the year, when the sky was as white as the world around and having enough firewood was the most pressing concern.

"Brother Cuthbald, what do you make of all of this?"

"All of what specifically, the impending war, your elven heritage, or the fact that I am sat here, potentially, with the future king of Mårcådiå?"

"All of those things, sometimes I wish I could just crawl back into one of those caves under the mountain and shackle myself to a bed for the night."

"You have had quite the adventure since you left those shackles behind, and in a relatively short space of time, but more important than where you have come from, is where you see yourself going?"

"What do you mean, Brother?"

"Do you see a crown upon your head, that is surely the biggest prize at stake, do you even realise that the king of Mårcådiå already has another son, he is your junior by just a year? After his, indiscretion, his father the king, arranged for a marriage with the daughter of, King Ina Wilsiga of Fālēaciā, the neighbouring country to the south, and she is a little firecracker, a worshipper of pagan Gods and everything the prince is not. The idea is that when both kings pass, the prince will become king of both Mårcådiå and Fālēaciā."

"Alas, why am I getting the feeling that this prince is not liked?"

"Because he is nothing more than a spoiled brat and a cad, and that is why they need you, my new friend, you are part of something so much bigger, the Reunited Kingdom."

The first day of Manous came with the first thaw of the year, water lay heavy, and mist hung in the low-lying areas of Kaldakinn, people everywhere were beating their hands against cold arms and then wiping the sleep out of their eyes, spring had come to the Shattered Realms, and with it the war.

Hundreds of troops from Ingolfsfell were wearily beginning their long march to the boats at Athenous, via the village of Kaldakinn, and Sheriff Magnus Steinolf was there in the thick of their send off, he was staying behind with a small garrison of his soldiers just in case the black guard tried an assault on the town lead by the queen in Østergård.

Soldiers from Langaholt under Chief Arn Sigewulfsson met with Chief Gufi Grettersson at his home village, Hundsnes, and along with mercenaries and displaced people, their ranks had swelled to over a thousand mounted and foot soldiers.

In Lōrnicā, Brenn, Zaryi, Willem, and Nariako met up with Chief Eric Wigheard and his army, including a detachment of volunteers from Beornica, he commanded in total nearly a thousand men, again many more than had originally been promised to Rogan.

The gap on the field of battle between the forces of Lōrnicā, to the west, and Gufi and Arn's forces just east of centre was to be plugged by the five hundred or so men that had been promised by the prince of Fōrren, yet there was no sign of them, instead for the moment, Gufi sent his combined force of fifty horsemen to cover.

Jarl Oswald and his army of Athenous had been filling boats all morning and so far, had managed to move near a thousand of his army of nearly two thousand warriors and militia, they were to hold the ground that was right of centre and to where the main thrust of the fighting would take place.

Rogan's composite army now comprised of three hundred elven rangers, five hundred elven warriors, three hundred of his men, and ninety knights from

Mårcådiå, along with thirty former royal guards under Captain Brecott and the Råvenniå northern militia, who numbered over a thousand.

The vanguards of each army converged on Athenous around mid-afternoon and they were taken straight to the boats embarking over the river Tawa, there to fill out to the western wing of the battlefield.

The plan had been to form a line of at least three possibly four ranks deep right across the battlefield, they would advance slowly until they reached a point just beyond the range of the Orsk flighted weapons and halt to re-dress the ranks.

At that moment, a small force of fifty warriors would enter the tunnels with Tukor as their guide and attack the Orsk from inside the mountain, the hope being that allies would rally to their cause among those who were captives.

The first assault on the Orsk lines was planned for late afternoon, it was to be nothing more than a feigned attack designed to draw the enemy out just so that their numbers could be counted roughly, but that was only part of the backup plan if the original plan did not come to fruition.

By the time that Rogan, and his bodyguard of three hundred, had reached the front lines all the other armies and their component units had reported in, via horse-carrying messengers and they were ready for the false attack.

However, the first group of fifty warriors to alight from the first boat taking Rogan's forces, who were led by Aethelric and who was guided by Tukor, had gone straight towards the crag that led to the tunnels under the mountain.

A high percentage of those fifty men had no idea what was waiting for them as they reached the vertical tunnel that the Orsk was using as a latrine, the iron gate that Trygg had jigged to stay open was still partially unlocked and it was Trygg who had the honour of opening it.

Waiting for them concealed in the darkness just out of the spread of Trygg's torch was a human warrior who did not give his name, nor was it asked when he came forward to present himself. He told Aethelric, that hundreds of humans and half-bloods had allied with all the settlements under the mountain.

"They will begin their attack, once they hear yours, and they can be identified by the white sheep skin throw they wore around their shoulders, in homage to Aatu the voice of the Gods."

Aethelric immediately dispatched his fastest runner to take the message to Rogan, and he asked if they could continue to the secret passage that leads to Berba-Shin's chambers.

Berba-Shin they were being told by the waiting warrior, was coordinating the rebellion from the top balcony and she had already sent a few of her folk to meet their maker.

It was around this time, above ground, that men and women alike, for this great army consisted of a third female warrior, and two-thirds male, all began to shout a great cheer, that rippled along the front line in both directions, for the prince of Fōrren had finally arrived with his army of three hundred foot soldiers and sixty, odd, mounted men, just behind the centre of the line.

Everything was now in place and Rogan was waiting only for word from Aethelric's warband. That word came literally as fighting broke out all along the battlements that the Orsk had constructed.

Messengers were hastily dispatched and they were given until the last one of them was out of sight, Then Rogan gave the order for the fake attack to begin it was to be started in the west and end in the east with the forces from Lōrnicā.

So, the warriors began to move forward, cautiously at first as they would be walking in range of the waiting Orsk archers.

When those arrows, did not come, not even one, every commander of men realised that the rebellion under the mountains had begun and that meant they stuck with Rogan's original plan.

The order had been that if the rebels had succeeded in their plot, then the advancing front rank of Rogan's army would hurl grappling hooks across the tar-filled trench which would be used to pull the stone-built wall down and into the trench, thus forming a ramp, so that the army could cross and join with the half-blood's rebellion.

Aethelric's warriors poured out of Baba-Shin's doorway and fanned out along the balcony, they needed to take the high ground and make contact directly with the Orsk shaman, Tukor had an inkling which way she would likely be, and so, he chose to go left with that group, sadly though by the time he had reached his mother she had been gravely wounded by another Orsk.

Tukor gave out a great roar, like an angry bear and he reared up and plunged into the mass of Orsk who had bunched up just beyond his mother's fallen body, Tukor fought with savage bravery, his sword whirled in the dimness of the cavern lighting, arms and heads of dismembered Orsk suddenly filled the catwalk. Tukor himself shortly thereafter succumbed to three arrows fired upwards from the ground below and one fired from the level that he was on.

Aethelric wanted to find the chambers where the women prisoners were held and for that, he had to make his way stairs, the rebellion was in full swing, and Trygg called for men to support Aethelric and another half dozen followed them both, suddenly it became a race against time as Aethelric pushed and shoved his way to where he believed some of those captive women had been chained.

Xu-Gor, the half-blood leader of the coup was in the first chamber where about thirty women were being kept, Aethelric ran into the tunnel leading to where he saw the half-blood standing, Xu-Gor was covered in blood from head to toe, and even the white sheep skin cover he was wearing was mostly drenched in blood.

"Who are you, half-blood, so that I might know to whom I speak?"

"Xu-Gor, but if you have come to save the human women then you are too late, they are all dead!"

"What? No, what happened here?"

"Hu-Man, you must understand that they were never going to get out of here alive."

"And so, what, what are you saying, that you have killed them all?"

Aethelric snarled, he was incandescent with rage.

"I have saved them from more misery, and any of their whelps that I found with them."

Aethelric raised his weapon above his head and screamed a primordial scream and charged straight at the half-blood insurrectionist.

Above ground, the fighting between half-blood factions was at its most intense, but it bought the time that was needed to throw the grappling hooks across the mote, and within minutes of those hooks finding purchase men grabbed hold of the ropes and began to pull.

On the other side, where the fighting was fiercest some of the white-wearing half-bloods had seen what the humans had been trying to do and they took to hacking at the wooden leg supports for the walkway above the wall, their plan now was to drop lengths of the walkway into the tar-filled ditch to assist with the humans, endeavours.

About one hour in and already Rogan's forces were streaming across the area where the ditch was bridged and aiding their newfound confederates. The plan had always been to put pressure on the northwestern corner of the Orsk defences, it was there that was a small outcrop of rock that the Orsk had used as a marker for the end of their line, but was also there that Rogan needed to get the elven archers, from that height they could help to secure this section of the battlefield.

About one hour in and already Rogan's forces were streaming across the area where the ditch was bridged and aiding their newfound confederates.

The plan had always been to put pressure on the northwestern corner of the Orsk defences, it was there that was a small outcrop of rock that the Orsk had used as a marker for the end of their line, but was also there that Rogan needed to get the elven archers, from that height they could help to secure this section of the battlefield.

7

The Bloodletting

Rogan was pacing about outside of his tent over in the northeastern section of the camp, the ground was supposed to have been frozen at this time of the year, and that was just as well because if the first week of spring was going to usher in warmer weather, then with this number of soldiers and horses, the whole battlefield will become a mud bath, the ground was already turning to mush.

The warlord was nervous, it was the calm before the storm, soon, very soon, thousands of men and women would be marching into battle, all in his name, and under his flag, and many of them would not be marching out again. Thoughts of making so many widows and orphans were beginning to weigh on Rogan's mind.

Ingrid Hallgerd awoke to the cold air, alone, and immediately pulled the furs back over her; she could see, however, the shadow of her lover pacing back and forth outside and there was nothing she felt that she could do to alleviate the pressure he was putting himself under. Perhaps, she thought to herself, *if I just act normal, get dressed and go outside and stand with him.*

Aatu was already outside pacing alongside his master as though he was his shadow. Ingrid laughed when she immerged from their tent, wrapping an extra fur around her to quell the biting easterly wind. "Look at you two, you're so funny together!" she exclaimed.

"I am happy for you women, that you find my predicament so amusing!" Rogan bit back.

Aatu felt the edge of his master's tone and turned to Ingrid and whined in sympathy. Ingrid paid Rogan's comment no heed, instead, she walked up behind him and gently wrapped her arms around him, as she moved her head towards his she whispered, "I love you!" in his left ear.

Rogan, keeping hold of her hands, swivelled his body around so that he could face her, and they kissed.

Aatu jumped up and barked, being careful not to knock them both over. "Oh, Aatu, are you jealous because I have the most beautiful woman in the world in my arms?"

"Do you see me like that, Rogan?"

"Of course, ah, but I also see a great warrior and a confidant whose advice I treasure!"

"Are you teasing me now?"

"No, I am not, ask Aatu!"

Aatu barked loudly and started to run around in circles with excitement. "See, he is agreeing with me!"

Ongar, who had heard Aatu barking, walked over to join his two friends. "Is he still pacing about all of the time?"

Rogan looked at his friend and just raised his eyes, in as much as saying, *Oh not this again.*

"What did I say to you yesterday, Rogan, it makes you look anxious, and that can rub off on our warriors!"

Ingrid, still with her arms around Rogan, squeezed him a little harder. "He's not wrong, my love, they hang off your every word, but only because they too love you."

Rogan had said already, to Ongar, more than anything why he was anxious, it was because he had heard nothing back from Aethelric's group after they entered the tunnel system with Tukor. "Yet," Ongar added. "It would have been difficult for them to have sent word back, we just have to trust in them that they will succeed."

Ascarli was making slow progress getting his elven archers up the slope that marked the end of the Orsk front line, the hill was not that steep but it was incredibly rocky, and as agile as they were the elven warriors were losing their footing constantly, but they kept going.

Ascarli took it as a positive, if they had been spotted either the Orsk was not taking any notice of them, or more likely Aethelric's group had their complete attention under the mountain. In the form of Xu-Gor's rebellion.

The way the cave system appeared to work was that each section comprised three separate warband communities under the mountain, each of those communities contained around thirty half-bloods and humans, equally, and they were led on the ground by whoever was their chief, and all three communities together formed one village under the rule of an Orsk warlord, and he had a staff of ten Orsk, for whatever administration duties they had to carry out.

The Orsk lived on the upper balcony areas in cave-like rooms off the back of each corridor tunnel, these would then have been linked at both ends with the corresponding upper balconies from the next village along, downstairs at ground level only the three communities were accessible to each other and there were no adjoining tunnels to the next village from any of those three.

The middle community was the only place that the Orsk could exit their section into the world outside, the two adjoining communities were closed off completely, it must have made it easier for the Orsk to contain and manage their charges with the minimal number of Orsk overseer's.

Rogan needed to secure the village at the furthest end and so is where he had sent Aethelric's group, it was the key, in his mind to rolling back the Orsk, from both inside the tunnels and on the outside, every village that was taken would then be re-enforced by a shield wall of warriors until a makeshift barrier could be put in place to both mark their progress but also to give the protagonist's a fall-back position should the attack falter, everything hinged on securing those key tunnels and their balconies inside.

Aethelric the Bard had no control over where Berba-Shin wanted to go, and neither could he order Toker not to follow his mother, whether she went right as they immerged from her room by instinct or design the bard did not know, but turning right meant that the two of them would have to deal with the twelve Orsk.

As this was the furthest of the underground 'villages' there was no connecting tunnel through the upper left part of the balcony so turning right was the only option. "Follow them!" Aethelric shouted while pointing his blade towards the Mother and Son. The twelve Orsk beat their swords against their shields and invited the fighters to challenge them.

Aethelric would have preferred to have loosened at least one salvo of arrows into the twelve as they stood clad in iron armour holding a menagerie of weapons. As it was there was no other choice than to attack, and so the battle under the mountain commenced, with men and women calling out their battle cries and charging forward with weapons raised high.

Down below the half-bloods and human women looked on with bated breath, would they become as Rogan, freemen, and women or would the Orsk prevail and return them to slavery? The Orsk guards on the ground floor opted to wait this battle out, like the others they were in no hurry to commit themselves to the wrong side.

The cave was bathed in flickering torchlight which favoured the Orsk who could see far better in the 'almost' twilight, and from the downstairs looking up the light caused a thousand dancing shapes across the walls and ceiling when there were fewer than fifty fighters. The clash of weapons rang out like a church cloister full of deranged bell ringers.

The twelve Orsk must have thought that Berba-Shin was trying to escape the humans as they lowered their weapons and stepped aside to let her and her son pass by them, before turning back to engage the bard and his group of attackers. Berba-shin stopped as she stood in the connecting tunnel and turned back to watch the fight, she too was now hedging her bets as to which would be the winning side.

Tukor saw his mother's sudden intransigence and begged her to help his friends but she would do nothing more than just watch and wait for the time being. The bard brought his steel blade down in an arc towards the first of the Orsk, the Orsk brought his sword up in an arc to meet the blow, but the steel shattered the iron and the Orsk was left holding nothing more than a hilt with a shard.

Oslaf, a Råvenniån militiaman thrust his sword forward, catching the Orsk between the side of his iron breast-plate and the two leather retaining straps, the Orsk gurgled as his lungs filled with blood until he choked up a great mouthful of the thick red liquid, before collapsing to the floor. Aethelric nodded in acknowledgment to his compatriot, for his quick thinking.

Osgar, another militiaman was not so fortunate as he received a nasty blow to the head from a hammer-wielding Orsk who pushed his way forward hunting for glory. Osgar helmet flattened under the heavy downward thrusting blow, slamming shards of steel down hard into his brain, and his legs dropped from under him.

Aethelric sliced his blade through the air and towards another Orsk, the Orsk was able to parry the downward blow with his shield but the sword continued downwards and severed his leg above the knee. That Orsk warrior could do no more than kneel and try to fend off more strikes but Winamac Tyren, a veteran guardsman caught the Orsk across his exposed neck, killing him instantly.

Berba-shin saw that the tide was turning in the human's favour and she drove her stiletto blade through the back of a very shocked Orsk, Tukor followed his mother's example and thrust his axe into the spine of another Orsk. While downstairs, the half-bloods and human women turned on their captors, by bringing their chained wrists over the back of the guard's neck and strangulating them.

Other Orsk who had watched Berba-Shin's treachery unfold from the other end of the tunnel now began a frenzied exercise in shield beating and cries of 'traitor', but they were ordered not to move from guarding the tunnel until reinforcement arrived. All through the underground villages panic was beginning to set in and calls for more Orsk warriors were heard up the supposedly secret narrow stairways that existed behind false panels.

Weonard was the next militiaman to be killed followed closely by two more Orsk, the twelve were soon reduced to four and they turned back-to-back to make a last stand, Orsk were the only creatures the bard had ever seen who fought to the death, many other races would have thrown down their weapons and surrendered. Berba-shin received a nasty gash across her face from one of the Orsk and Tukor on seeing his mother wounded, broke off contact with the Orsk he was battling and plunged his axe into the perpetrator of his mother's facial gash.

For his heroism, Tukor was struck in the chest by the Orsk he was originally fighting, the weapon of his choice being a war mattock which knocked the breath out of Tukor's lungs and he fell back heavily against the low railings that ran along the upper corridor as far as the next set of stairs going down before the Orsk could deliver the killing blow, he was stabbed in the back by Aluard Hogg, another of Kaldakinn's finest guards.

Soon the last of the twelve succumbed to the sword wielded by the bard and the freed prisoners had joined Aethelric's cause. "We need to block the tunnel up here and then push on to the next cell downstairs, re-enforcements should be waiting by the main entrance." The freed people downstairs, hands and feet still chained grabbed any piece of furniture they could and brought it up the stairs handing it on to what was left of the bard's forces, they in turn blocked the tunnel best they could.

The spare weapons were retrieved and after the half-bloods and humans were freed, they were given the twelve weapons. Others who did not receive weapons picked up implements from the blacksmith's table or cave excavating equipment like picks from the rear of the blacksmith's cave. While most of the human women stayed huddled in the first cave with their children, Zu-Gar offered to hang back and guard them.

Cro-Mar, a freed half-blood led the assault on the adjoining central cave, this was where the main entrance outside was located as well as a secret staircase going up another level. The whole of the area downstairs was filled with Orsk and if the half-bloods had not joined the bard, then they would not have stood a chance in this battle, as it was both sides were now equal.

The fighting was ferocious and bodies were falling regularly on both sides, Aethelric plan had been to drive a wedge towards the outer doors to let Rogan and some of his men in to reinforce his own, however, the Orsk backed themselves towards the doors, probably realising what the humans were trying to do, somewhere up the stairs more Orsk was able to come down and join the battle, the bard suddenly realised that his side was becoming surrounded, Trygg appeared as if from nowhere and shouted a warning to Aethelric.

"Look up there!" and as the bard looked he saw what looked like a single boulder-sized door move to one side while several Orsk slipped past, it was at that precise moment they both saw the grey-skinned women, and as they looked Aethelric received a blow to the back of his right shoulder, and another to his left leg, he stumbled and then went to ground, Trygg pushed his way forward towards his friend and fended off blow after blow while tried to crouch and listen to what the bard was trying to tell him.

"Go back out the way we came in, and tell Rogan!" he whispered hoarsely.

"Tell him what, about the battle, Bard?"

"No, about the women, we didn't even know about them or another level above the balcony…"

Trygg fearing the worse lepped up killing an Orsk warrior who was about to stab him, and turned to push his way through the throng of half-bloods and freed human lads. He was panicked into thinking this battle was lost and the bard would not get the doors opened in time, so he ran as fast as he could to retrace his steps, and alight the tunnels by the beach.

Berba-shin fell beneath the blow of another Orsk which sent Tukor into a wild frenzy, of hacking and slashing with his axe, killing the Orsk who hit his mother and two others besides. The half-bloods and humans along with what was left of the bard's forces were now being forced back into the first cave and Xu-Gor, who was supposed to be protecting the women began to pace up and down and shout obscenities at his fellow half-bloods, was panicking and cursing them for appearing to be losing the fight.

Tukor found the bard and single handily dragged his body back through the adjoining corridor, he was alive and furiously waving at Tukor to let him go so that he could rejoin the fight, but Tukor saw that he was wounded and took him instead into the cave where Zu-Gar and the women were.

As the Orsk in the central cave now all converged on the corridor, sensing victory they paid no heed to the half-bloods and humans they had corralled into the small cave that was their bedchamber, those companions made a decision that would tip the balance back in the rebellions favour, they saw an opportunity to grab weapons off the floor and out from the hands of the dead and they attacked the rear of the Orsk.

The melee turned feral, untamed, savage even, and suddenly it was the Orsk who was trapped between two separate forces, the fighting continued until barely any Orsk were still alive and bodies were piling up from both sides, so much so that they were blocking the ground level tunnel, and so to counter this the half-bloods and humans in the central chamber had to quickly climb the stairs up to the balcony level and move the makeshift barricade there to rejoin the fight.

Zu-Gar seemed to have completely lost his mind, his shouts and insults became louder and louder as the battle outside his cave raged, at first, he began striking the walls nearest to him with his sword, but when Aethelric tried to calm him down, and some of the women began to scream, it galvanised him into a reprehensible act of barbarism, as he started to butcher the screaming women.

The other chiefs of Rogan's army began to congregate around Rogan's tent when they were alerted of an approaching warrior by Aatu's howls, the warrior had come from the direction of the Orsk barricades.

"My lords," he began, between breathless pants, "I am Cro-Mar and I have a message from Zu-Gar, where can I find Ro-Gan?"

This magnificent barrel-chested specimen was a half-blood ally, he wore the white, albeit, blood-stained, woollen fleece around his shoulders. However, he was unlike any half-blood that either Rogan or Ongar had seen before, his skin had a deep tan hue, and his hair, the short stubbly amount that was visible, which he should have shaved off, was reddish-brown if it was not for two tiny teeth that protruded slightly from the corners of his bottom row of teeth, he could have passed as a fully human.

Rogan stepped forward and introduced himself, "Quickly, what news do you bring to us?"

"The first village, your old village, Nedrakah, is taken, your men have formed a shield wall on the upper right-side balcony to stop any reinforcements getting through, but they have taken many casualties and are badly in need of reinforcements themselves, our warriors have all but secured the outside and it is time for you to move in and section that area off, as planned."

"Captain Brecott, you heard our friend, let us get this first part of the plan secured." Brecott was to take his mounted men in first to back up the victorious half-bloods and the human warriors, each horseman would be dragging a log, and then a further fifty-foot soldier would be following them, each carrying lighter sections of wooden barricades that would be used to block off this area outside, afterwards they would split into two groups of twenty-five and one of those groups would enter the village to support the men already on the balcony areas.

Rogan quickly turned to Gunnar. "Send up a signal arrow for the elves, we need them to start moving across the lower lip of the mountain in support of Captain Brecott."

Gunnar tipped the point of his arrow into the burning brazier and waited until the cloth wrapped around it caught lite, it contained a mixture of ingredients the apothecary said would sparkle when ignited, and he pointed his bow skywards and let loose the burning arrow. Ascarli and the elves saw the firework-like signal and began to move along the ridge, Aylild commented on the flatness of this whole area, and one of the other elves, Finddras Springsky, called everyone's attention to what looked like new cut steps leading further up the mountain.

The steps on closer inspection were indeed newly cut, by something of great strength because it would not have been easy to fashion a stairway out of granite so easily, point of fact that was made by Finddras, was that surely it would have been simpler to construct wooden stairs, unless, said Ascarli, that the hands that made these cuts were not familiar with working in wood.

It was as Ascarli stooped to touch one of the flattened steps, that he was suddenly taken by a searing pain to the head, so forceful that it made him stumble for just a moment and hold the side of his head. "Father, are you alright, what happened?" Aylild asked, sounding very concerned.

"I don't honestly know, my child, it was as though I touched the stone and it triggered a vision." He said somewhat confused.

"What did you see, Father that could cause you to react this way?"

"Not so much what but, who?"

"You saw somebody outside of the ones we already know about?"

"Yes, it was a woman, and not the queen of Råvenniå, because she was stood at the very top of this mountain, right now, looking down on all of us, but she was shrouded in such darkness, and all around her were the black guard, but there was something different about even them."

"Perhaps we should try and share this information with Rogan, Father?"

"I have tried, my daughter, honestly, I have tried but it would seem that he has forgotten all of his skills for the moment and is relying on his strengths as a man because he is completely closed off to me."

"Silond, you must return to Rogan and report what it is my father has experienced, go immediately, but be careful the climb down will be as treacherous as it was getting up here."

"Father, would you like us to rest here a while?"

"No! we must keep pace with the men below, they are relying on our archers, urgh! I just cannot shake this feeling."

"Father let us put out two minds together, then I can share your burden and maybe I will see what you saw but from a different perspective."

"Be careful my daughter, I felt a great presence of dark magic."

Aylild placed her right hand flat against her father's left cheek, her fingertips resting on the soft flesh of his temple, and she cleared her mind and entered the memory he had just experienced. "I see her too Father, a woman dressed in black and crimson, but she wears a veil to conceal herself, wait, just let me see myself move it to one side, Ah!" Aylild recoiled and was then thrown backwards away from her father and it caused her great pain, both in her mind and her body as she hit the grown hard.

Two elves helped Aylild to her feet and another couple helped Ascarli who was again down on bended knee. "There is a greater evil on top of this mountain than any of us thought and with that great evil there is an even greater number of enemies, I am becoming more certain that we have not bargained for either of these things and as long as we are here that threat grows."

"What are you thinking Father, should we turn back?"

"No, my daughter we should not, we gave our oath to Arathorn Longstride and we elves are not in the habit of betraying our oaths, so we press on and whatever will be, will be, of that I have no doubt."

Ascarli saw that the humans and half-bloods needed their support, this delay although fleeting had knocked them back, and so he shouted out instructions for his archers to fan out along the ridge and pick out them half-Orsk who were rallying to re-take the ground that their comrades had just lost. Not a single elven arrow missed its intended target and a good deal of cheering could be heard from below as the half-Orsk fell one after another.

One of Captain Brecott's mounted men came riding back to Rogan's tent with a report from the fighters who were even now securing the caverns and tunnels. "My Lord Jarl, it is your friend Aethelric, we found him badly wounded inside a chamber where Xu and all the women were."

"How bad is Aethelric?"

"He has lost a lot of blood, lord, you should see him soon, they are making a device to carry him here on as we speak."

"How many women and children were saved?"

"None my lord, they were all killed, I am sorry to bring this heavy news to you, but something even more strange was that we found no Orsk bodies in that chamber."

There was no need to say anything further on the matter, and Rogan turned his thoughts to Aethelric.

"Ingrid, can you look for Ingulfrid, she should be over helping with all of the wounded on the beach?"

"Can I take my lady on my horse it will be faster that way?" asked the messenger.

"Yes, Ingrid, please go!"

"Rogan, that rider made no mention of Tukor or his mother, yet it would seem that they have searched the whole area to secure it."

"Gunnar you are right, but we cannot keep sending a runner every time we hear or don't hear from inside the caves," Rogan replied.

Gunnar apologised, but Rogan said it was he who should have said sorry, Gunner was just pointing out the obvious and he overreacted.

Runners did begin appearing from other units asking if it were time to pull back as the fighting was dying down across the other side of the tar ditch, in some places the half-bloods, as they were being nicknamed, were winning, and in others the half-Orsk still held the upper hand. Rogan said that they had accomplished what he had set out to do, and so he gave them all instructions to pass on down the chain of command to begin the withdrawal, but slowly and cautiously, men in retreat could very easily be panicked.

The withdrawal would take most of the rest of the day, except for the area Captain Brecott was defending, Rogan wanted to hold on to just that one village, it was where Ongar and he were held captive for five years in Rogan's case but for all of Ongar's life for he was born there, it was to send a powerful message to the other half-breeds and humans that stayed loyal to the Orsk, and to the Orsk themselves.

As mid-evening approached so did the elven messenger, the elves who Rogan had almost forgotten about such was their stealth and effectiveness. "What news from my good friend Ascarli," inquired Rogan enthusiastically.

"There has been a development my Lord." Silond Silverleaf revealed.

Rogan grimaced as he asked what it was, his elven intuition breaking through. Silond recounted the whole episode with Ascarli and Aylild and Rogan felt the dread well up in the pit of his stomach like acid bile.

Ongar picked up on something Silond had said. "What do you mean when you said 'they were not like the half-bloods'?"

The elf said that it was not spoken so to as offend, it was a statement of truth, the black guard is not half-blood like Ongar and the others of his kind. "So, what is it exactly Ascarli thinks they are because he clearly hasn't said that they are like the older Orsk either?"

Rogan, remember what we were told when we first spoke with the Orsk, they said that the black guard was the future of Orsk kind, not that Rogan even knew what that was supposed to mean, but is this somehow what Ascarli now 'felt'.

"Ongar, I don't know, but I think that we were lied to, by everyone, but mostly the Orsk, and that whatever secrets still lay in the kingdom under the mountain will have to wait until tomorrow when we launch the proper offensive."

"What about the rest of what has been told to us about this vision of the woman, and her power, shrouded in darkness?"

"Halla, as yet we have neither heard nor seen anything of either, we must stick with our plan and we can deal with them as and when, wizards and witches will have to stand in line for now."

"Yes, Halla, the mountain reaches high into the sky, whatever hides that far up is truly a long way from bothering us right now." Ongar pointed out.

"So, we should ignore them?" The warrior asked.

"No Halla, I am not saying that but we are already spreading ourselves thinner and thinner, we can ignore them until they cannot be ignored, then we will deal with them at that time. Until then, I need to be making my way into the caves and I need to be seen by the Orsk spies, because where ever I am, then that is where the Orsk will focus all their efforts, which in turn will relieve pressure on the rest of the line out here, and a distracted enemy is a half-beaten one."

Ingulfrid was found bloodied and her clothes a mess, not that she had been in combat but that she had worked tirelessly with all the wounded, to some she had been their partner, to others their mother, and yet others whose hand she held, she was a comfort. Ingulfrid could be proud of the work she had done and many of the wounded would walk from this battlefield because she cared for them.

Ingrid saw near exhaustion etched in Ingulfrid's face and she told her to go rest while she took over tending to the wounded. Ingrid had never had to deal with such sights before, there were just so many broken bodies, but she was a tough shield maiden and she had also survived capture by the Orsk, at least that is what she told herself as she reached the first outstretched hand that beckoned her.

Ingrid could not get over the smell of death that hung in the air, it was a charnel house down on the beach where rows of dead or dying were being laid on makeshift cots. The smell of blood mixed with excrement and urine was almost as overpowering as the sights she now witnessed, and she longed for Brother Cuthbald to have been here, but he was a principled man and he remonstrated with Rogan and the others how war and vengeance belonged to God, and only he had the right to take another's life.

It was while Ingrid was tending to the wounded on the beach and as one boat after another came and went full of the bodies of the warriors who could be moved that Trygg suddenly appeared, breathless and covered himself in blood.

"My God, Trygg, are you wounded as well, why do you come from out of the rocks though?"

"Ingrid, you need to get a message to Rogan, and no this is not my blood, don't worry, I'm fine, really I am."

"What message, Trygg?"

"We saw a strange thing when we were blockading the tunnel at the top of the walkway, we could see, but not clearly a set of wide stone steps that led upwards, to yet another level, and it was then unless our eyes were playing tricks on us, women!"

"Women, you mean the human prisoners, like us?"

"No, these were like Ongar, but they had, you know what's!" Trygg made a gesture with his hands to indicate that these half-bloods had boobs.

"I mean there was just a couple of them looking down the stairs but they were grey-skinned and there was a flash of two white teeth that stuck out in the corner of their mouths."

"And you could see all of this, even amid battle, and with only sparse torch light with which to see anything at all?"

"Yes, Ingrid, I know what I saw and it scared me, quite frankly."

"My God the thought of it, we do not know the half of it, half-blood females! come we must take your news straight to Rogan, but first, you must do just one thing for me, please."

"Yes, what is it, Ingrid?"

"For God's sake, go bathe yourself in the sea you stink worse than a pig languishing in its excrement!"

For Rogan, it was a moment of truth, walking back into the tunnel that led to the village of Nedrakah for the first time as a free man, it was a moment to look one's demons straight in the eye and say, not anymore, today I take back control over the rest of my life. Ongar was stood at Rogan's side and he too found this place to be somewhat unnerving and a place he had hoped he would never have to see again.

Rogan spent a few moments standing in the middle of the main cave where the stairway ran up to the balcony above, with its high vaulted ceiling, dry clawing warm air, and the smell of death that had become trapped inside. This place was nothing more now that a glorified mausoleum. He would gladly pull the whole lot down, the mountain, and the memories of what this place had come to represent to him, and those who survived still with him to this day, and then his thoughts turned to Aethelric.

"My Lord Jarl." It was Atli. "My Lord, we have recovered two bodies and we are unsure as to what to do with them?"

From deep within the cave system, screams and cries and other strange noises emanated, all distracting Rogan for the moment. "What? What are you talking about Atli, show me?" Rogan was still lost in the swirl of mist and death and the past, as old memories fought new ones in his mind's eye.

Atli took Rogan over to where just two bodies lay covered in coats, and which had been kept separate, away, from all the others that had been brought out. They were the bodies of Berba-Shin and her beloved son, Tukor and Rogan just fell to his knees and began to cry, tears raced down both cheeks for the two creatures, both unique in this world who had been reunited in death, and it was almost too much for him to bare, it is at times like this, that life amongst the living can be one of the loneliest places on earth.

"Bring two coffins up, Atli."

"My Lord?"

"Atli, dispatch someone to bring two coffins up, I want these two to be transported back to Brother Cuthbald in Kaldakinn, seal the lids after they have been cleaned up, and send back a messenger too, Brother Cuthbald will know what to do with them both afterwards."

"Yes, my lord, but…"

"Atli, please just do it for me, and for them, for Tukor, I want him to be treated as one of us, he would have been so delighted to have finally been excepted among us, as an equal."

"In that case, do you want me to treat everyone the same, with coffins and the like?"

"Tukor became a trusted friend, tell me Atli, did you not observe, see beyond what your eyes were seeing, he was one of my trusted friends, and while, yes, I would like to afford a coffin for all of those who have made the ultimate sacrifice. I fear though that by the end of this war there will be neither the wood to build them each a box nor will there be enough left alive to do the job, now go, do what I have asked."

Ingulfrid was still sitting at Aethelric's stricken body, holding tightly his left hand, and stroking it from time to time. "Has he regained consciousness yet Ingulfrid?" Rogan asked in a gentle voice.

"No, my lord, he has not," she sobbed, "and I fear that even now he is lost to me."

Rogan gently placed a soothing hand on the back of Ingulfrid's head and neck, as he stood above her, inform me if there is any change, or if you think of anything that we can do for him, or you, now, I am sorry but for me, the grieving time is not yet, there is still much for all of us to do.

It had been decided that the single corridor that connected the upper balcony and this village with the next one along should be blocked and that the real offensive that was to begin in earnest tomorrow, should be outside, especially given that the elven archers were of more strategic use from their vantage point on the flat land above.

Warriors were told to fetch the thick roughly made benches that were now strewn about the main cave. "Put them against the corridor end and brace them so that the Orsk cannot break through, and then when that is done, station twelve men up there to guard the barricade." Then Rogan next wanted to be shown into the chambers where the women had been so brutally murdered.

The bodies had all been removed but the blood and the stench had not, a myriad of flies took to flight when Rogan walked into the chamber on his own, his first reaction was to gag for the smell was almost too much, especially in the confines of the already humidity of the caves. Rogan turned to one of the men outside the room. "Did you say both Aethelric and Xu were found here together, and no other Orsk or anyone?"

"No, my lord, that is just as we found them, with Aethelric's weapon lodged firmly in Xu's body, it took two of us to remove it was so firmly embedded."

"Hmm, then we must conclude that it was Xu who killed all of the women and Aethelric discovered him going about his business, this is not the outcome I wanted." He said more to himself than the man who stood guard.

"Rogan? Rogan, where are you?" Captain Brecott was shouting.

"I'm here?" Rogan answered as he left the women's chamber.

"Rogan, ah, good there you are, we have placed the barricade across the gap between the mountain and the tar trench, and the elves are on standby above and men are waiting for their orders."

"Good, where are your men, Ricsige?"

"They have taken their horses to the rear of this section and are watering them and giving them each a brush down, the work here was not easy on them, they smell fear and danger unlike any of us and so need extra special care and attention."

"It is not easy on any of us, never mind the animals we use, but I understand old friend, and you do a fine job."

Aatu howled at that comment, and Rogan bent down and put his arm around the beast's neck. "It has been a tough day on us all, man and beast alike, you are right and I am being thoughtless." And with that, he buried his head into Aatu's shaggy mane, and Aatu reciprocated the love by rubbing his head on Rogan.

It was Sister Wenyid's turn to root out Rogan next and she was concerned about the tar-filled motte. "What would happen if this was set alight?"

"I am not sure to whose advantage setting the trench alight would be, is it more likely to favour the defenders or us?"

"If rather suspect, it depends on how deep the trench is, for instance, if it is only a couple of feet then the tar would surely burn straight off if that were done while we were crossing the rubble bridges, our soldiers would be badly burnt, if however, it was any deeper, then it might become completely impassable for a longer period?" The warrior nun observed.

"I can only think that the Orsk dug it out in the first place for a very good reason, although I doubt that they thought of it all by themselves, Orsk aren't renown for being defence-minded, do you have any thoughts on it?"

"No, but I would like to test its depth while there is a lull in proceedings, with your permission, lord?"

"Silond, Ongar, Gunnar, come with Sister Wenyid and I, we are going to test the depth of that tar trench outside."

Ongar was the one who grabbed hold of a spear and began pushing it gently into the trench. "Ongar, perhaps it would be better if you were able to go a bit further out, more into the middle?" shouted the nun.

The half-blood pulled the spear from the glutinous black gloop and stepped across the fallen wall where the stone had become a walkway across.

Once he had reached what he believed was the middle, Ongar once again began sliding the spear into the mire. "How long is that spear?" the sister asked.

"Eight feet but I have yet to touch the bottom."

"So, we are saying that if that lot goes up, anyone who is caught between that trench and the bottom of the mountain here will burn!" Gunnar stated.

"One thing is for sure, if it goes up it will burn for days, possibly weeks or months and the flame would be so intense that it would destroy all of the rubble bridges and any of the wooden structures." Added the sister.

"Did the Orsk not think this through properly it would be suicide for them, all of them the full length of the mountain."

"I think you already know the answer to both those questions, firstly, the Orsk do not think for themselves, they are instructed, and secondly and most importantly every last one of them is expendable, so perhaps the better question is who wanted this here and why?" Silond added.

"What are we to do about it though, I can hardly have the men drain it with buckets or try to fill it in with spoil?"

"No, you can't, but we must find a way to cover the area nearest to the barricade we have set up between us and the enemy, then if it is set alight then it won't affect us as much as them, any idea anyone?"

"Can we lash the wooden planks together and slide them over it, then cover the planks with a light coat of rubble, not so heavy that it sinks the whole thing, but enough to snuff out the flames before they took hold of the wood?" inquired the nun.

"Sister Wenyid, you are a saint! Set to and get that organised," Rogan was already turning away. "And one more thing, thank you!"

Next, it was important that the outside barricades had been constructed properly and that was where Rogan headed now. "How is it going, everyone?"

"It's quite Rogan, they came out spoiling for a fight just as we were putting the wooden spikes out, but your elven friends sent them a message that it would be better not to venture out, and they haven't bothered us since except for the odd stray shot from someone stood just inside the tunnel, over there, but the angle is too tight so they miss every time."

Rogan could see that four wooden hex shapes had been placed at intervals of two paces apart, and then a single long trunk had been nailed to them where they stood, then behind them had been placed several large barrels so that there was no gap beneath and that it formed a solid barrier from which his men could purchase some cover when the enemy did attack.

Night was fast approaching and Rogan was pleased with what they had accomplished so far, the pressure was off those thinly spread soldiers on the other side of the trench, all Orsk's eyes would be firmly fixed on their former captive and Rogan believed that when they attack, the main thrust of it will be where he was, both because they will have viewed Rogan as an oath breaker for returning and because he had taken his former village, Nedrakah, and that would sit heavy on minds of the Orsk.

Rogan instructed the men to post a strong guard while telling the others to set campfires, inside the caves and get hot food and then rest up for tomorrow was when the real work would begin, and the only employment that will be required will be that of butchers because that is precisely what work of this nature would be butchery.

Trygg caught up finally with Rogan, having circumnavigated the whole of the cave system in the east to return via the front entrance to find his lord. "Lord, I have strange news to tell…"

"Speak up boy, the hour is late and I grow weary…"

"We found what we believe to have been a secret stairway going up into another level above the upper balconies…"

"…and?"

"That is when I saw two female grey-skins, you know with their things hanging out!"

Ongar came over to ask if Trygg had been drinking. "Come here, boy, and let me smell your breath!"

"I am telling you they were female half-bloods!" the youngster insisted.

"Impossible," stated Ongar, "you know this to be true, Rogan, there has never been a female half-blood, not ever!"

8

The Butcher's Bill

Ascarli posted guards at five-foot intervals to form a half circle around where the rest of the elves would be spending the night. The long flat ledge where the elves were stationed was far more open in terms of there being little or no cover, than any of the other parts of Rogan's army, neither could a fire be lit for food or drink to have been heated, hard tac and juice would be the order of the night.

Somewhere, just beyond even Ascarli's ability to use the gift of 'far sight' lurked the enemy, every elf felt the cloud of malice that resided at this place. For those who would sleep, on rote, it would be a restless night, elves can tap into the world around them, when they relax, they become at one with the heartbeat of their local vicinity, be those animals, or even the flora and fauna.

The camp was set up opposite the clefts in the rock that rose high above their position, if there was anywhere that a hidden enemy might spring a surprise attack, this would be the place, although the truth of the matter was that Ascarli 'felt' that this staircase hewed from the rock, had not been used since such time as it was originally cut, otherwise, he would have had his forces pull back to a safer place.

Sleep comes to us all at some point even if that sleep is restless and short, our bodies desire it and we must succumb to it eventually, Ascarli was no exception this night or any other, his eyelids were heavy and his body craved it. Aylild went over to where her father had chosen for his turn on guard duty, she had sensed the great burden that was upon him, he felt the weight of responsibility for every individual under his command.

Ascarli felt his daughter's presence even before he could see her, it brought a measure of serenity to him in the most hostile of places. He could even hazard a guess as to why she had come over to him when it was her turn to sleep. "Father, let me take the rest of your watch, please you look exhausted."

Aylild watched her father's lips as he tried to formulate the words he wished to say, but the truth was he was shattered. It was to him as though he had thrown a protective shield around his entire group to protect them from the dark forces that were at work in this place, and in truth, while awake he could do precisely that, but at what cost to himself. *Fathers!* she thought, as she perched herself upon a small rock and readied herself for the long night ahead.

Not one half-hour had passed when Aylild smiled, she felt the presence of her betrothed before she felt his arms slip around her waist. "You should not be here, my love…" she said but not openly, as humans might, this was the elven way, 'mind speak'.

"Neither should you, your duty doesn't start for another two hours."

"I couldn't sleep, and I know my father is exhausted, not that he will admit it, so I offered to take his place early, truth be known I could not sleep anyway even if I tried."

"What troubles you, my love, is it this place or the thought of battle?"

"Wyrran, it is both!" Aylild turned to her love and he gently cupped her face in his hands.

"Tell me, and I will help you to dispel any thoughts of darkness and death that linger at the edges of your mind."

"That is the problem with this place, every waking moment it's there, the creeping doubt, the thought that you, that I, may never see the beautiful green grass and the pink blossom trees of home, again."

"That is her, she is trying to twist your thoughts." Aylild and Wyrran pulled apart, that voice belonged to neither of them.

"Father! I thought you were asleep, and yet here you are sharing my innermost thoughts with Wyrran."

"How could I sleep when you two love birds sing so loudly!"

"I am sorry, sir, it is all my fault…"

"No Wyrran, it isn't, the fault is all mine, I should never have let you both come to this god-forbidden place, even now she seeks you out…"

"Who, Father, who seeks us out and why?"

"The evil that is in this dark place, she sees the bright of your light, your love, where she exudes only hate, you two are like a beacon of hope in a desolate landscape, and she is trying to home in on you."

"Why do you keep saying, 'she'? Father, do you know who it is…?"

"I don't know for sure, no, but I have a feeling, it's faint but when I feel her power reaching out, I get this tiny window to look through, and I see a woman."

"Is she human?"

"No, she has extraordinary power, no mere human could handle so much, they would be consumed, literally, but she can channel it…"

"What shall we do, Ascarli?" Wyrran asked.

"Just while we are up here and it is quiet, stay apart and try not to think of each other, you are both exceptional warriors, you do not need to worry about each other, and maybe her mind's eye will turn its attention elsewhere."

Looking up at the stars, when he had laid back down to rest, even an old elf like Ascarli was made to feel young, how long have they been there he pondered, the seat of the angels, and the one true God, Ělyāh, who sat above them all. Ascarli wondered what his God was thinking when he saw all his children at war with each other.

What was it that the humans have written down in their holy books to remind them, written by one Iesū's apostles, Mattityahu, in chapter ten, verses twenty-nine and thirty-one, "Two sparwō sell for a coin of small value, do they not? Yet not one of them will fall to the ground without your father's knowledge. So have no fear; you are worth more than many sparwōus." Ascarli pondered over that passage of scripture for a moment.

A sparwō although directly translates to a sparrow, in the scripture could have meant any small bird of which there were more than a few varieties at the time when the lord Iesū walked the earth.

Ascarli drifted off into a deep sleep, but his dreams became darker as a thick black cloud rolled into the corners of his mind, Aylild suddenly gasped, she was wide away and on guard duty but she felt herself being sucked into the void, that was her father's mind and the more she resisted the more it pulled at her. Panicked she tried to cry out to Wyrran but her voice and her mind were being taken from her, until her resolve to fight it was broken.

Have you ever clung tightly to the side of something only for you to feel it slipping out of your grasp, and then the sensation that you are falling into some endless abyss, that was how Aylild was feeling right now. Ascarli was unaware of the presence of his daughter he was too busy straining every physical muscle in his body to halt the fall that was only in his mind.

Until, it stopped, just like that. Then Ascarli realised that where ever this was, his daughter was also there. "Father, what is happening, have you any idea where we are?"

"No Daughter, I was about to ask you the same question."

"You are both here because I commanded it of you!" said the ethereal voice.

Both the elves twisted and turned to see which direction the voice came from but they could see nothing or nobody, it was as though they had been taken out of time and space and supplanted into nowhere.

"Oh. Ascarli, you seem confused, have you forgotten me after all this time apart, should I be hurt?"

"Ophelia Catula?" Aylild whispered the name.

"No, my child! Do not utter that name for it is an enchantment of seduction just to do so."

"You are too late Ascarli, my love, as we speak your daughter has fallen into an endless sleep, from which only I can awaken her, but you already know that don't you Ascarli Northstar!"

"Why are you here, Daughter of Lōthōs?"

"Where else did you think that I would be made welcome, but in the realm of dreams, after what you said and did to me?"

"My God! Women that were centuries ago, and you knew that we had no future, together, once you began to meddle in the dark arts."

"My father is the God of this whole earth, and you accuse me of dabbling, I am the embodiment of my father, I have his power coursing through my veins, in me is both light and darkness, but they do not corrupt me, they empower me."

"I suspected it was you once I felt your presence earlier, his whole thing, it is you, isn't it?"

"I am the queen of Obreā, and you have entered my lands, my domain, and do you come as an ambassador or do you come as part of an army, and the army of invaders?"

"I am here at the behest of my friend, but you already know all of this, so why act so surprised, did you honestly think that humans would bend to your will without putting up a fight?"

"These humans are fickle and frail why do you care what happens to them, and tell me Ascarli Northstar, have I ever encroached upon your lands, even though some might say I had every right after what you did to me?"

"If I hurt you, I am truly sorry…"

"Oh, you don't know the half of it, elf, but you will, especially when you get to meet my real children, these others you fight are but a distraction, and as I said, it is you who have entered my lands as an invader, but you will not leave, none of you, and I will watch as you suffer, as you watch those you love destroyed."

"You are quite mad, Daughter of Lōthōs, quite mad."

"Quite the contrary you see time has taught me a harsh lesson but now indeed, I am quite the forgiving type, if only you had stayed around long enough. We digress though, Ascarli, let me see, for old times' sake, for the lives of all your warriors, let us make a deal?"

"Hurry, witch, speak your vile words, and let me be done with you once and for all!"

"If you agree to leave now and take all of your elven soldiers with you, then I will spare you all, and let your daughter live, but you must just leave right now and don't tell your little mortal friends, that would spoil the surprise I have in store for them, later."

"You are crazier than a mother goose with a fox in her sights if you think any of that is going to happen, enchantress!"

"You know, you used to say such sweet things to me, especially in my bedchamber, and now you are so cold, so distant, but not as distant as your beloved daughter is right now, say your goodbyes and kiss her one last time on the cheek, she is now lost to you Ascarli Northstar!"

The connection broke abruptly and Ascarli found himself sunk and on his knees out of sheer exhaustion, but he was able to see his daughter, as he raised his head, she was sitting on a small outcrop of rock as she was when he left her, still watching, and waiting on guard duty. "Finddras!" he rasped. "Finddras, check on my daughter, will you please?"

"Yes, of course, my lord." The elven archer had said while rousing himself from his slumber.

"Lord! I am not sure what has happened, Aylild sits as a statue with her eyes glazed over white, what kind of magic does this to an elven princess in the presence of her father?"

All the elves were awakened and Ascarli told them to be extra vigilant, he would not say why, even he did not dare to utter that name, the name of his first love, for to do so would mean all those who thought it would become ensnared in her intoxicating beauty, like a fly in a spider's web, there until she cocooned you and then consumed you completely.

"Wyrran take my daughter straight down to the beach and commandeer a boat, then take her directly back to Avanore, and pray to the one true God that you make it in time, only there will we have any chance of saving her, please, go quickly."

With that, Wyrran and Finddras made a stretcher from their cloaks and gently lifted the lifeless form of Aylild and laid her body carefully down before picking up each of the cloak's corners and carrying her away off the mountain slope.

The beach, even in the early hours of the morning was a hive of activity and it seemed like every boat within a hundred leagues was here, those which had arrived recently were debussing their human cargo, soldiers, and those that had been there a while were having their cargo hold filled to the gunnels with the wounded and those who had contracted sickness from the unsanitary conditions.

The two elves were looking for a small boat, one that required only space enough for the three of them. So, they placed Aylild's body on the bank just beyond where all the other wounded were being lined up ready for transportation and they began their search for just such a boat. It wasn't long before they found one which was the ideal size, it was captained by a man who had been bringing supplies over from Athenous, and who was just about to depart.

After explaining their plight and offering, the man a remittance in coins he reluctantly agreed to take the three of them back across the water, they would have liked to have journeyed further around the coast but the man said that he had other more pressing duties to carry out for the war effort.

A third elven archer was dispatched to seek out Rogan and to let him know about his sister, Ascarli stressed the need to impart to the jarl that she was under a spell that could better be treated in her homeland than here on the field of battle.

Later that night the elven archer was not the only visitor Rogan Ragisson would receive, nor was it the only news that would sow yet more confusion into the hearts of his warriors.

Ongar woke Rogan shortly before dawn, not two hours after his previous visitor with the news about his sister. "Rogan, we have visitors!"

Rogan was not sleeping by any definition of the word, for he had tossed and turned every second since being given the news, his thoughts trying to reach out to his sister in the way that she had taught him, he remembered her saying that distance was no obstacle, and yet try as might, he could not reach her. "What is it Ongar, trouble?"

If by trouble, Rogan meant that the Orsk had launched a night counter-attack then that would surely have been a comfort against the news he was about to receive. "My Lord Rogan, my name is Tiberius Visellinn, of the Lōrnicā royal guard, and I come on business most urgent!"

Before Rogan had managed even to sit up straight on the furs that he had used for a bed, he felt the sense of trouble and was asking the new man to speak candidly. "I am here to inform you that our alliance is in danger of breaking apart."

Now Rogan was on his feet, wide awake and attentive, he asked one of his guards to fetch him a bucket of water.

"My Lord, did you hear what I just said?"

"Yes, yes, but what do you wish me to do, run around like a headless chicken flapping its wings and unable to cluck?"

The guard brought a wooden pale full of ice-cold water and Rogan dunked his head in it before gasping at its frigidity. "Now, tell me slowly and carefully what has happened and then I will know just how to answer you."

"My lord, earlier this evening a woman walked casually off the mountain, amid the fighting, and all about her stopped fighting to watch her, she was…well, enchanting and she walked across the debris which was placed as a bridge across the tar trench and off she went into the camp of the prince of Fōrren."

"Prince Tostig?"

"Yes, my lord."

"And then what happened?"

"She spoke briefly with him in private and then turned about face and walked back just as casually across the motte and up the side of the mountain, it was as if she was able to glide across the ground, my lord!"

"Did anyone present recognise her, do you have a description so that I might ask the elves for instance?"

"She stood 5' 7" tall, her hair was jet-black and so were her eyes, yet her complexion, her skin, was as pale as the driven snow, she was quite the most beautiful woman, and she was dressed in a long flowing gown made from black velvet, with a sort of long red shawl, oh, and she wore a crown on her head, like that of a queen."

"Was that all? It is a remarkable story, but what was the point of it, Tiberius, tell me?"

"The point, my lord, is that everyone stopped, just stopped everything that they were doing, both sides, we watched her walk in and then walk away. Prince Tostig then came outside and briskly called for his army to up sticks and move their camp!"

"Move their camp, where too?"

"Further back, and he waved his hand southwards."

"How far back are we talking?"

"Almost to the river Tawa's edge, my lord, and I don't think that they wanted to stop there, it was as if they were in a trance or under a spell, one which was broken as soon as they touched the water."

"Did anyone else try to approach them, or question their motives for such a move?"

"Not until they all stopped at the river's edge, that was when they seemed to be in such confusion that the forces on either side of them sent emissaries."

"...and?"

"Now they are refusing to return even to their camp."

"Okay, Prince Tostig was a holding force to be kept in the rear anyway, yes, it's a problem from the point of view of morale, nobody will want to look over their shoulder in battle and see that there is nothing in reserve."

"Yes, Lord, so what are we to do about it?"

"What we cannot do is replace so many warriors by stripping other units, but I have an idea, guard! Bring me Leofstan if you please, he was to be our reserve here on the right flank, now Tiberius, these men are mounted knights from the royal house of Marcadia, do you know what that means?"

"No, my lord, forgive me for I do not."

"It means that they are worth ten of any man or woman in this entire battlefield, did you know that they are blessed by our God, Ělyāh, they even carry with them bone fragments of holy saints, they will plug the gap if we spread them out in a single line." Persuaded Rogan.

"How many of these knights are there, my lord?"

"Blessed knights remember! and there are ninety of them, but as I said, they will fight like there are, nine hundred, of them if they are called upon to do so, now will that fill the gap?"

"Yes, my lord, and thank you, I will assure our commander of your plan, and what will you do for a reserve here on the right?"

"Fighters are coming off the boats every time they come across to pick up the wounded, they can soon be arranged into battle formation, and while they may be mercenaries, they will already be familiar with their expected duties, but my force is already a reserve, we have warriors fighting under the mountain ahead of us."

"Excellent! Now Ongar, who is next, now that I am wide awake?"

"It is someone from the beach, Ingrid sent him."

"Step forward, man, I do not bite!"

"Pardon me, my lord, but I have a message from Ingrid Hallgerd."

"Yes, yes, I know Ingrid, very well do you know that we are practically family?"

"Lord, I did not know that she er, never said."

"Well, never mind what is the message?"

"The boats are returning from Athenous full of the wounded we have sent them already."

"What! Why is that, that makes no sense, did she give a reason?"

"Yes lord, they said that they cannot take any more wounded the town is becoming swamped with everyone's wounded, they are complaining that they now have more wounded than people who can care for them, and there's one other problem…"

"Please, spit it out!"

"Coin, sir, they keep asking who is going to pay for everything they consume."

"What, are they serious? Do they not realise that there is a war going on?"

Atli stepped forward with what he said might be a solution.

"Please Atli, speak, as though I don't have worries enough this day."

"Lord, why don't we organise the wounded into two different groups? Leave those who are unable to care for themselves in Athenous, and let the ones who are 'walking wounded' continue to Ailgin, the journey should not be too arduous as we laid the new road, and Ailgin did prosper from all that extra trade."

"Atli, take a dozen warriors, no more, and a bag of coin, remind them how well they have fared so far, and how they may benefit after the war when men pass through their town with pockets full of treasure!"

"Yes, my lord, and I'll be sure to emphasise the latter." Atli went calling for Sigrunn Hallkatla to pick out the other ten who should ride with them. Horses were in great supply down around the landing area as most of the first day's fighting had taken place on foot. Atli was secretly relieved that he was able to get his love away from the carnage.

There was just one other who was waiting patiently to speak with Rogan, it was a female elf ranger.

"I am Padrien Birchwood, lord, and I come with grave news from Ascarli. We have been visited by an enchantress…"

"Visited, my lady, I'm not sure I understand?"

"As you may be aware, we elves can attune ourselves to the frequencies of nature, we call it the dreamscape, it is a place of great beauty and serenity, or it should have been, last though Ascarli was attacked in that realm by someone he identified as the enchantress."

"Yeah, all this elven ability beyond our world is still very new to me, but was he hurt in any way?"

"Not he, no, it was your sister, Aylild, the Princess has been put under a powerful spell, she has fallen into some kind of deep malaise, from which she cannot be awakened, even now as we speak, she is being taken to the boats where she will go directly back to Avanore."

"Do you need me to find you a boat, will she be alright?"

"The boat has already been procured, I believe, it is a small supply boat so it won't hamper your efforts to remove your wounded, Ascarli is greatly troubled by her condition but he knows who the enchantress is and how to counter the spell, more than that he wouldn't say."

"Did he say where this enchantress is, and if she is a threat to our forces?"

"Another woman, an enchantress, where are the Orsk in all of this?"

"I am sorry, my lord, but I fear you have lost me when you say; 'another woman'?"

Rogan briefly explained the visitation some of his troops received.

"I believe they are the same, lord."

"Who is this woman that she can just stroll around on a whim, and poison the minds of men and elves alike."

"Why is it only now that we are finding out about her, have the elves been keeping secrets from us?"

171

"This is the first time we elves have found out about her too, please don't think that we would hold things back if we knew our serious, they were."

"Return to your lord, with this message, The prince of Forren has left the field of battle after an encounter with your enchantress, and stress that word, no if there is nothing else, I wish you a good day!"

The elven ranger nodded her head in recognition and then left.

"Do you still trust the elves, lord?"

"Ongar, if my sister, Aylild, knew anything about this enchantress then I am positive that she would have mentioned her sooner, concerning Ascarli, I have to believe that he knew nothing of her presence here, more than that we will have to find after the fighting is over."

"Very good, lord, shall I go rouse the army, now?"

"Yes, allow them time to eat and drink and do what soldiers do before battle, once we begin, every section should attack one after the other starting with ours, and remember, I just want those on the other side of the tar trench to pin the Orsk down while we link up with Aethelric's command and go from village to village, once we have cleared each village section, then the men on the other side of the trench can come across and join us."

"We just need to be mindful about the middle, it would help to know what Prince Tostig is planning, does he intend to march his men home, or does he think to rejoin us, if he is under some sort of enchantment, should he be trusted, or what?"

"You could send Gunnar; he was the one who first spoke with him?"

"Good Idea, Ongar, can I leave that with you?"

"Of course, lord, have you given any thought to all the 'white Orsk' who are coming over to our side?"

"I hadn't given them any, no, do you know how many have come across to our cause?"

"Reports are coming in that there are hundreds, strung out along the whole battle front, many waited until dark and came over, none of the commanders knew what to do with them and so they have been sending them back to the beach area."

"Then we must call them all together and put them under Leofstan's command, I didn't like the idea of just having a handful of mounted men in the centre, if we break there, God forbid, then our forces will shatter and the war will be lost."

172

"As the Orsk has the advantage of being able to overlook our army from the mountain, do you think they will spot our weakness, and give us trouble?"

"I don't think anything about those ruddy Orsk, as you know they prefer to hit a problem head-on, but I am kind of wondering about this woman, the enchantress, anyone who can ruffle Ascarli's feathers is going to be a force to be reckoned with, let's just hope that whatever game she is playing it won't concern us until all other matters have been dealt with first."

"Rogan, you sent for me, how can I help?"

"Ah, Cro-Mur just the half-blood I wanted to see, did you participate in the Orsk games, in the arena, I mean?"

"Yes, if you mean the coming-of-age games, everyone has to compete in that at some point, I was in a group just below you in age, I was still living in the chamber with all the women when you fought, but we all heard about your success."

Rogan seized Cro-Mur about the shoulders and asked him to get down on one knee, then Rogan drew his sword from its scabbard, and held it out towards Cro-Murs right shoulder, Cro-Mur wondered at this point if he had disappointed Rogan and he was about to relieve him of his head!

"Rogan, is everything alright, I mean what are you doing?" asked Ongar in a very concerned voice which caused everyone else who was looking on to stop what they were doing.

"By the powers vested in me," Rogan began to say while holding his sword as straight as he could. "I appoint you Cro-Mur as war chief of all the half-bloods!"

"Eh?"

"From this day forth, you shall be known as 'Cro-Mur the undefeated', now arise and embrace your jarl."

Cro-Mur did not dare move a muscle, he had no idea what was happening, even when the men watching began to cheer, men it appears always like to cheer, but for what reason, as yet remained a mystery to the half-blood.

It was left to Ongar to say, "I think you are supposed to get up now Cro-Mur, I mean Cro-Mur, you have just been knighted, at least that is my perception?"

"You are correct Ongar, Cro-Mur you are now the leader of all the half-bloods and I want you to round them all up, staring down at the beach, then rally all others behind Leofstan and his mounted men. They are the fancy-looking men on horses at our centre, once you arrive, give yourself time to get your lines in order, now one last thing…"

Rogan removed a thick gold chain from around his neck and placed it around Cro-Mur's neck.

"Take this as a token of your new rank, and tell you, people, that there will be more where this came from after the war is over!"

Ongar watched as the new war chief left in search of his charges and then he cocked his head in Rogan's direction and smiled before shrugging his shoulders and asking what was there still to do? Rogan just asked quietly how he did as that was the first ever knight thing he had ever done, Ongar said he had no idea either but when next he saw Leofstan he would be sure to ask him, as he was the resident expert of all things knight related.

Cro-Mur wasted no time finding the other half-bloods, as it was where he had barely stepped back over the tar trench then he found Ron-Omir, Sar-Onar, and Gram-Agall all just milling about, they were informed of Cro-Mur's new status and each congratulated him, before falling in line behind as they came back over the tar-filled ditch and set off towards the beach area in search of their fellow countrymen.

Rogan asked Ongar to fire the flaming arrow which would signal the war had begun.

Men from Athenous who formed part of the army that was to the left of Rogan's starting point now marched forward in the hope of drawing the next warband of half-breeds and Orsk out of the second underground village, the tunnel opening was about a hundred paces away from Rogan's new front line.

The plan was to entice the Orsk and their supporting half-bloods into making a run straight for the barricades over the tar pit which would take them right past the left flank where Rogan's men were crouching, with throwing spears in hand.

The Orsk it was thought would have no way of knowing that the first village under the mountain had already fallen, Rogan had dismissed the notion that there might be a secret door that lead to yet another level after spending so many years inside the cave system, he believed, wrongly, that the two levels he did know about were the only ones, in fact, in the end, it was only through Trygg's insistence that he reluctantly agreed to leave a guard of six just inside the mouth of the first cave village at all.

When the Orsk and half-bloods who reminded loyally, came it was with numbers, far more than would ordinarily have been in one village, and they were chanting war tunes and by the time they left the full safety of their main tunnel they were in a frenzy. Rogan watched as they split into two separate bodies, one which charged forward to the battlements in front of the tar-filled ditch, and the second which peeled away towards where his forces were hiding.

On the flat plateau above, Ascarli and his elven archers waited for each elf with a bow in hand, poised to lose their volleys when the opportunity arose. As the Orsk warriors, inter-dispersed with half-Orsk came straight towards Rogan's positions, he stood and shouted to his men to throw the first of their three spears, the Orsk responded by holding up their shields in front of them.

That was the signal for Ascarli and his elves to open fire from their elevated vantage point, seventy-two arrows, tipped with elven steel bore down on the exposed shoulders of the charging Orsk, biting into flesh and through leather coverings without resistance, felling over half of the pack, those who were lucky enough to be struck on their iron helmets or iron chest armour still felt the sting of being hit, enough to make them think about how they should best defend themselves from a second attack.

Rogan's first rank of spearmen had far less success as the javelin-like spears slammed mostly into the large oblong shields, however, where the thirty or so spears hit multiple shields at the same time it became quite a cumbersome weight for the Orsk to carry, and many therefore let go of them. The elves left three times the dead that Rogan's attack had.

The Orsk and half-breeds who ran straight towards their defences at the tar pit had the upper hand as the forces they faced were barely able to pull any of the defences down and that soon became a slinging match between the two opposing forces. In the heat of the battle, the defending Orsk and half-bloods stuck rigidly to their task and did not think to look back and see how the other part of their forces were doing.

Rogan then gave the command for his second rank to throw their spears, almost at point blank range, this time gutting the attack that was heading their way, then came the order for the final rank to engage what was left of the enemy with swords. The elves upon the ridge on seeing that their services were no longer required turned their next arrows towards the rear of the Orsk defending their battlements above the tar pit, they targeted exposed arms, legs, and neck parts, where the Orsk felt no need to completely cover that area in iron.

Wounded Orsk and half-bloods littered the ground but other Orsk just left them where they fell, they had no facility or training to deal with such ones, in open battle they would have been left, as they were being here. Afterwards, those who were deemed capable of recovery would have been patched up, those thought of as too badly wounded would have been dispatched with a blade under the chin.

Ascarli sent one more volley of arrows into the rear of the Orsk ranks and then instructed his elves to move along to the next section of tunnel openings, there to await Rogan's next order set of orders. Rogan stationed fifty of his men directly outside the tunnel that led to the second village, and took what was left of the other half towards the Orsk on the battlements, Aatu, who had been held back until now was running alongside him.

The Orsk and the half-breeds were losing too many warriors and finally turned to face a new threat, and one giant of an Orsk, a creature who stood over six feet tall stepped forward to face the on-rushing charge with so much courage that Rogan almost admired him, but to Aatu he was just a blockage that needed clearing, and he bounded towards this leader flattening him as he leaped towards him at the last moment.

Seeing their leader go down so heavily under the attack, and realising themselves who that warg was, and who therefore was with him the rest of the Orsk line faltered, and in that split second, they sealed their fate. If they had charged forward, they would no longer have been stood on the wooden platform over the tar pit. What they did not know was that the forces across from the pit had thrown grappling hooks across and caught hold of the wood-stathes holding the platform up.

The tug-of-war that followed saw the aggressors pull the thick timber legs from under the platform, toppling it and all the Orsk on that section into the sticky black morass, from which they could not escape, their heavy iron armour saw to that. Once more those who looked on saw no glory in watching the Orsk, and half-breeds flounder before being pulled under to their deaths.

Rogan did not want to lose the momentum of the attack and started shouting for his forces to join up and focus on the next tunnel, the fifty who were lined up across the mouth, with Gunnar in their midst began the slow march forward. The occasional missile was thrown from within, and then a great shout went up somewhere inside, the half-bloods had seen their moment to strike and they did, in a similar fashion to the first village, with the chains on their wrists and with discarded weapons from those who had already been killed in the entrance.

The attack inside was led by a man Rogan had met only a couple of times before, called Thara-Dack, who was a brave warrior, one who the captives would follow, and as the first fifty men of Rogan's front rank ran down the tunnel, they were met by a hail of arrows from the upper balcony, which was aimed at the rebels. That was quickly followed by a squad of around fifty Orsk warriors with iron armour and weapons, charging down the main stairwell.

Once Rogan, Ongar, and the others had caught up with the front rank, Ongar suggested that they use the fire-pots to dislodge those reining arrows down upon them, but Rogan wanted to save what they had in reserve for when they finally met the black guard. For the time being, it would be hand-to-hand and along with the newcomers joining in those Orsk who had poured down the stairs were now being dealt with.

The Orsk archers on the balcony were eventually commanded to join in the melee downstairs, and in the flickering light, the buttery in the second underground village began. It was hot work, in the main cavern as cut bodies released a lot of warm gas and the floor became incredibly slippery with all the blood and guts. Rogan could do nothing more than to encourage his men to press forward, and so the slaughter continued.

Aatu went straight for the Orsk who were blocking the left side cave entrance first, bringing those beasts down and the half-bloods would be free to pour out into the main chamber, after which he made his way over the right tunnel. Thara-Dack thanked the white warg for his quick work in freeing his comrades, not even knowing whether the creature could understand him or not.

The fighting went on for most of the morning until the Orsk numbers had dropped so low that it became a massacre, as they simply refused to surrender, afterwards Rogan turned his attention to the upper balcony and the tunnels that led to the balconies on either side of this main gallery, Aatu was the first to run up the stairs, and as he did so he caught the scent of something that piqued his curiosity. Rogan was not far behind his warg. "What is it boy, what have you found?" Rogan could only see the warg scratching at the back of the wall, quite why he had no idea.

Aatu began barking and howling loudly, he was becoming quite agitated. "What is the matter with him?" asked Ongar as he made his way up the stairs.

"I have no idea, Gunnar will you take your warriors left, and Thara-Dack would you take your group right with the rest of my housecarl?"

Aatu, who had until now gone about his work precisely and without fuss, began his low guttural whine, signalling to Rogan that he should take the time to listen! "What is it, boy? What am I missing?" The warg, who was the size of a large dog by now, leaped up and down and twisted around a few times while continuing to make smaller, shorter whining sounds.

Ongar picked up one of the lit torches that were spaced out along the walls and he brought it up close to the area that had Aatu in a tizz, and while neither he nor Rogan could see anything out of the ordinary, they saw that, when held over a certain place the flame flickered. "What does this mean, Rogan?" asked Ongar.

"It means that maybe Trygg was telling the truth, there is a secret door at the top of each staircase."

Ongar brought his blade to bare in the place where it made the flames flicker, then he prodded the area with the tip of the blade until it stuck in the rock. "What is it Ongar?"

"Look, Rogan, I can drag my blade down this tiny ridge, it does appear to be a doorway!"

"What do think, if it's locked, should we just post a guard and leave it, at least until we have cleared the tunnels completely?"

"Lord Rogan?" shouted a female wearing the royal guard uniform.

"I am up here!" replied Rogan.

"Lord, I have been sent by Captain Benardin Faucon to let you know that we have cleared the battlements outside right down to the main central cave, what would you have us do next?"

"Secure what you have taken, bring some of the warriors on the opposite side of the tar pit, and then tell your captain to take his forces down to the beach for a couple of hours respite, if you are anything to go by my lady you've had it tough out there."

"Thank you, lord, I will convey your message immediately."

"Who was that beauty?" inquired Rogan.

"That beauty will cost you your head, lord Rogan, especially if I catch you ogling her…again!"

"Ingrid! You know how I have eyes only for you, I was just thinking out loud for one of my men…"

"Darling you are a better fighter than a liar, and it's just as well!"

Aatu barked his usual agreement with Ingrid and Rogan merely patted his head saying; "Bad dog, remember who your master is!"

"Absolute not, Rogan, but we certainly make some protective armour for Aatu, like Leofstan's horses, they all wear armour and are even used in battle as weapons against a tightly packed enemy, just say, yes, and I will have men re-ignite the Furness's in our old cave, we could even use some of the discarded weapons and armour from the fallen to melt down."

Next to appear looking for Rogan were two of the half-bloods who had been fighting for him. "Tan-Cred and Cro-Mar how are you doing, is the centre holding up outside?"

"We are fine my lord, but we are also losing men faster than any other warband."

"Why is that, my friend?"

"Lord, we don't have any armour, unless we pick it up off the dead, and if we reach for the armour worn by humans, we are receiving abuse from the living, but the armour the Orsk wear is far too heavy and restrictive."

Ongar intervened; "Lord, why don't we let them restart the blacksmith's fires in our old village, surely then if they collect all of the iron armour, they can smelt it down and make steel for themselves, using the Orsk clay moulds?"

"Alright, but first we need to reset our defensive line, the barricades have taken a hammering, you go and get those fires breathing again and I will organise this mess, and tell the men to re-seal the upper corridor, we don't want any counter attacks coming through there." Exclaimed the jarl.

All this extra work would mean another day lost but Rogan knew that the defending Orsk was not going anywhere, they were surrounded on three sides by his army, and in their rear was the ocean. As yet there was no sign of this enchantress or the heavily armoured black guard, in fact, Rogan was beginning to think that if this witch was anywhere, it was much higher up and she was very much alone up there.

The Orsk seemed to have a great fear of the ocean and the waterways that surrounded their realm, they would only cross either by a boat, and yet they were not boat builders nor were they workers in wood, they could carve the stone in a rudimentary way, and they could forge iron, but water as always held an innate fear for them. Now was a good time to pause and reflect thought Rogan.

It took a while but when it came, the news that the forge in the cave at the back of where Rogan and Ongar were held was up and running, it was welcome news, Aatu was back to his happy playful state and the warriors who had been fighting were glad of the break in fighting; no soldier—no matter how well-trained—could wield his sword all day long and doubly so if he was wearing armour.

Rogan headed back to his old village under the mountain to check on the forges. Virtually every half-blood and human male had been taught to use the forge by the Orsk and Rogan found an inner piece revisiting his old place of captivity, where he worked hard and honed his muscle.

"Ongar, how is it going, I could feel the heat from the main cave…"

"They are just seeing if the forge is hot enough yet."

There was no real way of testing just how hot the forge was, it was a skill that the blacksmith learned by reading the coal and the colour of the flame, it had to be seven hundred and sixty degrees Celsius to be just so, the metal that was to be used also needed to melt down so that it could be placed in a mould before it was ready to be shaped, heating this way was a dirty business, and Aatu watched and waited as both Rogan and Ongar.

Later still when all the pieces had been checked and passed inspection the task of fitting it all together was given to the women, leather work was their domain under the rule of the Orsk. Now though at least they were being offered a choice, and most of them grabbed the opportunity to be part of the war effort. Unbeknownst to either Rogan or Ongar, the half-bloods had made some lightweight steel armour for Aatu and the women were going to work on fitting it around his head and torso.

Aatu was loving the attention, if not the armour, he found it a little cumbersome, he was a creature of the wild and this was something he would never have countenanced in the wild, however, he took it for what it was, an expression of other people's love and appreciation for him.

When the fighting resumed the following day Rogan had put together a most audacious plan, Aatu, now looking like an armoured hedgehog was to be sent into the main entrance, on the ground floor of the cave, and then run up the main staircase and round to the corridor on the upper balcony where Ongar would be waiting for him, then Rogan and his vanguard would rush in and form a shield wall on three sides to engage the defenders, once they had done that, they would expect Ongar's troops to have at cleared the balcony so that they could then aid Rogan's three shield walls.

All the battle-hardened warriors watched in awe at Rogan and Ongar explaining the plan to Aatu, and they were even struck each time that Aatu jumped and twirled around after being given very specific instructions. Rogan then went through the same idea with the men and when it reached a point where Aatu was involved he did his little routine.

Sending men and women into hand-to-combat with an enemy that held both the high ground and the element of surprise was foolish, to say the least, and Rogan even wondered what the bards would sing, when they reached the part about a warg being key to the attack plan's success, in their sagas and songs in the future.

Just before dawn on the following day, the reflection from the rising sun on the distant clouds was cause for a solemn moment of reflection for all, but particularly as they thought about Aethelric the bard and his badly wounded body, which had finally been moved on to a boat for transportation to Athenous. "Blow the horn and fire the flame arrow, and let us get on with the slaughter!" Rogan said as he tried to shake the images from his mind about one of his closest and dearest friends.

The barricade was being removed on the upper balcony and at the same time outside they were pulling one of the spikes, and log traps back to let the first group of thirty warriors and Aatu through.

Aatu set off like a whippet curving his run into the mouth of the tunnel and then focusing in on the stairs that were ahead of him, at first half-breeds only tried to hit him with arrows and when that failed, or rather they failed to halt his mad dash, one or two of them tried to hack at him with their swords, each blow bouncing off his armour causing no damage and at the same time unsettling the wielder of the weapon.

There were those of a more challenged disposition who tried desperately to catch the warg with their bare hands, his armour was covered in tiny sharp spikes which ripped their hands to pieces, they would not be able to wield a weapon for quite some time.

Behind Aatu came the warband, thirty warriors forming quickly into a testudo, while up on the balcony, Aatu had just made contact with the first archer and as that archer reached out to grab the warg, his hands were shredded on the raised spikes and sharp edges, and he fell back in agony, and the sight of the blood jetting out of his wounds was just enough of a distraction for Ongar's group to pour through the corridor to the left of the upper balcony.

Aatu swung around knowing that his part in this mission was over and now it was time to demonstrate his abilities especially to their half-breeds and their human sympathisers. Ongar was now in the new cave up on the balcony and he immediately ran to one of the defenders and smashed his war-axe down hard on the Orsk warriors' shoulder, the Orsk attempted to parry the blow but his arm was not as quick as Ongar's stroke was, and the axe buried its self, deep into the flesh, almost severing the Orsk warriors' arm from his shoulder.

Aatu launched himself at another Orsk who was attempting to draw his bow while pointing it towards Ongar's back, Aatu hit the Orsk with such force he broke through the barrier that sat three paces above the balcony walkway and fell to his death, Aatu adroitly turned, twisting his body to miss another arrow which had just fizzed past him, this time he was on the archer in the blink of an eye, his jaws wide and his teeth bared, tearing at the iron chest armour the defender was wearing, his powerful jaws crunching through the brittle metal as though it were bone, and the victim's chest at the same time.

Aatu's jaws clasped another Orsk's neck in his powerful vice-like jaws and then snapped his head clean off his shoulders, shaking the severed head left and right as he tossed it over the remaining railings. Some of the humans, who were supporting the Orsk were throwing their weapons down and putting their hands high above their heads, they had witnessed something so powerful that not even the Orsk scared them anymore, but it would be to no avail, Rogan roared with bloodlust, "No prisoners!"

Out of the thirty men it took to complete the capture of the new cave system, on the ground level, Rogan had lost a further six, Ongar had not lost any, but that was largely thanks to Aatu's savagery, the Orsk and their comrades lost their appetite for fighting as quickly as they lost their lives.

Rogan sent runners to inform the chiefs on the other side of the tar trench that once more it was safe to move forward. It would be after this battle was over that Rogan resolved to rotate the men who had helped liberate the first to cave villages. The fight was not over yet, there was still the thought of secret doorways and passages beyond, and there were women, and prisoners to liberate, although sadly some had taken their own lives during this terrifying ordeal, and others were murdered by the Orsk in a last act of revenge, but several were grateful to Rogan and his forces for setting them free.

"Ongar, get your men to block the balcony at the far end. I will use my men and the reinforcements that should be coming over the tar trench to scour the lower levels." The layout of this village was the same as the last one, and the warriors now began to have a feel for where to go and what to expect, another four men were lost securing this whole section, and once again Rogan called for the barricades to be placed as before, and to tear down anything that stood above the tar trench.

Soldiers poured forwards, some with axes to chop up the wooden supports and others with spades to backfill the tar trench section by section. Everywhere soldiers and their leaders were deservedly congratulating each other for the minimal loss of life and the rapid capture of the second village under the mountain.

9

The Enchantress

The main entrance to the kingdom under the mountain was situated in-between two other villages on either side, on the evening of the fifth day Rogan's forces along with Gufi Grettersson and Arn Ironside respective armies delivered the final blow to the Orsk on the left flank, both villages were taken and all that remained was for the soldiers on the right flank to catch up, it was calculated that they were about a day behind.

Ascarli and his group of thirty-four surviving archers came down from the ledge above the double doors via two sets of stone stairs that ran down either side in a curved pattern that followed the line of the rock.

Rogan was quick to embrace the elf and his warriors reciprocated the welcome with all of the other elves. "The other half of my command should be joining us here tomorrow, my friend."

"Do you why they are delayed, Ascarli?"

"The Orsk on the right flank was less eager to poke their heads outside once they saw the might of the combined armies, so it has taken longer to flush them out, and a great many more human lives lost, I am sorry to report, lord Rogan."

Rogan and Ascarli stood looking up at the letter that had been carved out of the sandstone above the doorway. "I know what you are thinking young jarl, but first let me give you a gift."

"A gift, what could this be so late in the day?"

Ascarli wore a small bag around the base of his back, and he shuffled it so that it perched above his right hip, unbuckling the leather strap, he apologised, "I wish I could have brought a more, old friend, but what with everything else we brought with us this was only adding to the weight."

"What are they, some sort of glowing stones?" Rogan reacted as Ascarli picked one out and handed it to him.

"We call them 'elf stones', you might know them better as crystals, these are only small and so won't stay lit up like that for long, a couple of days maybe. I thought they may help once you enter the main cave complex here."

"Would you mind if I gave them out to my warriors?"

"No, no, not at all, that is why I brought them with me. I noticed your warriors like to wear various trinkets around their necks; tell them to tie these on as well, they will illuminate their surroundings far more than the torches they hold, and they will free up that hand."

"That is a very thoughtful gift, Ascarli, thank you."

"Rogan, you will face evil as you have never known before, and it lurks in every corner, at every turn, this crystal will at least make them more cautious of leaving their shadows."

The cave mouth was around twenty-four feet wide and equally as tall, it was been hued from the sandstone bedrock at the base of the mountain and then closed off with enormous solid oak double doors, braced with iron slats. Gunnar was the first to point up to writing after being given a crystal. "So, what do you think?"

"I don't; superstition that's all, Gunnar, you know I must have walked past this very spot hundreds of times and never noticed it once!"

"Hey, you!" It was Ingrid. "What's everyone doing?"

"We are taking a breath while the army of Lornica catches up, I have sent men to harry the enemy's left flank but the fighting is contained within the third village under the mountain."

"It seems strange now, thinking back, but none of us women were taught their speech I think Solveig was the only human female I ever heard who was able to hold a conversation with the guards."

"You didn't miss out on much, we called it the language of the dead."

"Can you translate it, my beloved?"

"Damned are all those who enter, dead are all those who try to leave."

Ongar looked at the words and then very quickly looked away as though even reading them in his mind were to put a curse upon himself, he saw others carefully trying to translate them in their head and he held a hand up. "Don't waste your time, for it is the tongue of the necromancer, and you will only bring misery down upon yourself by trying to say those words!"

"Xupnox uko uii htejo fte onhok, xoux uko uii htejo fte hkc he iougo," recanted Tan-Cred as if those words were etched upon his heart.

"No, you fool!" shouted Ascarli. "Rogan, get out of here now, before the gates open."

"What, why, what is going on—" Rogan's sentence was cut short as they all turned and looked towards the double gates. The doors began to creak and wail on their hinges, and dust filled the air and small pieces of sandstone fell to the ground with dull thuds, and the doors began to open, slowly, inextricably, as if by magic.

"Pull back, all of you!" the elf master bellowed, and Rogan, feeling the panic well up in his friend, turned and began waving the men back to their previous positions.

Ascarli called upon his heavy infantry to move forward and block the road leading out of the main tunnel, up until now their services had not been needed, and so have been held back in reserve. Now everyone watching was treated to a spectacle that few others have ever witnessed. Two hundred and fifty heavily armoured soldiers drilled to perfection.

Row after row, rank after rank came standing in lines ten wide and twenty-five deep, had Ascarli done this to deflect attention away from the double doors? Rogan wondered. But his question was about to be answered for him as the large oak doors opened wide.

The chanting was the first anyone became aware of, the vibration through the floor which cause yet more debris to fall, as a thousand iron-shod boots stamped down hard on the ground. Ascarli called out a command in elvish and his soldiers changed their stance, from one of standing straight to that of a fighting stance, their bodies slightly crouched, right legs back one pace, shields out, spears down, and pointing straight forwards.

Then came the cry, like something had been unleashed from the bowels of the earth, a reverberation that shook every man, woman, and half-blood, so that they had to hold their hands over their ears, but the elves stood unmoved, perhaps they had covering within their snug fitted helmets that drowned the sound out.

Then came the monstrous black tide, equally as well-drilled as the elves, it was the first wave of black guard and they crashed against the spears and shields like the incoming tide on the breakwaters. Once those gates were fully opened it was as though a giant snake had opened its jaws wide and vomited forth the contents of its stomach, the smell was toxic, the air turned darker and everyone present realised that something truly terrifying had been unleashed.

Ascarli quickly signalled to the elven archers who were still stationed above the doors, and they lined up so that every one of them could have a clear shot, and with that first minute they had released over a hundred arrows, the air was full of the sounds of grunting and groaning, but strangely no sounds from the wounded and dying. Bodies began piling up and soon it would be impossible to fight at all, Rogan noticed that when the elven arrows bit home they fizzed on contact with the jet-black flesh of the black guard.

Moments began to feel like hours, as the watching warriors stood in subdued awe, the elves were not just holding back the black guard they were eradicating them one rank at a time.

By midday, the fighting had slowed to almost an impasse, not because either the elves or the black guard we weary, because they had already fought on long after any human or half-blood were capable of doing, but because the bodies of the fallen were like a wall between them, so much so that they blocked the doorway to the main entrance completely.

Ascarli ordered his heavy infantry to step back several paces, and from somewhere inside the darkened cavern a voice called out the same command in the language of the dead, "Kohkouh hon muyoj!"

"What now, Lord Ascarli?" asked Rogan.

"Now we wait, get your men prepared though, I fear that whatever has been released we haven't seen the half of it, yet." The elf lord delivered those words with cold precision, not even once making eye contact with the jarl.

The sound of horses' hooves on the soft sandy earth broke the momentary quiet, it was Captain Ricsige Brecott of the royal guard. "Lord, we have a situation."

"Speak quickly while we catch our breath, captain."

"Prince Tostig is refusing all requests to move off the beach, and his army is now blocking the ships from loading the wounded."

"Gunnar tell me truthfully have we replaced the number of warriors in Tostig's army with half-bloods that have come over to our cause?"

"I would say so, yes, and then some, lord."

"Captain would you please take this message back to the prince: 'Thank you so much for all your support, the battle is all but over and we expect you will be eager to return to your homelands with your army.' Sign it, Jarl Ragisson."

"That's very generous of you lord, after all the prince has hardly moved five feet in any direction…"

"The prince is either a fool or a coward, neither of which is of any use to me now, but I have no wish to make him my enemy, this piece of parchment that I write gives him an honourable discharge from his duties, and we shall remain allies."

Prince Tostig Godhelm was preoccupied with his visitor, Queen Ophelia Catula. "You are about to be dismissed…"

"Dismissed, my queen, from what?"

"As we speak, that upstart Rogan Ragisson seeks to send you home with your tail between your legs, he believes you to be a coward!"

"Then I shall teach that cur a lesson he won't forget!"

"Oh, my word, you can be quite the aggressor when you want to be, but what plan do you weave in that mind of yours, prince?"

"You think I don't see his warriors languishing about around the fallen battlements, I shall march right up there and put them all to the sword!"

"I fear, my prince that you will waste so many a young man's life, leave his forces to me, instead I have something far more delicious for you to do, and I expect all of the losses will be his, and his alone."

"Tell me, my queen, for you have but to speak and it shall be done…"

Ophelia smiled, a satisfactory smile, as she placed her right hand gently on the cheek of the young prince. "You are my very special friend, and I promise for your loyalty to return you home a king. But for now, I need you to accept the jarl's request and then I shall tell you what it is I need you to do."

"It has come, stand fast my friend!" warned the elven master.

Rogan barely had time to convey instructions and the great doorway burst into life. First, there was a thick black cloud of swirling smoke than from its centre grew something resembling a black hound with eyes a blaze, that kept on growing until it filled the cave entrance. "Fire at will!" shouted the jarl.

A thick dense cloud of arrows peppered the beast followed by a forest of thrown spears but not one tip pierced any part of the creature, instead, it was as if it had no substance and could not be hurt. Then the elves loosened a volley of their arrows from above the beast as it emerged from the cave, and those arrow heads did bite and the creature reared up in pain and roared its feelings before spewing fire from its mouth, left to right across the rocky outcrop, The elves had to dive for cover of being engulfed in flame.

The beast did something quite unexpected, instead of attacking the forces arrayed in front of it, the creature stooped its head and began consuming all of the dead bodies that blocked the mouth of the cave, greedily and without concern for the armour those figures wore, black guard, Orsk, half-blood, elf or human, scooped up great mouthfuls and chomped them all grinding them down to dust, but it did not swallow a single morsel it produced a cloud of dust which seemed to fall from every angle of its mouth.

Rogan's forces stood like they had been turned to stone, it was both a mesmerising and intoxicating sight, and they realised just how insignificant they truly were, Ascarli held his heavy infantry back, he knew that they could hurt the beast, but he did not want them to incur its wraith, hurt it his elves might, but he was convinced that they could kill it, nor did he think that it had been summoned to fight, it was nothing more than glorified cleaner.

After watching as the spirit hound crunched and crushed, its final mouthful it disappeared in a puff of smoke, a cloud of dust that threatened to choke those near enough to inhale it. "Hold your breath!" called Rogan, although it was an order that was not required. Moments later the cloud had dissipated and the doorway was wide open and completely clear, but before anyone could react, they began to swing shut, until they were completely closed once more.

It was as though a spell had been broken and everyone snapped back into the present, Rogan called on Ongar, "Where is Halla Greilanda?" Halla was Ongar's lover but she was also captain of fifty swords.

"I stationed her over on the left facing the men of Lornica, shall I recall her, lord?"

"I was going to send her to aid them in person, how many of her command remains?"

"About thirty warriors, lord."

"Gunnar, take her what remains of my housecarl that should more than bring her numbers up, send them to reinforce the Lornica attack, and let us be done with these cave dwellers, so that we may concentrate on this main entrance."

Ascarli bent down to speak with Aatu, "Now, I know that you too have a gift that is like 'far sight' You sense things in the shadows, in dark places where my vision is severely limited, so I need you to stand at the very front of my formation and let me know if those doors are going to open again, can you do that for me?"

The elf stroked the back of Aatu's head as he spoke the words to him, and afterwards, the warg barked just once, in recognition. Once again Ascarli called on his heavy infantry to form a line across the closed doorway, their number had been reduced by upwards of fifty it several rows shorter than it was. Rogan offered some members of the royal guard to help bolster the numbers but Ascarli told him to keep them back, and out of the sway of the enchantress's reach.

While there was this uneasy peace, Jarl Oswald and his entourage made their way up from the beach, he was complaining about everything and everyone, nothing seemed to be in his favour. "Ah, lord Rogan, there you are!"

"Jarl Oswald, I was not expecting to see you this far in land, have you brought welcome reinforcements, perhaps?"

"No, no, nothing like that, goodness me we are doing all we can for the wounded you keep sending us, you know we now have more of them than people to deal with them, my town is in utter chaos!"

"Then tell me, why have you come here, surely not to take warriors?"

"Oh goodness no, I am here with a message from his eminence the bishop, and the town people."

"Go on, I'm intrigued seeing as though you have already done so much, and emptied my coffers like no other!"

"Erm, well, let me begin by saying what a wonderful privilege it is to be here today, 'we' stand on the brink of something truly historical, a victory over the Orsk, and their ungodly off-spring," Oswald had certainly got Ongar's attention.

His inflammatory statement had brought some gasps and surprisingly some nods of agreement from those who gathered to listen, he continued, "I have been authorised by the bishop of Athenous to tell you all that any of your brave warriors, who have fallen in battle, will have a place reserved for them in the cathedral's cemetery…" As he paused, he began applauding what he had just said, and again what was more alarming was that those who agreed with his words began clapping themselves.

"For a small remittance, of course, blessing…and coffins don't come freely, unfortunately," he added through the noise of applause.

"I knew this would be a pitch, that weasel and his boss the bishop care only about the coin!" Rogan scoffed, but Ongar seemed incensed.

"What about the brave half-bloods, without their help we might not even be standing here having this meeting?" Ongar was seething, it was almost as though he knew what was coming next.

"Well, nobody here doubts the input that your, ahem, that those friends of yours have given to this most wonderful cause, however, and I do not say this to be disparaging, there are only a limited number of burial places, and I think we must all agree that those places should, rightly, be reserved for the human contingent of the fallen, as we do not have any of your kind in residence, to tend to the graves, now what do you all think?"

Once more the nonsense that Oswald spoke was lightly applauded.

"Well, that is most concerning Jarl Oswald, because half-bloods were among the first casualties that were taken to the beach area for transport over to your town." Rogan pointed out.

Many more, although not applauding what Rogan said, did themselves mutter support for his words.

Oswald looked horrified. "Surly Rogan Ragisson, you did not expect us to deal with those, those…ahead of our kinfolk, no, most certainly not, they were taken for transportation to Ailgin, along with Atli and his women!"

"That explains why the boats were so slow removing the wounded then, some were even returning with them still unloaded from your side." Ingrid who had spent a lot of the day trying to tend to the wounded, stated.

"With all due respect lords, ladies, and gentlefolk, we are not here to argue over the wounded or the dead, we are here to prevent anymore needing to be evacuated off the beach, let us talk now about the plan to continue the war," Leofstan remarked.

Rogan flashed a hard stare at Jarl Oswald, and for the first time since he bestowed that title on him, he wished that he had not. "Thank you, Jarl Oswald, I am sure, those here who have applauded your words will in private seek you out and talk with you some more, do send our thanks back with you to your bishop."

The jarl did not immediately move, he stood firm as though he were expecting something, Rogan looked at Ongar, and Ongar nodded his head ever so slightly. "Ah, Jarl Oswald, how very remiss of me, I believe I should send a little something back with you to share with the bishop, Ongar, tell me what funds do we still have?"

"There are a couple of small coin pouches left, my lord."

"There take this with all our gratitude, oh, and one last thing, Jarl Oswald, please take those men of Forren back with you, surely you can talk them into staying in Athenous to help with the wounded, and the burial of the dead. Now if you do not mind, I have a council of war to convene!"

Oswald bowed graciously as he snatched at the coin pouch, jingling it a little to test its weight. "Thank you, my friend, and I will be sure to consult the prince as I depart."

Prince Tostig had not that long ago read the message he had received from Rogan, he was relieved in as much as he was not required to fight, but he was also upset that he felt it had all been a bit of a waste of his time, so when the jarl of Athenous put the proposal to him that he travels back with him to help with the problem of the wounded, he was suddenly much perkier. "Empty all of the boats!" he demanded.

That even took the jarl by surprise. "Tell me Jarl, how do you expect me to cross the channel with my men, should I instruct them to swim?"

"Just to be clear, lord prince, you will help with our problem once you arrive in Athenous?"

"Of course, now hurry we must make haste…"

Ingrid watched in shock as all the boats began returning their wounded and dead back to the beach, while Prince Tostig stood by and watched, at least the jarl showed a modicum of concern. It was three hours later that the prince was able to start loading his warriors and as he stood on the bridge of the centre boat, he shouted to those on the beach, "Don't worry we will send the boats back tomorrow!"

A wounded warrior with a bandage over one side of his face did try and bring a message about what was happening on the beach to Rogan, but he had already called for a meeting of warrior chiefs and specifically asked his guards not to be disturbed. The wounded warrior was told to clear off or return to his unit for duty. So, he returned to the beach crestfallen, the lady Ingrid had relied upon him and he had failed.

Chief Wigheard of Lōrnicā was the first to speak after all of Rogan's introductions, "May I say how pleased I am to be here, especially since our flank hit that little snag earlier this week, thank you Rogan for sending your housecarl, and the lady Halla."

"Tomorrow, I wish to assault the main gates, but I don't want any nasty surprises like that huge devil dog, and with that in mind Ascarli has given me an idea, he gave me a sack full of these organic lights, and they are imbued with the power to light up in the darkest of places, so my idea is that we hurl them inside once we have got the door open once more."

"First we should need to open the doors open lord…"

"I believe they will open by themselves once the incantation is read aloud, from over the door."

192

"Won't that bring that hellhound back to eat us?" stuttered Henri Damours, one of the royal guard captains.

"I am hoping that by throwing the 'elf stones' inside it cannot manifest itself again, they don't just light up an area they purge it of evil, it should disrupt whatever control the enchantress has over her warriors," Ascarli added.

"Alright chiefs, captains, and sergeant-at-arms, we need to make sure each warband is back up to strength, fifty warriors in each, even if it means using some of our reserves to bolster units."

"Lord, what about the guards we have left in each village?"

"Rotate them, and use the half-bloods even if it means integrating them into some warbands..."

"Lord...!"

"Sinhadd, if you are about to remind me that some of our men do not want to fight alongside the half-bloods then I will lump them all into a vanguard and send them in first tomorrow, is that clear, everyone?"

"Lord Rogan there is er...a man outside who is insisting on speaking with you."

"Winamac, I said no one disturbs us!"

"Lord, please...!"

Rogan rolled his eyes before asking everyone present to excuse him. Outside stood a mountain of a man, seven feet in height and covered in an unusual amount of body hair. "Thank you, Winamac, I'll take it from here."

The man with the unusual amount of hair stood at least seven feet tall and had huge arms and legs and a great barrel chest, Rogan's immediate thought was, that he was glad he was on his side, this man-beast.

"Lord Arathorn, you will not remember me, you were just a small boy of eight, if I recall correctly when last we met, and from what Leofstan has been telling me, you go by the name of Rogan Ragisson now, but where are my manners, my name is Beadurolf Moonstone."

Most of the others present who were not directly connected to Rogan and his escape from under the mountain, immediately went down on bended knee, for they knew exactly who this man was, King Beadurolf of Beornica, from the realm that sat just to the southwest of Fōrren, and immediately above Mārcādiā.

"My Lord King," Rogan began, "please forgive my insolence. I had no idea you were here, even if I knew of whom you were, tell me, how may I be of service to you?"

The king held up a hand to stop Rogan. "Please it is I who am here because all those years ago, you did me a great service, and I said back then that there would be a day in the future that you would call for my help, and I would be there. I am a man of my word, and I do not come alone, with me are sixty of my finest warriors."

"Excuse me, lord king, but you are not wearing any armour, and neither it appears to do any of those who came with you, would you like me to find some for you?"

"We do not need armour, my dear fellow, you see our skin is like hardened leather and when we charge into battle, not many of our enemies stay alive long enough to get that close."

Rogan wanted some time alone with his new guest but there were shouts from the elves on the plateau above the main cave entrance, Ascarli mere stated; "Someone is coming."

"Coming Ascarli, from where?"

The elven archers were pointing upwards as though the person was coming from further up the mountain. "He is carrying a white flag, lord!"

"Allow him to proceed, if he is from the Orsk, then they might have had enough of fighting and want to negotiate a truce." Offered Rogan.

The Orsk took nearly a quarter of an hour to finally make his way down the hillside and when he arrived it was noted how well he spoke 'Ingolandic'. Rogan invited him to join the group, while Ongar watched him like a hawk. "My Mistress seeks a truce with the one known as Rogan Ragisson!" he declared, not knowing which one of those present was the jarl.

"Why does your mistress want a truce, and more importantly who is your mistress, and why should we have any faith in her, anyway?" asked the Ongar, while still looking like he wanted to start a fight with this individual.

Ascarli dreaded this moment but he felt compelled to step forward all the same. "She is the most powerful enchantress in the whole of the Shattered Realms, and possibly the world, what you humans would call a 'demi-goddess'. Even to say her…no, even to think of her name is to have the spell already cast upon yourself, simply to say that she is the daughter of Lōthōs, does not convey the nature of that woman!"

Suddenly amid the group, there was a gust of wind, like a mini tornado, that whipped up just a few feet wide and not so many feet higher. Pots and pans were sent flying, helmets were dislodged from heads and weapons jangled on leather

194

straps from belts, and then just as quickly as it came, it disappeared and was gone, anything flung into the air dropped back to earth. The room stood in stunned silence.

"I take it your mistress, this one we call the enchantress can hear our words, is that correct?"

"It is!" said the one who called himself, Grak-Lak.

"We came here to put a stop to a diabolical and heinous business, that of Orsk males repeatedly raping human women who had already been sold into slavery against their will, and we believed that the head of this insidious order was none other than queen Helga Arnbjorg, of Råvenniå, yet we now know that she was but a willing lieutenant. Cease this practice at once, free all your slaves including the half-bloods and we shall walk away with them."

Grak-Lak turned to face Rogan after he had finished speaking, but when he opened his mouth to speak they were not his words, but hers, "You have twice felt the might of my invincible black guard warriors, and they were but a small number, the world is changing Rogan Ragisson and you must adapt to that change or be swept away in the current, now, hear my proposal if you will, take what you have won so far and leave my lands. Whatever business I conduct, and with whom I choose to do it should be of no concern of yours, I allowed you your freedom when first you left, and yet here you are once more, meddling in affairs that do not concern you."

"You are manufacturing soldiers and hiring them out to the highest bidder as mercenaries, yet you ultimately keep control of them, that sounds awfully like a plot to dominate the whole world to me!"

"Are you always this dramatic Rogan Ragisson, I am merely a woman who enjoys the benefits that having coin brings, all my mercenaries are loyal to their buyers, but again I see no reason for you to stick your nose into these matters."

"You do not deny the raping and kidnapping of innocent women as part of this plan?"

"They are the very dregs of society, I like to think that I am doing them a favour by taking them in, ask any of your women, ask Ingrid Hallgerd where she was before I secured her tenancy?"

"That is enough!" Rogan spat. "Get out of my sight before I gut your lackey and send him back in tiny pieces!"

The Orsk threw the white flag on the ground, turned away, and began walking back the way he came. "Lord were you not a little hasty with the enchantress?" A young man who came with the army of Lōrnicā asked.

"I am sorry, but I do not know you, we haven't been introduced?"

"My fault lord Rogan, this young man is Ordmaer Odda, prince of Lōrnicā, and I am commander Tiberius Visellinn of His Majesty's royal guard."

"Even so, Your Highness, you are a little young to be offering me advice on the matter of war."

"I mean no disrespect, lord Rogan, but I imagine that we are of a similar age, and I am a prince!"

"Have you ever been involved in a fight, lord prince?"

"That's hardly the point, I have been schooled in all of the classical wars…"

"Stop your bickering, this is just exactly what she does, the enchantress, she sows discontent, we are here to support lord Rogan Ragisson, and we all follow his orders, that is all." Snapped Ascarli.

"Okay, you all have your orders, now regroup our forces before morning, get some food and drink, but not too much, and rest for tomorrow will be the hardest day, dismissed!" Rogan railed trying to keep his voice sounding calm.

"Lord!" It was Ongar. "We have a luxury of warriors from all over the Shattered Realms, and they are already bickering behind your back about which army or warband should be in the vanguard, it is such a privilege and many of them came here to make a name for themselves, not to sit back in reserve…"

"Your point please my friend, it has been a long and eventful enough day."

"Let us split the forces into a three-pronged attack, we know where the corridors end in each of the side tunnels, so why not put Lornica in the left village and Råvenniå in the right and each have their warriors knock through into the central cavern, the walls up at the end of each balcony can't be that thick, neither can the walls directly below, if it works, we can have warriors moving into that central chamber very quickly from all sides."

"I did have an idea of my own but kept it to myself, Ongar, after we get the main gates open again and after we have lit the main cavern up with those 'elf stones', I was going to have us throw as many of the fire-pots inside as we could before the main attack is sent in."

"Lord, why can't we do all of them, especially if we use the fire-pots to mask the noise of the men breaking through the side walls?"

"Ongar, fetch the king of Beornica back to me, please, and I will run my ideas past him first."

"Rogan as I see it my warriors are equally as agile as the elves, but you need them outside in case of unforeseen problems, let my sixty warriors take the fire-pots and throw them inside, I mean, just look at us, everyone built like a brown bear, if we throw the fire-pots and then withdraw the enemy might even be stupid enough to come out after us, then the elven archers can have their say from above."

"If all goes well, would you be willing to take all sixty of your warriors in first, I mean it doesn't sound like a lot and we have no way of knowing how many warriors the enchantress has at her disposal, surely shouldn't I add lord Leofstan to accompany you?"

"My people and I are called Babau, which is a word that doesn't translate well in Ingolandic. Chief Wigheard, who I count as a dear old friend, would have you believe that my people can shape-shift our form into that of a wild bear, but alas, ad if that enchantress is half as clever as she makes out, she is, then she will well know the stories that are told about my people, and her feelings, hopefully, her fears, will translate down to the lowest ranks in there, that's got to be worth something!"

"I was planning to allow the half-bloods to lead the second wave of attacks through the front entrance, I certainly get the impression that they want to play their part, and in a way, this is their realm, how do you feel about them, lord king?"

"I can only imagine what slaughter awaits us all inside, whatever order you send the different races in, I have already felt, as has your friend Ascarli, there is far more we haven't seen that is yet to be discovered, so think carefully about how many warriors you commit to the cave system, that mouthpiece of the enchantress came down from above but on the outside."

The following morning came around far too quickly and many of the warriors had been up since before dawn, they wanted to trade words and items with each other to be given to loved ones should they not return from the forthcoming battle.

Rogan had taken the time to briefly visit each unit that was in place and ready to go inside first as part of the three-pronged attack. "Prince Ordmaer, I understand that you wish to lead the attack via the upper balcony?"

"Yes, lord Rogan, that is correct, and as you can see I have chosen eight of my biggest, strongest warriors, who work in shifts of four, to smash threw that wall as quickly as possible, and I shall be backed up by fifty of the royal guard,

Commander Tiberius Visellinn as eight equally large and strong warriors to break through below us, and we shall try to make our breakthrough at the same time, he has the other fifty royal guard, then we have two hundred warriors outside with a further one hundred militiamen in reserve."

Rogan shouted "Good hunting!" as he left the prince of Lōrnicā, because he had already spoken at length with the king of Beornica, he merely waved as he passed behind his forces and instead, Rogan went to speak with Cro-Mur the half-blood leader of the rebellion forces.

"Cro-Mur, we have no idea how many black guard are inside and we can only guess that the interior is the same as all of the other cave villages except that this one will probably be much, much larger in every sense, I want you to give us a signal if things are not going well for you inside, and then move to the sides of the walls in there, because I will order Leofstan to ride in with his armour horses and relieve your position, but try and support those who go in ahead of you first."

"I understand lord, and thank you for allowing us to have our warbands."

"There are so many of you, the ones that had been attached to other units had already filled their ranks, it just made sense to put the rest of you together."

"And who will relive us if we also come unstuck, Rogan?"

"Arn and I will bring our forces together and attack on foot, between us we must still have at least five hundred warriors, eh, Arn?" interjected Gufi Grettersson, chief of Hundsnes.

"Gufi my dearest friend, I was wondering if you hadn't stayed away for some reason?"

"We both did, Arn and I, this is your great day and we didn't want anyone looking in any other direction than yours, I hope the captains who represented us handled themselves well?"

"Of course, they did, as well you both know, so you are to be back up here in the centre, yes?"

"Yes, with three hundred and fifty warriors. Arn will take the village on the right, he has already broken his army down into seven bands of fifty."

The two men came together in a heartfelt embrace, both patting each other on the shoulders several times. All that remained was for Rogan to see Arn and after that visit the warriors who had come from Athenous, they were chosen to sit this battle out and stay in reserve, alongside them were all the mounted men from each of the other warbands except for Leofstan's knights.

Sometime in the early morning just as all the warbands were marching towards their starting positions, Ingrid suddenly appeared and with her Aatu, who seemed agitated. "Rogan, shhh," she put a finger to her lips, "come look for yourself before you alert the others."

"Ingrid, whatever is the matter that you creep about in this manner and just before the main attack begins?"

"To the beach, we must hurry, come, and don't stop to speak to anyone!"

Rogan ran after Aatu and Ingrid and the three of them were observed by just about the entire army, many men might have sniggered to watch them run in the way they were. "Perhaps they have last-minute words before the battle?" quipped one anonymous wag.

When they climbed down onto the beach where all the wounded had been evacuated from it was an absolute tip, and Rogan wondered if Ingrid wanted him to bring men here to clean it up. Then when he saw where she was looking, he suddenly snapped out of his malaise and ran back up the dunes to find a guard who possessed a horn. "Sound the alarm, quickly!" Rogan cried in a loud panicked voice.

Several warriors from the rear guard of the men of Athenous began to look around in confusion and alarm. One of Their horn-blowers dutifully obliged and by putting the horn to his lips and blowing a soulful single noted sound.

Sergeant-at-arms from every warband and unit were dispatched to the horn-blower including Ongar, Gunnar, and Halla, they all came running from every direction, but before they could process and the thoughts of why the alarm was being sounded, they all began, one after the other to stand and gape towards Athenous, the town across the river Tawa.

Rogan walked over to the rear rank of the warriors nearest to him and began addressing them; "Men of Athenous," he began, and they turned to face him, and then they too witnessed the most shocking sight, "we cannot all get back across the river in the boats that we have."

"I propose that I cross the river with a strong force of one hundred warriors, the rest of you must stay here and form the reserve for the battle later today, I guarantee that I will find out who has caused this and together we will hunt them down and make them pay for what they have done, you have my word!"

Athenous was ablaze, and the biggest fire of all was up at the wooden cathedral.

10

The Longest Day

The simplest solution was to take fifty men from Gufi's warband and a further fifty from Arn's, what was not so easy was convincing Ascarli or any of the other leaders that this was a good idea. "Rogan, I understand your desire to see this done right, but by you leaving the army ahead of this battle today, I just think it will be bad for the morale of the men."

"Ascarli, what would you do, split me in half?"

"Send Gunnar, Leofstan, or any of your other trusted lieutenants in doing so you will demonstrate just how important Athenous is and at the same time steady the nerves of the army hours before battle."

"Lord Rogan, he is right and you know it, let me go in your stead, please," implored Gunnar Helgisson.

"My mind is made up, fetch me once the men have all been loaded into the ships, Athenous did not just set itself on fire!"

Ascarli mouthed to Gunnar, *Leave it with me*. And Gunnar went off towards the beach where there was already a steady column of men filing that way. "He's right to send only men from Råvenniå, those who are from there were against excepting half-bloods into the army, even know rumour is rife that the fire was set by the wounded half-bloods."

"Ingrid, he is the only one of us who can keep this coalition together, if he goes this alliance goes with him, it's that high stakes, look around you, you can see it in their faces, they will lose without him being here!"

"I will talk with him, Ascarli, but I will make no promises."

Ingrid found Rogan standing on the shoreline as he watched the one hundred warriors load onto two of the remaining three ships that were still moored on this side of the river. She approached him from the rear and wrapped her arms around him, "You know I would follow you into the darkest vision of hell, my love." The last two words were whispered sweetly into his left ear.

Rogan slowly turned around in her arms until their noses were touching, and his eyes stayed looking downwards, he knew why she was there and what she was intending to say, he knew that she was right and that his stubbornness was the only thing keeping him to his word, he even wondered if he should give the army another day off, in this foreign land, while he determined what had happened in Athenous.

"Return with me to Ascarli, let the men see that this is the place you need to be, here with them, on this most important of days…" Ingrid's words rolled off her tongue as if coated in honey.

"Where is Gunnar?" was all Rogan said; he knew when he was beaten.

Gunnar was the last man to board the ships and as he stepped on the boardwalk leading up from the beach, Rogan put a hand on his shoulder. "Watch yourself, this could be something as simple as an outbreak of disease and that is why they have fired the town, or it could be an outflanking manoeuvre by the enchantress, she is certainly clever enough to be able to."

"I was thinking of, what if queen Helga had broken through at Ingolfsfell with what remained of her blackguard, lord?"

When Gunnar sailed and Rogan made his way back up the beach and to the front of his army with Ingrid proudly at his side, all the watching warriors, from all the different races, cheered loudly, and Ingrid beamed from ear to ear, as did Ascarli secretly.

The two boats carrying Gunnar and one hundred warriors had barely put out to sea when a strange bumping noise could be heard from all along the starboard side of the boat. "What is that sound?" was a question on many lips but it was not until someone leant over the starboard side that they got the answer they were looking for. "Lord, it's bodies!" said one of the warriors grimly.

The bodies had been stripped of everything except their undergarments and any bandages that had been applied while still alive, they were not bloated either which meant that they had only been in the water for a short period. "The tide is coming out from Athenous, lord," stated one of the other warriors who must have had some knowledge of how the tides work.

Gunnar had wanted for the main sail to catch the wind but it seemed the wind had other ideas and so reluctantly Gunnar had to give the order to man the oars, reluctant because he knew the bodies would snarl the oars and unsettle the rhythm, but there was no other way, no matter how sickening this was.

The boats had reached about the three-quarter mark when the smell started to waft over them, it was like overcooked bacon and smoked fish, and many other far less pleasant odours, whatever the combination it had the warrior oarsmen tearing strips of cloth from undergarments and wrapping them around their lower faces.

The town had been built from wood, imported from Hundsnes mostly with only a very small number of buildings using stone at least for the ground floor, like the tavern, but not one of those buildings was still standing, everything had been consumed by the terrible inferno, now only the scored black skeletal remains of this new town poked from the dirt, like open-handed fingers on a dead man.

As the wind blew, it whistled and caused unstable buildings to creek and rattle it was a place of the dead and one where Gunnar and his charges would not have been at all surprised to witness the dead rise and reach for their souls.

The boats hit the piers about three hours after dawn and no warrior had to be given orders to leap out of the boats and form up. Their silent manoeuvres matched the emptiness of the town. Gunnar stood on the bow of one of the boats and began to bark instructions; "Right, we search street by street look for survivors and clues to who did this, this fire was no accident, nor was it to purge any sickness, this has the hallmarks of a raid!"

Edward Holm, Gufi Grettersson's master-at-arms, stood on the stern of the other boat and waited for Gunnar to stop before he too gave orders. "I want group formations, now, sixteen bands of twelve, the remaining eight sergeants-at-arms, you will act as a go-between for the bands and to report back to me; what are you waiting for, have at it, men!"

Gunnar took charge of a band of twelve warriors and told the others that he would make his way up to the bishop's cathedral. "Come on my group there might yet be survivors up there on the hill."

Bodies filled the streets like human litter, posed as they were killed running in all directions, some tangled together others clinging together, and yet others alone, but in death they shared one other common trait. Those people had not just been put to the sword; they had been cut to ribbons in a frenzied attack.

Mangled black bodies lay in burnt-out buildings just like those out on the street, some in clutches of other solitary, men, women, children, and livestock, nothing remained of the living. Gunnar wondered if this was what bishop d'Athenous had described hell as being like, and it made him wonder where was the Kristosian God now?

Gunnar realised that with most of the menfolk being across the river in Obrea, all these bodies would have been their women and children and any males would most likely have been the wounded. As Gunnar and the twelve steadily but cautiously climbed the slopped approach road to the cathedral, it was possible to feel the heat still from this immense building as it snapped and crackled in the dying embers of the fire.

The group stopped about a hundred yards from the actual building, it would have been suicide to get any closer, and no amount of water was going to save the seat of God, a place to which he was to view the destruction of the Orsk. Albert Cartwright, the sergeant-at-arms, pointed to where a large crucifix hung above the altar. "Is that meant to be that way around?" questioned Gunnar.

"No lord, it has been hung upside down, but that is not all, there is someone nailed to it!"

"Is that not the Lord Iesu?"

"That is the body of a person, look how it is burnt, and it has a chain hanging around its neck."

"Oh no, I recognise that symbol, it is the same as a necklace Rogan gave to Aethelric the Bard."

Alti Hælæifsson and Sigrunn Hallkatla arrived on the far side of Athenous with a warband of twenty-four warriors, every one of them carrying some wound or other, but they had all seen the flames from as far away as Ailgin, and they insisted on forming up to go investigate. Hugue d'Athenous's body was found on the path immediately outside of the ruined cathedral, he had been nailed to a wooden 'x', and his body was riddled with arrows.

Gunnar saw Atli and shouted a greeting over to him and the two separate groups came together, there was a short period of joy tinged with sadness as all three of the old friends hugged and exchanged pleasantries. Gunnar outranked Atli and Sigrunn, Sigrunn being a shield maiden and Atli a sergeant-at-arms, Atli was the first to offer to cut the bishop down but it was Gunnar who offered for his warriors to dig a shallow grave.

"Atli, did you see anyone while on the road up coming here?"

"No lord, we saw the flames on the horizon about four, maybe five hours ago and we formed a warband to come investigate."

"So, you have no idea who could have done this?" Gunnar quizzed his friend.

"Judging by the level of destruction, I would say a small army came through here, but have you found any bodies of our enemies?" exhorted Atli.

"Too early to say, I have groups searching the whole town though."

"If they came by boat, then they might have left the same way, except for the fact that the harbour is full of boats, all those who answered Rogan's call, and who have been transporting troops across the river and returning with the sick, wounded and dead."

"All of this so far leads me to believe whoever did this came by boat and left on foot, and there is one easy way to check, there is a coastal track just to the west of here, it connects to a small settlement called Broch, it's the only other way to get to Fōrren without going through any other villages."

"Fōrren, are you suggesting that this is the handiwork of Prince Tostig?"

"Tostig met with the enchantress and shortly after moved his warrior back and away from the fight, Rogan sent him home, his troops used those boats, at the docks, to get here, so who else?"

"Then we must find those tracks and be sure before we report this back to Rogan. An army of that size will have left an impression in the ground as it is still moist in places from the thaw, we follow and we make sure before reporting back to Rogan."

The incantation spell was read aloud once more and the great double doors began to open just as before.

King Beadurolf Moonstone, along with his sixty warriors, was gathered outside with the 'elf stones' in hand, poised to throw them inside as they charged forward; what was apparent and somewhat confusing to all the other warriors who waited patiently alongside them, was the fact they carried no weapons and wore no armour other than a loose-fitting leather ensemble.

Ongar turned to Rogan and whispered, "This should be very interesting, especially if that main cavern is filled with blackguard like we think it is. I just hope Cro-Mar and my half-blood kin are up for their supporting role."

"Do you want to join them, Ongar, I will understand if you do?"

"It would be a privilege to join my brothers, Rogan, and can I trust that you will be at hand should we meet resistance?"

"Of course, but you will have support from both flanks by that time, now I must sound the charge; look, the gates are almost fully open!"

The Beornicans broke out into a jog and then a sprint and before you knew it, they had disappeared inside the huge cavernous centre cave. A bright white light began breaking out all around the central cave as the crystals were being tossed, and then came the loud crash, like a thousand clay pots being smashed upon the floor, it was the 'shapeshifters' slamming into the well-drilled and disciplined 'testudo' formation of the blackguard.

An order was given in the speech of the dead, "zkuyo ceakjoigoj!" telling the blackguard to brace themselves, and they did, holding their eight-foot spears out front and their shields tightly interlocked. The Beornicans could appear to change at will as they hit the front rank of black guard they were already in bear-form, and hacking and slashing at their opponents trying to find a way through the thicket of spears.

Several of the Beornicans had fallen before Aatu pelted inside the cave after them, using their huge bodies as a ramp on which to step before catapulting himself onto the interlocked shields that protected the black guard from an assault from above, but there was no metal yet made that could withstand the pressure that Aatu's bite brought to bear as his jaws clamped around the rim of one shield.

Slowly but surely, Aatu prized the outer edge upwards until it 'popped' out of the holder's hand and he found his way down into the midst of the one-hundred-strong unit. Within seconds, Aatu was chewing and clawing at all of those around him while at the same time using his large muscular frame to push the individual guards apart.

Suddenly, the blackguard was exposed to the Beornicans in brown bear-form and their long spears were useless to them many clattered to the floor in quick succession as the black guards withdrew their swords. Those early casualties the Beornicans suffered were their last in this encounter as they joined Aatu in eviscerating the black guard with such savagery that their masters, who watched in silence from above, were themselves shocked into a state of paralysis.

Once the half-bloods saw that the black guard unit had broken, they too ran forward to join the melee, swords flashing in the combined artificial crystal light and the many torches, to those onlookers outside the cave, looking in, they would have seen the incredible show of shadow fighting as huge elongated figures danced out across the walls and ceiling, the ritual dance of death.

Ongar found himself pushed into the shield of one of the black guards, so hard that it winded him, but the crush from behind and the pile-up of bodies already forming in front of those blackguards, stopped him from falling over. The temperature inside the cavern was rising and it was getting hard to breathe, mixed with the smell and the blood it was already becoming overpowering.

By now, there was barely any room to move and the whole war effort was threatening to collapse into two shield walls pushing and shoving, with neither being able to succeed in driving their side to victory. Swords, axes, spears, war mattocks, anything that could inflict pain or injury was wielded desperately in a final attempt to break the deadlock.

The black guard attempted to rally when it became obvious, they were unable to hold on to the side chambers since the left and right flanks of Rogan's army had broken through the cave walls on either side.

Black guard soldiers scrambled over the dead and dying in a vain attempt to join as one cohesive unit, however, all the bodies that were stacking up everywhere prevented them from doing so, and the real battle set in, attrition. The black guard had nowhere left to go, and as was expected they asked for no quarter and they gave no quarter and the erosion of their forces became a formality.

Rogan would have preferred to have pulled his troops back and called for surrender, watching so many dying, so needlessly would haunt him for the rest of his days, but he had no control over either side, what was going on inside that centre cavern was feral, undisciplined, and savage, with severed limbs being used as basic weapons when other forged weapons had broken or been knocked from hands, neither side recognising one from the other.

On another day, their strength and fortitude could have been praised but not on this day, Ongar knew if this stalemate continued his people would suffer gruesomely, and so with every ounce of strength he had left he reached for and found a discarded war-axe. Curling his bloodied fingers around its shaft he used it as a level, hooking the double blades under the shield that he was being pressed up against by a black guard soldier.

Slowly, surely, inch by painstaking inch, Ongar felt the weight of that shield shift, before its owner was even aware, it was moving upwards, and it caused a ripple in the front of the enemy shield wall, and a sword blade was rammed forward at his side, the point of which nicked Ongar but found purchase in the side of the black guard. It was enough, with the weight of bodies behind, still pushing and heaving so that it caused the creature's innards to spill out.

The newly reformed frontline of the blackguard suddenly peeled back like the skin of a piece of soft fruit, and air rushed back in to fill Ongar's lungs, and he gasped! Sweat poured from his brow as he lifted his tired arms time and again, as though he had entered a world in slow motion, another jet of warm blood sprayed across his face and down his front, mechanically he lifted his right arm again and again, stopping only when it encountered another body.

What nobody was paying any attention to was the sandstone pillars, they too were taking a battering by mistimed weapon swings, or bodies being pushed into them, nor did they take notice of the periodic falling stones from the roof. At first, it was just a shower of dust but soon enough it was a large chunk of rock that drop straight out of the roof and into the middle of the melee, and shield or no shield those caught there were being squatted like flies.

Ongar heard his raspy voice yelling that the roof was falling in but, in the noise, the smoke, and the complete and utter chaos of the battle no one heard his words nor did they take any heed of the falling rocks from the ceiling it was not even as the first section of balcony collapsed on to both sets of fighters, it was only when the second section fell and the black guard had been obliterated that anyone stopped fighting and began looking for the exits.

The next part of the ceiling to collapse was that over the main entrance and as it went it sent a great shower of broken rock and dust, spewing out of the main entrance along with a huge woosh of hot air and the cries of those caught by it, every warrior in the third wave of the attack, Rogan included, had no choice but to pull back away from the cave.

Ongar spotted that the first stairway that had collapsed had done so in such a way that it had formed an almost perfect ramp leading up to the adjoining corridor upstairs, and he pulled himself to his feet and he pushed through the tight body of half-bloods and the scattered Beornicān survivors and he forced his way to the base of the broken stairs and he began to climb, past the fallen bodies and falling sandstone, Allies seeing that the fight was over started to follow Ongar, others were fortunate enough to return to the cave villages on either side through the holes they had cut.

Ongar saw a hand coming from somewhere above his head covered in thick sticky liquid and his initial reaction was to bring his weapon to bare, that was when his eyes met those of Cro-Mur. Cro-Mur had also guessed what was happening and already climbing upwards to get onto the balcony when he spotted Ongar and came back to help him.

As Ongar moved further along, so Cro-Mur reached down to help another of the half-bloods to gain purchase to freedom from what was fast becoming their mausoleum. The 'elf stones' were being buried and the wall torches were extinguished by the flying dust it was becoming a race against time to figure out an exit, during what felt like an earthquake, but was more of the roof caving in, a small fissure opened in the wall at the top of the collapsed stairs.

That was when Ongar saw something different out of the corner of his eye, something that should not have been there, it was another set of stone-cut steps that led upwards to another level above the one where he was standing. The good thing appeared to have been the lack of falling rocks on those stairs, so they were leading away from the collapse, Ongar just needed a way to bridge the gap between the last step and the balcony where he was.

'Going up' was certainly not on his mind, because if the roof was all coming down then 'out' was the better option; however, what swayed Ongar now was that there was very definitely the shadow of a figure standing at the base of the newfound stairs, and the figure was holding a torch in one hand, and a small bundle that was moving in the other.

Cro-Mur asked Ongar, "Why have you stopped? We must find a way out!"

Ongar said, "I think it is a woman holding a baby!"

King Beadurolf Moonstone bounded up the broken staircase with a large oblong black guard shield in his hands and he rammed the top edge of it, where there were two flat iron spikes, into the base of the bottom step, an action which caused the figure to retreat further up. Ongar offered his hand to the king of Beornica and pulled him up, now they had a way to step across to the stairs.

Ongar instructed Cro-Mur to get as many of his people out as he could, but not to forget to save himself, it was getting impossible to speak now as the crescendo of noise was getting so loud, Ongar pulled a torch from its bracket on the wall and handed it to Cro-Mur. "Here, use this to show others the way." And with that, he was away up the stairs.

The woman, as it turned out, was not a woman at all; well, not in the everyday sense of the word she wasn't, she was a female half-blood, the first that Ongar had ever seen and her beauty, even in such a setting as this, was captivating— her skin was a lighter shade of grey than his own, and the baby she held was different again, its skin was jet-black, and if it weren't for the fact that its eyes were wide open, Ongar might not have seen anything other than a bundle of clothes.

The female spoke to him in black speech and he had to do a double take, she had told him that there were others like her upstairs but they were scared. Ongar wondered what others she could be talking about, not to mention a whole secret level above the only two he had ever known.

The new woman took hold of his arm and pulled him towards a wide-open space at the top of this new set of stairs, and it opened right in front of him and on the opposite side to where the cave-in was occurring. An open space with corridors leading off both sides, it was almost a replica of the village system below.

Soon more warriors were climbing the lower set of stairs and Ongar knew he could not stay where he was or it would form a choke point, so reluctantly he followed the beckoning women. Ongar allowed himself to be guided to the first room, on his left, and to his shock and horror he found that the room was not a room at all but another cave village, he was in an underground pyramid of sorts.

Everywhere was lit up, just like it had been below, and he could see terrified half-blood women, some huddled and holding their children, while the ground beneath their feet trembled, Ongar quickly tried to count them as it looked like there were hundreds at least, and he had a sinking feeling, in the pit of his stomach that he was not going to be able to save any of them, they were still trapped inside here.

Ascarli felt the surge in the airway before he saw or even could have understood what was happening on the mountain way above his head, but it concerned him enough to vault towards the elves on the flat ledge above the main doorway. Although they felt the ground tremble, sway, and buckle, where they were standing seemed to be stable, the sandstone rock was thick and where it was collapsing was ten or twelve feet beneath their feet.

"We should get off this ledge, although I don't think it will collapse, whatever is breaking up beneath us threatens to cut us off from Rogan and the rest of the army." The elves who were a sensitive race did not need telling a second time and they turned to the track which Ascarli had used to bring himself to their level, and they began streaming down it.

Abruptly, it seemed from the outside looking up that the top of the mountain exploded, except for the fact that there was all the noise but none of the debris, it felt like the whole of the mountain range had some kind of aftershock. Rogan looked up high into the sky where he thought that he should see something; instead, what he did see confused him more than ever.

A thick black tide, like floodwater, began to cascade down the face of the rock. Rogan could only see the three sides from where he stood; however, he could see everything in its path turn to black. It was like he expected a larva to flow except this was not larva flow, it was something viscous, animated, and very much alive, and it was rapidly converging on the stone-cut steps like it had a purpose.

Ascarli saw Rogan was looking up for some reason and as he hit the ground level, he turned and followed his friend's gaze, instantaneously connecting to the enchantress once more. The elf saw the black mass from afar, then up close as though something had taken hold of him and dragged him forward against his will.

The black mass promptly became soldiers, hundreds, no, thousands of heavily armoured soldiers with one single purpose in mind, that the destruction of Rogan Ragisson and his entire armed forces. Had this been the she-devil's plan all along, to gather all opposing factions here to this one point in time and history, and wipe them out entirely?

"Rogan, you need to get out of here, pull everyone back to the boats, there is no way we can fight that many black guard. I sense there are thousands of them, and they will crush us if they catch us here on this island."

It was Captain Brecott who was shouting now above the noise of the ground as it buckled and trembled. "Rogan, they are coming around from the left!"

Rogan seemed unable to move, as he watched the horror unfold before his very eyes, she, the witch on the top of the mountain had played him superbly, set a trap and he had walked straight into it eyes wide open. His dearest friend, Ongar, lost, trapped inside the main cavern as the earth gave way, Aatu also. Not even the calls from Ascarli telling him that the black guard was advancing down the right flank too.

Brecott instructed two of his men to drag Rogan back, at least until they had cleared the tar-filled ditch, panic started to set in as the warriors who had been held in the rear watched in abject terror at the unfolding situation. "Rogan! Snap out of it, man, tell us what to do before all hope is lost!"

By now, it seemed as though the black guards were seeping out of hundreds of concealed exits all over the mountain face. Soon the first thousand or so black guard had reached the top of the main entrance and began fanning out. Where it had collapsed, it now formed a gentle slope down to ground level, forming a slope with which the black guard could march down and strike at the very heart of the Great Army.

"Shield wall!" Rogan called, in a vain attempt to slow the enemy down while the villages on either side of the main chamber emptied of their fighters, as each new warrior emerged from those side caves, Rogan saw just how bad it had been inside, many of those warriors came out supporting an injured comrade.

Rogan's heart leaped for joy when he saw Aatu, at least he thought it was him, no longer white but a bloody mixture of sandy brown and crimson red. "Aatu, over here, boy!" he called and Aatu came bounding over towards him. Running diagonally in front of the base of the new slope, Aatu paused. First, he looked at the solid black wall clanking down towards Rogan and his forlorn hope, then he turned his head to see Rogan; in that precious moment, Aatu connected with Rogan and he made his mind up.

Row after row continued to be added to the ranks of the enemy and it was at that point that Aatu stood legs set apart and howled like he was calling out to the Gods, but when they stayed silent, he vaulted forward and sprang on top of the nearest testudo formation. Rogan shouted for his pet to stay but it was too late— he was lost in the ritual bloodlust that gripped all fighters eventually.

Men, elves, and half-bloods watched as the warg tore metal apart with his teeth and dislodged shields with his claws, he had become an unstoppable force of nature, and that gave a glimmer of hope, and in that slither of daylight, Rogan, knowing what his next order could mean to his dear friend, called for the back row to launch their spears.

The evening sky turned to twilight as hundreds of javelins soared upwards before changing trajectory and plunging back to earth, ripping great welts in the body of blackguard. The warg somehow managed to hop, twist or wriggle out of the way of the thin throwing spears, he was by now at one with his craft. Aatu was dancing this way and that, one moment he was on top of the roof of shields the next he was down amid the tangle of black guard.

Rogan again watched as the creature jumped from one testudo to another, leaving the way open for the allies to focus on that previous group before moving across to the next. Again, as Aatu landed on top of the next testudo he clamped his jaws down hard on a shield that he had prized loose with his snout. The body of another blackguard was lifted off its feet and then shaken like a ragdoll before being tossed to one side.

By now, the first testudo of blackguard were buckling this way and that and it was time for Aatu to leap across to the next testudo and for Rogan to order his spear-throwers to hit the second group.

The third testudo of black guard was already bracing themselves for the attack and the centre wobbled under the weight of the beast as he landed this time, after pulling up one of the horizontal shields he bit down on the black guard below but the warrior managed to skew where Aatu's jaws clasped around his helmet and as the warg reared backwards to pull the warrior up four others around him instead pulled him downwards.

The warrior himself lifted his own feet off the ground and momentarily dangled as Aatu fought to pull him free, instead though he was pulled down into the centre of the enemy formation by those pulling on the other black guard. Rogan paused before giving the command to throw spears, he wanted to give Aatu time to jump out, but as the seconds ticked by, he lost sight of the warg and the black guard reformed their front with reinforcements from behind.

Brecott said, "We have to torch the pit now or they will be over it and we will be finished!"

Rogan could no longer hear the captain his eyes scoured the enemy unit to look for signs of his friend, but there were none, yes, he saw black guard rise and fall and the ranks trying to move out of the way, but it was not Aatu who was causing this, it was Rogan's men who were throwing spears.

Brecott turned to Rogan and shouted that they had to get to the boats now! And evacuate from the beach, some of the men who had been sent there earlier had got the last remaining boat off the beach and were readying it for the sail.

Rogan had the men form a shield wall on the ridge above the beach and he was told about the last remaining boat, he knew then that it would take a couple of hours to navigate the channel and another couple to return, hopefully with more boats—he needed to buy more time.

Ongar was gone, Aatu was lost from sight, Gunnar was over the water already and Rogan was starting to feel the loneliness of command. Ascarli noted the feeling and came to stand with him, as did Tiberius Visellinn, and with him others from the royal guard of Lōrnicā.

"Everyone, get back, retreat!" Rogan called at the top of his voice before turning to one of his men-at-arms, "Dress the ranks, and don't let them panic!"

"Rogan!" It was Ingrid, she was terrified and caught hold of his arm. "The boats, there are none. Tostig took most of them and Gunnar the others, we are stranded."

"I was led to believe that there was at least one boat, Ingrid?"

"They have just put out into the channel…"

"Then we must do whatever we can to hold back this enemy until they return with other boats."

Rogan's mind raced for a solution, as he knew that they could not keep their shape constantly retreating in the face of an advancing enemy, the ground was too uneven, there were bodies still that had not been removed, and equipment like carts and wagons; the army could do with eyes in the back of their heads. Ascarli picked up on that thought and sent all of his archers around to the rear.

"Fan out and walk them backwards, call out to let them know of obstacles!" Ascarli called, not to his elves for they had that 'magical' mind connection, even Rogan felt it as the words formed first in his mind. Ascarli called out so that the other warriors would understand what he was trying to do.

"Lord Rogan, there is no way we can win this, look at them there are thousands, it's like hell itself has opened, and the boats, what shall we do?" Prince Ordmaer Odda of Lōrnicā begged.

"We wait for the right moment; look, their front ranks are just navigating the tarpit, Your Highness."

Ascarli spoke next, "Rogan, do you still have those fire-pots?"

Rogan did not need further conversation, his 'far sight' allowed his mind to connect with that of Ascarli's and he saw the elf's battle plan. "Lock shields, fourth row, get ready to throw your fire-pots!" Rogan bellowed, and the command was reciprocated all along his lines until all those who had fire-pots took them in hand and lit their wicks.

Rogan waited for everyone to be far enough back from the tar-filled trench and then he called for all the warriors holding the fire-pots to throw them at the trench. Hundreds of black guard were already picking their way across the rubble and readying themselves for a fight. Some of the fire-pots plopped into the black goop and began to sink, others hit the wooden structures and burst into flame, a few even broke against some of the black guard warriors and set them on fire.

For a few agonising moments, nothing much happened until one tiny drop of burning fuel dripped onto the surface of the tar pit, and then with a mighty 'whoosh', the whole thing ignited. The sheer heat from that initial ignition consumed every black guard soldier within a twenty-five-foot radius; it was a truly horrifying spectacle, but one which brought about instant relief throughout the allied army.

Nothing and no one was getting past that wall of fire until it burnt itself out, which could be days, even weeks. Rogan's plan had bought them time, for now. "Right, we form up on this ridge warband by warband in block formation, all the other warbands that cannot fit up here, down to the beach and make ready for when the boats return."

That night, Rogan went from one warband to the next, making sure that the bulk of warriors had eaten and were resting, pickets had been posted and he was walking to the next warband; he reciprocated this action all through the night to bolster morale, make sure everyone knew the plan and to help take his mind off possible future events.

Ascarli eventually found him out and clasped a hand on his shoulder. "I know what you are going through, my boy, and I am grateful for the honour of serving alongside you; this war was just and you have scored some small victory, leave this place and know that the black guard is trapped here, blockade the top of the river Tawa and let no ship pass this way again."

"What should I do with the rest of the army once we land at Athenous, lord elf?"

"Send them home to their families, but keep a core with which to march on the capital, there is still black guard on the mainland that needs to be dealt with."

"Will you stay with me, your elves, I mean?"

"I was thinking of asking you if we could take some land in Råvenniå, your sister is a wood elf at heart and her betrothed is the captain of my archers; perhaps they could find a nice spot over by the river Tawa at the edge of the forest perhaps?"

"I would very much like that, Ascarli. What about the men from Lōrnicā?"

"Their prince is weak, he came here in his father's stead but his heart is not in it, especially after witnessing firsthand the horrors of war. I think he will offer to leave you some of his warriors but then he will slink back to Lōrnicā with his tail between his legs."

"What about King Beadurolf Moonstone? He must have lost over half his command in those caves, I feel dreadful about that."

"He knew what he was getting himself involved with when he rallied to your cause. I am afraid though that this battle was his last hoorah, his people are sparse and could ill afford to lose so many, he will remain your devoted friend though, of that I have no doubt."

"How did Leofstan fare?"

"He lost about a quarter of his command, but again he came here for you, but not to leave you here, his sworn duty is to return you to Mārcādiā where he firmly believes a throne awaits you."

"Well, that's not going to happen!"

"Then he will be your loyal servant and friend until you change your mind!"

"That just leaves Gufi and Arn."

"Two who love you as only fathers can, and who will support you to the end. Gufi's warriors took a beating getting through the right flank, Arn's warriors were held in reserve and felt guilty, it is they who line up behind you now."

"Oh, where are my warriors then?"

"They are down on the beach taking time to rest and recover, they will be the first to ship out when the boats return."

"Do you honestly think we will make it across the channel before the fire dies down?"

"I know we will, Rogan!"

As the first boats returned full of warriors, they saw that Athenous was nothing more than a blackened skeleton of burnt ruined wood, it was no longer a place to find shelter, and with no natural forest nearby, the town was to be abandoned—at least for the time being. For the bulk of the army, now began the great retreat.

Rogan was the last man to leave the beach, his boat was already loaded but he wanted time to take one last look; his heart sank for the friends and good warriors whose bodies he was leaving behind, for whatever words Ascarli had spoken, his heart was broken and it felt like a massive mistake. Once his boat docked in Athenous, Gunnar jumped aboard, as everyone else disembarked.

"It was that jumped-up little prig, Prince Tostig; he butchered everyone and torched the town, we followed the tracks of his army around the edge of the channel, he avoided every settlement until he found fishing boats that would get his warriors across the river, then he did the same to the settlement as he did here."

"He did this for her…"

"The enchantress?"

"Yes, but he will answer for his crimes, not straight away, for our army is on its knees right now, but he will pay nonetheless—that much I promise."

The war was over.